SPY NOT

BY

GEORGE V. HENDERSON

To Marilyn

Best wishes

THE PUBLISHER

August 16, 2002

FIRST PUBLISHED 1999 BY THE PUBLISHER

SECOND PUBLISHING REVISED EDITION
2000 BY THE PUBLISHER

ISBN 0-9685032-0-9

The Publisher 1999
17-700 Mcleod Rd., Suit 272
Niagara Falls, Ontario
L2G 7K3

This book is dedicated to my wife,
Carol and my kids, who have put up
with me over the course of this long
journey.

Spy Not

Chapter One – 6:30 A.m., Tuesday Morning near Drake's Seat, St. Thomas, US Virgin Islands

The Findings

Officer Francis Ernest Mann slid out of his cruiser and let the early morning wind frisk him, finding all the moist areas on his six-foot-two body. A moment later he meandered over to the edge of the winding, hill road. His view of Charlotte Amalie, and its harbour, was breathtaking. This vista comprised of cruise ships that glittered like gigantic, white elephants in the morning sun, the yacht basin with its hundreds of masts and vibrant sails, over to the question mark tip of Hassel Island. It seemed only aqua blue, lincoln green and sky assailed the eye. Beneath him the white buildings with their red tiled roofs marched up the hills. Feeling like a king on his castle top he breathed deep and exhaled noisily. He was alone and it was a great day to be alive.

He reached the top of the straight drop and looked down at the over-turned Taurus thirty feet below. Lucky it hadn't hit the Rasta's cinder block bungalow with its tin roof. The tourist guides loved to tell their wealthy charges that the roofs were tin so that when the hurricanes tore them off, it was easy for the owner to chase them down, drag them back and nail them on. Ah well, as long as everyone was happy.

There were no skid marks, but that was possible. The tourist might have been drunk. He certainly was dead. The air bag had opened and the safety belt was on. However, the roof of the Ford had come up to meet his head; breaking his neck as the car had landed on its nose and flipped on its back while sliding down the yellow grass slope near the road.

Below, another police cruiser and a local tow truck were sizing up the problem so that the vehicle could be removed from the Rasta's property.

The Rasta had heard ' the mighty thunder' (Fran chuckled) but nothing else. The man was already dead when the Rasta had 'gone and looked right away'. The ex-Jamaican shook his dread locks, "Auta to cage dem tourists at night, mun!" was his contribution to the investigation.

There was no wallet. Fran figured the Rasta had it but finding it would take a search and he had no warrant. You couldn't bully the Rasta. They had already tried a little subtle pressure.

There was a business card though. The corpse belonged to James Sutton, late of The Bank of England.

The lack of skid marks, began to bother Fran.

On second thought, if Mr. Sutton had been going too fast, even over fifty, his trajectory would have cleared the road below and not stopped until he hit the harbour. No! too far. On the other hand, Sutton should have been able to stop at a slower speed.

Fran made a mental note to add these thoughts to his report and enjoyed the caress of the early morning Virgins wind.

7 AM, Tuesday Morning, Water World, Coki Point, US Virgin Islands.

The aqua blue ocean dazzled the eyes. Deep royal, edged in lesser blues, with its white outline, painted the distance between St. Thomas, St John, the Cays and Tortola. The view seemed to spread its glory for James Claten. Jimmy was young at sixty-five. He thanked God for every day he had to look at the sea and sky, to feel the wind, sun or hurricane. It was all the same to the transplanted North Carolinian.

'So Long Pier, was a port of call for local sailing yachts.
Today the owners were away and Jimmy was about to catch his lunch and supper too, maybe. He

chuckled. Reaching down with weathered black
hands he pick up the fishing rod and red Kmart
bait box, before slowly trudging to the end of the
pier.

He seated himself, shaded by a battered straw hat
and began to bait his hooks. Out of the corner of his
left eye he saw it. His face paled as he realized what
it was. The sharks had gotten the head. There were
terrible slash marks on the neck. Only an arm and
the torso bobbed by the pier support. He was first
clutched with terror but Jimmy had seen death at
Seoul and other less prominent places in Korea. His
first action was to search for sharks and was
rewarded by a gray flash only yards away. A big,
white-tipped dorsal cut the water then disappeared.
"Jefferson bring the hook, hurry Jefferson!" The
twenty-year-old who looked after the pier was
stacking gear in a shed at the far end of the dock
immediately grabbed the gaffe hook and ran to
Jimmy.

11:30 AM Sunday, London, England

The death was officially designated as an accident.
There was a short clip in the Daily News, the local

Virgins newspaper, with no name listed for the deceased. The police took fingerprints off the remaining hand and looked through their own files. Nothing!

The next step was to check in with CIA at Langley, DEA, NSA and the armed forces computers.

The CIA computer interfaced with Interpol and Interpol interfaced with the European military computers. Four days later there was a match. William Bailey, it seemed, was once of the Royal Lancs ,a British subject, and a past employee of Epsylon Computers. The remains were held over for transportation to the United Kingdom.

A report went to Epsylon of the accident. There seemed to be no next of kin. Epsylon already knew about the death. The Royal Army had noted the X-1 tag on the Bailey file and informed the Secret Service. Theodore Boothby - Staters or Granny Staters looked at the computer copy of the police report courtesy of the CIA. You could get a lot out of the Yanks if you were willing to help out.

Once again Granny marveled at the computerization of the world and its consequences.

Granny Staters was thirty-six but looked younger. He was lean and well muscled. Granny played tennis, golfed and worked out regularly. He did smoke, a filthy habit but one he could not break, nerves you see.

Granny lived in a four hundred year old farm house, one down from a manor, in Wendover on Run and commuted to London each day. As Director of Epsylon, his movements and disappearances were covered with his neighbours. He didn't talk much about work, company secrets you know, and only periodically had to fend off a chum's need to have his computer repaired. Granny knew only that computers worked and that was sufficient. Epsylon made a good profit on the gadgetry it produced, which in turn made its cover that much better.

China blue eyes ran down the limited details before him. His long elegant fingers removed a Players Filter from its packet and placed it into his fine linear mouth, then slid up the length of his pencil straight nose to scratch the bushy blond eyebrows. These in turn held up his short, broad forehead and meticulously styled blond hair. His most interesting feature was the chin, extending like a concrete buttress, making him look forceful and tough.

Bailey wasn't the name of course, it was Lacy, John Lacy. Not from the Lancs, the Cold Stream Guards actually but long ago and far away. John had a sister. Staters would have to call. The official notice of her brother's death would come from above but Granny had known John in Geneva. Thinking back, his wife knew the sister too. Went to the same school, he thought. Granny would have to ask Silvia when he went home. It would be infinitely easier if he went over with Sil. Of course opposition could be watching. But who?

Who would kill Lacy? His orders had placed Lacy in the British Virgins concerning what? I'll be damned, turtles. Some bloody Leather Backed turtles. The British Virgins were trying some sort of variation of the St. Johns 'scuba with the turtles' frolic for the greenies et al. However, underwater explosions were killing the endangered breed.

It seems the tourists could snorkel with the Leather Backs, the largest of the sea turtles. Some of the largest weighed as much as 1,200 lbs. A few of the turtles had migrated to Tortola, probably to get away from the bloody tourists. Someone in the Governor's office figured they could steal a march on St. Johns, where the Leather Backs lived a protected existence in a National Park. Here was an attraction that made money and was good for the environment. Of course dead turtles tend to clog up the works, so he had been asked to look into it because the problem might be in the American Virgins.

Lacy was due for a rest so Granny had given him two days on the islands. Well, longer if he could organize it, maybe a week before circumstances pulled the plug or well something else came up.

Maybe Lacy went out to frolic and ran into a shark or had a heart attack the shark finding him. Granny lit the Players and dragged deep. Leaning well back against the red leather of his chair he let the smoke drain slowly out of his lungs.

The scenario was wrong. Sharks very seldom attacked people, then usually just those on the surface. The flipping of the feet or any turbulence made them think the individual was in trouble. Blood in the water was the primary reason for an attack. There were very few reports of shark contacts around the islands or perhaps the local press kept it out to soothe the tourists. He would check but it was thin.

The CIA, for all its faults, wouldn't kill turtles or Lacy for that matter. There were the Russians of course, the old enemy. No! They had about as much interest in the British Virgin Islands as Brighten seaside hols would to the Royal Family.

Of course American nuclear submarines provisioned periodically at St. Thomas but that was common knowledge.

Breakleaf, the senior intelligence man for the Governor and the local service representative said there were no suspicious types on the island outside of the package tours. These seemed to provide only the usual family groups and holiday fun seekers. Certainly no explosions on or near the islands, although the turtles seemed worse for wear.

Lacy's first, and last, report, confirmed Breakleaf's input.

That old chill caused the hairs to prickle at the back of Granny's neck. Something was not right in paradise. Granny had to know what that something was. The question was who to send?

There was an audible squeak as his pedestal chair turned to allow Granny to look out on the drab court from his second story perch. Away from the traffic, a single oak tree centered his mini world, protected from the rest of the city by an almost hidden gateway. A small garden surrounded the oak, a colorful but dying foot warmer, even this late in October. Granny loved the court, it changed with the seasons but was seldom blemished with people. Like a Chinese garden it was serene to the outside world, IRA bombs and national cowpox.

Nothing changed in the court other then the small business owners.

His people kept close tabs on these intrusions. He was, through the tinted, armour plated window with its sound scramblers for the over curious, just another worker in another business. The modern oak trimmed office was the face, while behind it, packed into cubicles, the rest of the North American branch of Her Majesty's Secret Service plodded away.

Who would he send? There wasn't anyone, well, of course there was, Granny gave an audible sigh. 'If I take someone from something else.' He of course could go. Nothing like a week in the Virgins. He allowed himself a sarcastic smile, wouldn't they love that down at White Hall? Sir Mortimer would have a good laugh just before Granny was flayed alive.

The Queen was in Africa and that meant he had lost people to compensate elsewhere. Then, of course, there was the blow up in Brazil that had tied up more agents for how long, he couldn't tell. He turned to his computer and brought up the US file. The list was surprisingly short. No one wanted to be a spy anymore, that was the trouble. With the dear old Russians gone there was no major threat, everyone knew the drug lords were too big, the local toughs too small.

The brainer, who had come up with the plan to advertise postings for MI 6 in the London Times should be deballed and boiled in oil, in Grannies' opinion. Oh! From a marketing stand point, the concept was brilliant, international recognition, the story picked up in the media in every country in the world. Millions got the message the firm was ahead millions of pounds in free publicity, barring the Major Boris git who hacked into the Web site. It was flawless. Of course what it dragged up was something else. Granny remembered exhaustive months of vetting malingering, psychotic nuts. Bring me your eager masses ready to spy. Everyone from the elderly and disabled to witless and stupid. Granny had enough of that lot in his command for a start.

Oh they had found some good people but at what price? Only God and White Hall knew.

Nationalism was dead. The old glory of spying gone. There were no volunteers to go trudging on to the bitter end to save the flag and Queen. Patriotism was softer. University graduates went into business not the Service. The ex-military was still the best source of people but they looked the part and made poor operatives. No! Some local with a good business cover, who could leave at a moments notice that was the ticket. .

Granny picked up the golf ball, which sat on a small Egyptian obelisk, and handled the small white sphere. The ball was lucky. Stater's hole in one. A horrible shot that the wind had taken on the twelfth at Veering and deposited in the hole after a purely miraculous run across the green. Granny smiled as he remembered the crack of his number one Penick , 325 feet to the green, a bad shot gaining legs and the wind, with its height, just enough. His heart soared up with the shot over the roughs, a thing of beauty. The staggering moment when it went in. The elation! There are no words to define a hole in one. The pats on the back, drinks until drunk. What a day! What a day! Far too few of those now that he was lumbered here.

The ball reminded him of something else. What about the Virgins? Yes, Sidingham, a monster of a course on the northeastern tip of Tortola, very private, very plush, owned by William (Walley) Sidingham . Those who played Sidingham were not the average tourist. Japanese and US corporate types paid thousands of pounds to take on this man killer. The front nine were edged on the ocean and presented a fairly steady course but the back nine were created on islands and rocky outcrops that

were greened and defended by sand traps
that would swallow you up. Along with dumping
half your balls in the ocean and a wind that changed
like a whirligig, the Marquis De Sade eighteenth,
which was a blind dog leg and a good 800 feet,
could destroy any golfer. Finish under par and they
gave you the Victoria Cross.

The course was a Mecca, a Holy Grail to golfs'
challenge seekers and busy all year round. It had
two positives, one the owner was adamantly Queen
and country and two, the marketing of this gold
mine, which it didn't need, was done by one of his
couriers. One Michael D'Iverville McFurson , a
Canadian from Niagara Falls, Ontario.

Jolly O'! A small business man with a clean cover
and someone who at least knew the ground, if not a
great deal about field work.

Granny picked up the phone, deep in the bowels it
was answered.

"Listen get on to Scotland Yard and have them
check out the Lacy funeral, make sure there aren't
any watchers, also check his sisters house, just for a
few days. Send off a message to Dr. M. in Niagara
Falls ....

Chapter Two - 2:00 P.m., Monday, Niagara Falls, Ontario, Canada

Maple Leaves and Rum Punch

The E-mail chat box " Brit line" offers the caller the opportunity to leave a message for, or to interface with, other Brits. Discussions are about gardening, the weather, the horrible fall of everything British and so on. Among the little messages between grandmas and others, there are orders to various members of the American branch of the British Secret Service. Obviously in code and obviously changed regularly from chat line to chat line hidden by hundreds of other callers.

The message was longer then usual, I down loaded it and placed the printer sheet on my desk while I went over and got the white copy of Harold Lasiter's, Bonmon. The numbered sequence of words now had to be removed from the book and then vetted through a standard code chart.

Wonderful, McFurson was off to the Virgin Islands.

I hadn't seen old Sidingham for a while. Walley would want a new brochure in keeping with my cover and his deal with Granny. Just for the record, I'm a good marketer and Granny uses that ability periodically to get locations for my many trips. As a central courier I move a lot of things around.

Interestingly enough, the amount of computerization has made 'by hand' delivery of information a lot more popular. There are no real secrets in a world of computers, spy satellites and other technical gadgetry.

Lots to do. I would tell the wife I was off to Cleveland. No secrets, just I didn't want to worry her. I'd tell her about the Virgins on my return, as a needed side trip. The wife was always on about money and making sure that clients paid travel expenses. Travel and financing are standard with the Firm (Secret Service). With other customers I had already signed, travel expenses were required. Sometimes, however, I had to invest my own funds in business trips and that was when the fat hit the fire. We weren't wealthy. The house was middle class and needed work. Three kids, one almost in University cost lots and we didn't have much put aside. So she had the right to worry. I had lots of life insurance, on this job it was required. I didn't tell

her what I was worth straight out. She probably
would have bumped me off herself, the sweet old
thing.

I left my house, office with its computer and stacks
of paper. Out into a beautiful October day . The sun
had been kind this fall. The maple next door was
bright crimson. Our birch was well into its yellow
turnover. The air was crisp, smelling of leaves, the
moist earth and perhaps just a dab of the odor of the
Falls, although they were a fair distance away.
Niagara Falls has a unique metallic smell that seems
to extend from the mist as the water hits the rocks
hundreds of feet below. Less kind city residents
might suggest it was an excess of pollution in the
water.

I felt that stirring when something new and
exciting was about to take me away from the
mundane, that twinge up the spine, the slight worry
pang .

Being a spy does not make you superior. It just
makes you different. I drove the Civic over to the
local post office. Parking my Honda on Queen St.
our slowly deteriorating main drag. I entered the
neo-Victorian, Victorian building.

Box 104 opened. Inside, with some flyers and an
opportunity to lose money on a free trip to Florida,
was a simple brown envelope sent the day before
from Kitchener. I returned to the car and opened it.

The envelope contained 1,000 dollars in US currency, tickets on American Airlines to St. Thomas, in the US Virgin Islands and reservations for the Dolphins, a condominium come hotel near Coki Bay, the place where Bailey had been found. An alternate British Passport for a man named Phelps was there with my picture conveniently attached.

Tuesday dawned bright and early. I kissed the wife and packed the car. She commands me to take care of myself. The Honda carries me back to the QEW, in almost darkness.

The QEW is a major four lane highway which connects Toronto and the border at Buffalo, New York.

People looking into my little white car would see what? Well at forty-eight, a dark haired man with very little gray. A rounded face with kind brown eyes and a prominent nose. The mouth is slash like and gives the face toughness, perhaps experience helps here. The cheekbones are high, there is native blood in the family, these complement a prominent cleft chin.

Dressed in a Brooks Brothers' Gray suit (There is an outlet mall in Niagara Falls, New York. It was the last of a line and on sale), a white cotton shirt with a wine red tie designed with blue plumbs, blue wool socks and black Nunn & Bush loafers finished the design. The suit is a wool tropical weight and would be comfortable for the short time I wore it in the islands. My lined raincoat provides warmth but isn't intended for wear after the Toronto Airport. The end result is just about what it should be, a faceless business type.

St. Catharines passed away down the gray highway. Endless road construction continues to create an eight-lane Superway to support the increased traffic for our new casino in Niagara Falls.

The Burlington Skyway provides a spectacular view of Hamilton. Endless smoke mars the sky from the steel firms that crouch on the bay side with their many support industries. Then up through Burlington a lake view, green lawned, bedroom community. Oakville comes up next, another lakeside denizen. At one time the largest number of millionaires in Canada lived behind the immaculate gardens and mature trees.

Beyond the Oakville Place, a huge shopping mall which flanks the highway, comes the turn into Mississauga with its industrial parks and mobs of look a like houses. Now you are really in Metro Toronto, a huge city, which had been ordered by the Ontario Provincial Government to absorb its smaller neighbours. Four million people moved in its streets and were part of its evolution to an international megalith.

Dixie Mall looms up on the right. At 120 km it is passed and you sling into the cutoff for HWY 427. The sun is full up now but watery on the four lanes of asphalt to Pearson Airport at the western tip of the city.

The car is dropped off and a small bus takes travelers to beautiful Building One to wander about for a few minutes before the 7:15 flight. I find a United Cigar store and purchase the latest Time and MacCleans.

My hatred of planes and airports is undying but then flying is part of the job. The mob of travelers moves like a great ameba, parents telling children this is going to be fun, afraid it might not be or worse. Young lovers kiss in the open, unafraid and alive. Huge numbers of business types like myself, killing time, talking or sitting alone, absorbing lost moments, which will never come again. Herds of Chinese, Japanese, Indians all interacting at pace and together.

I wait 15 minutes before boarding and wander over to watch the jolly group that will share my cigar in the sky. Lots of West Indians, more business types, some Indians or expatriate Islander's of Indian extraction, one or two that look Arabic, little chance of someone grabbing the flight but you never know who you'll find on the plane. The individuals you have to look out for, are the ones whose air luggage arrives without the passenger. After all you don't want to be there for your own explosion.

I was also looking for something else and found it, a mother and baby. This is the most feared of problems for the passenger, especially loud annoying children on a four-hour flight. In my case it was perfect. Siting down I opened my magazine and smiled at the blond, blue eyed eighteen-month old sweet heart who, smiled back. Mummy was pleased someone had noticed.

"She's beautiful," I commented. Our conversation covered the child's age, the fact that they were also going to St. Thomas her husband worked at the

Coast Guard base, he was American. Her parents
lived in Mississauga and had just dropped her off.

Telling a little about myself, we listened for the
American Airline call. Linda, the twenty something
mummy, was through the metal detectors before I
followed .US Customs passed on me, we pre clear
in Canada to destinations in the US, open border
and all that.

No hidden guns and so forth? Well, yes for the so
forth but they wouldn't find it. Guns were
impossible to take on a plane and a dead giveaway.
The new plastic weapons were still a little less then
perfect.

As I expected, Mummy was given a wide birth by
the rest of the crowd. The flight was pretty full as I
slipped into the third isle seat. She smiled, happy
someone would talk to her and I grinned back. Her
soft blue eyes indicated a pleasant companion.

The baby, Cass, was enamored of the big man
beside her, great blue eyes looked up with a smile.
Smiling back and making an appropriate noise made
her giggle. Having three kids gives you all the tricks
of the trade. .

The 737 trundled down the taxi way and turned

into the runway .The pilot gunned the engines and the plane went straight up, hammering the occupants into their seats. He then circled out at thirty five thousand and headed to Miami. This let all of us breath and our ears pop.

Cass and I continued our passing friendship. Her mother who was at first a little nervous, was won over as we shared pictures of families. Mine were from various locations, certainly not my own children. Cass let me hold her in my lap and finally went to sleep on my chest.

Hell of a nice guy, aren't I? Well no! You see, if Mr. Lacy had been fed to the sharks, there would be someone waiting at the airport, on St. Thomas, to see who showed up.

If Linda needed help out to the taxi, it would give me a cover. The opposition, if it existed, would be looking for either a team or individual out to evaluate the problem. Linda's husband who worked at the Coast Guard Base would be unable to pick her up. Even if he had, a nice introduction to some locals, would do wonders to allay suspicion. The more cover I had, the better my chances.

The stop in Miami to change planes was mercifully short but allowed me to walk off three hours of sitting. Miami airport is depressing with its mobs of tourists corralled in holding areas until the plane left or until the bus came to transport them off to some discount package fun in the sun week. I stepped into the corridor leading to my plane and left the noise and crush behind.

Cass got a little upset on the second leg as we skimmed around Cuba and she cried. Mummy tried but no good. Carrying her up and down in the isle for a while finally made her sweet round face with its pug nose burrow into my jacket and with a contented burp, which stained my suit, she went to sleep. Linda was frantic. She would pay for my cleaning bill. No, that's OK. This was going far but then sometimes it's the small things that keep you alive.

One of three things were going to happen or perhaps had happened. One, the competition had left. That would make sense if they had tortured Lacy or, more humanely, given him a truth shot. They would know what he was and presume that there would be others. Two, the competition couldn't move or Lacy had died before he talked. The opposition would then depend on the fact that we didn't know much and that we wouldn't find out enough to trouble them before whatever was planned would happen. Three, Lacy had made a mistake and been eaten by sharks by accident. I don't think so Tim.

Who else would be blowing up turtles to start with? Treasure hunters, stupid ones, might to find a wreck or uncover it.

If the competition couldn't move, then I was in trouble, because as soon as he got close to anything they would cause me to have an accident.

The sea was so blue, the green of the four main islands that make up the Virgin group seemed dimmed by its majesty. Slowly St. Croix, St. John, St. Thomas and Tortula got larger with Puerto Rico, a ghost on our right wing only sixty miles away. Finally the airport offered itself and with a light bump the metal bird returned to earth having broken the laws of metal reality.

I helped Linda with her things, letting her carry Cassie, who made faces at me over her shoulder. My old brown briefcase with my lap top hidden inside in one hand, a diaper bag, general accessories and a make up bag in the other we set out.

The airport personnel smiled thinking we were married or at least attached.

While waiting for our bags we chatted and I looked around. There he was. If the Mona Lisa

described the beauty of woman, the smile, the
mystery that defined man's dream of the female
soul, this face did the same for death.

The slate gray eyes were checking out a thirties
executive. His evaluation was so obvious it
surprised me. The eyes were dead like the portholes
of a man who had been in prison too long, who had
lost the luster of life to the gray walls until they
were simply mechanical for vision. The face was
international, thinish, with a short military cropped
pepper salt hair cut. A short aggressive forehead fell
to fine eyebrows. The overview was a hard empty
expression on a lined, pinched road map face. A
broken nose and small tightlipped mouth set in a
grayish ash link skin. A slight dusting of tan said he
had been on the islands for a little while.

The frightening part of the apparition was his lynx
like positioning in the chair, as if with the absolute
minimum effort, death could be dealt.

The man was wearing a green and white striped
polo shirt, which exposed steel hard muscle on his
forearms. The hands were large and strong, stone
cutter's hands. The blue polyester pants made him
no local.

If this was the opposition, I was upset. Usually
watchers tend to be the low end of the line.
Certainly the hardest to spot. This was a first line

thug, a thinking animal, no games here, no subtlety and no mistakes. I cadged short looks at him as I got all the bags together, flagged a porter and directed Linda and Cassie out into the 85 degree heat. At the door I aimed my copper identification bracelet at Mona and pushed the small plunger. The camera hidden in the nametag had him.

Mental note, make sure that this man is checked out. He could be a marine on leave or just some tough passing through but he is far too interested in the passengers. His location in the lounge made it obvious he was a watcher. I scanned the rest of the airport building. It was small and no one else stood out. Maybe I was wrong but if he was here, tomorrow I would know.

The national taxi of the Caribbean is the 1985 Toyota Van. Looking like a little elephant, it stands in shimmering rows ready for the customers who exit into the tropical heat. Rule one, make sure yours has a working air-conditioner. Taxies do not leave without a bum in every seat, to wit full or over full and bodies that packed together tend to smell after a while. Luggage is packed in the trunk, on top or where ever.

One fast glimpse of Mona Horror and away. But just a moment, Horror nods. One of the black porters helps the young thirties executive that was being eyeballed inside, into a private cab. One of the porter's callused hands took the tip. The other pulled out a bright yellow handkerchief and wiped his face. The dusty blue Cavalier pulled out and followed the targeted exec. I placed my wrist against the window and snapped the license plate number

My, my, my! I sat in the van with Linda and listened to her small talk about rising taxes and the problems with the locals. Linda is a little afraid, two white men from South Carolina , were shot to death in their own driveway, by locals. Visit paradise then leave it or else. The limited number of jobs and a limited temper with whites are a bad combination. Especially in a place where guns are so plentiful. Of course the tourists were safe they need the money.

The Toyota left Cyril E. King Airport and turned right into Charlotte Amalie. I made sure we weren't followed. It was a short trip to the small bungalow where Linda and Cass got out. Everybody waved and I sat back into the comfort of the van for the tour of the city.

We trundled down back streets, watched as the children dressed in there blue school uniforms wandered home together. Only one or two white faces among the black throng but no fighting, just smiles. We stopped at two bed and breakfasts in the port then made out toward Red Hook by way of the cruise ship row beside Havensight Mall. A Princess, Carnival and the Diamond were in. Throngs of passengers scurried about the shopping pier cleverly built next to the landing for last minute gifts and souvenirs. The ships left early to be in St. Martin or where ever tomorrow.

'Tourists', an old Virgin man once told me, 'got three types of wealth. They got cash wealth , they got credit card wealth , they got traveler cheque wealth and they all come here to give it to me,' as he sold another T shirt. Yes, bring the wealth but go home, its too fine a place for you here, just a visit and home so you come again. Don't look too deep or you will see us so poor. Maybe you get just a little twinge of conscience around dinnertime.

Along the Red Hook Road finally through the town and out on to the South Bay road with stops at the Marriott and so forth. After what seemed like hours there was a small circular drive with a car park to the left through the palms. The large blue sign stated The Dolphins.

We drove around the wide lawn and the central fountain where three metal dolphins frolicking in beautiful multi shoots of water. The van finally stopped at the clean, modern front desk and foyer of the white stucco building.

The bellboy grabbed McFurson's heavy nylon bag and he was whisked into a huge silk gray room with television and pink flamingos marching across two queen size beds. Oh! Heaven! Mike paid the smiling young man and collapsed on the bed as he left.

Chapter Three - 3:42 P.m., Tuesday, Red Hook, The
Dolphins, St Thomas US Virgin Islands.

Broadening Travel

 I lay on the bed for about 15 minutes and breathed
the luxurious cool air-conditioning. A complete
stretch includes, the extenuation of the arms as far
as possible, while doing the same with the legs, so
that the majority of your body is off the bed. In fact
until you can hear the joints pop. This I did with a
pleasurable grunt of the same sort my father used to
make.
 Relaxed and at one with myself, I started a review
of earlier today. The opposition was going to be
tough and I was way out of my league. On the
benefit side they didn't know I was here, that was
positive. Further, my cover was excellent.
Tomorrow I would see Breakleaf and with a little
overnight computer magic have the situation more
in control.
 At least I knew what I was up against. While the
opposition was professional, it wasn't national pro.
More local thugs than people backed by a national
government.
 I finally got up, stripped and walked over to the
sliding door to peer out. I like being naked as my

body hasn't gone completely to seed or at least not in my estimation. Discretion being the better part of a lawsuit, I only looked through a crack in the drawn drapes.

The hotel was made in the form of a great half bow. Sliding doors from the rooms exited on to a concrete walkway. This was overhung by balconies and by a sky blue awning, which extended out over the sand. Cinderblock walls extended out to the water to provide complete security and privacy for the guests. Golden sand slid down a gentle slope to the sea. Paradise gives few invitations so I pulled on an orange Speedo boxer, grabbed my towel, slid back the door and walked out on the beach.

The wind blew in softly, allowing the 87 degree heat to balance perfectly .The water was even better, warm as a bathtub and about three feet deep. I swam out as far as possible, then back three or four times. Exhausted and happy I dragged my body back up on the beach. With this sun I couldn't stay out long without a sunscreen. So back to the room, rubbing myself down my towel.

I heard a bird like whistle, of some sort, not terribly tropical, to the right. While trying to figure out what that was, I noticed something move in my

room. Better check the room number to make sure
it was mine. A little embarrassing walking into
some else's place. No! It was my room.

Time to call security but not yet. I at least wanted
to see who the competition was. I stood by the door
and peered into the darker interior. It took a moment
for my eyes to focus to the light. There was a
movement, in the small sitting room at the entrance,
away from the beach door.

A girl, came into view about eighteen, short
perhaps 5'.1", but well built. I personally like a
good bum, she had that, as well as superb breasts.
Her blond hair was in a long pageboy. My intruder
had a pixie's face with high cheekbones and a full
mouth, the type that could create a stunning smile.

At present her hard blue eyes were evaluating
varied small items from my bag. A thief!

I hate thieves. I mean if you have to eat, that's one
thing but this one looked very well fed.
I slipped in, moved over to the wall and leaned on
the partition at the entrance of the room.

She sensed me, turned with a gasp and took two
steps back. Her small hands were at her sides. She
wasn't armed. The only thing she wore was a red
and white checkerboard bikini which covered just
enough.

"See anything you like" I motioned to the small pile of things she had accumulated on the bed.

"I was just looking. The door was open." Her voice was high and nerve twisted. The blond tensed her body and I noticed she had repositioned her feet. I look formidable at six feet, even with some extra weight. Also, I knew I had locked the door, hadn't I.

"Word is, the Charlotte Amelia jail isn't bad but back here who knows where they'd put you!"

"You're not going to call the cops?" she said her voice flat, middle American, as her eyes widened and the pixy face lost its colour. There was real fear now.

"I don't like thieves." I added a nasty twist to the last word.

She looked around quickly for an escape route. If she had run I would have let her. Then she stopped as if she had made up her mind about something.

"You like what you see, right?" Her voice went soft, more assured. Her right hand removed the string from the bikini top over her shoulder exposing a full breast. The nipple, I noted, was peach coloured. My body was reacting, as it should, badly.

The second breast came out.

"You like me don't you?" She said this more to reassure herself, then asking me. Her body tensed as she moved forward reaching out a hand to touch my naked chest. The bra was off. I calculated the position of the chair at my right.

"Take your pants off." My voice was harder then I expected and colder. She stopped, hesitated and then reached down to place a thumb under each string and dragged the little piece of cloth off her hips. A soft blond eye winked up at me from between her legs.   My next move was planned. Before she had her pants from around her knees I slid to the right and sat. At the same moment I caught her arm above the elbow and pulled her over my knee. This one she hadn't expected. She squealed and I brought my hand down on her bottom. Once, twice, three times, her hands stretched back to protect her derriere. That was fine with me, I simply grabbed them at the wrist and smacked her about four more times making her bum bounce the last two times. I then let her off.

Like a cat she didn't fall, being low to the ground came in handy. We confronted each other over five feet of carpet.

"You bastard she hissed, you mean shit, why did you do that?" Her hands rubbed the insulted part of her anatomy. My thief wasn't crying, but close to it. She wasn't giving me the satisfaction.

"I don't like thieves and I don't like being taken fo:
some drooling old half-wit who will do anything fo
a touch. You, on the other hand, are lucky that's all
did. The next guy you run into may not be as simple
to deal with. I won't call the police. You're way too
young to go to jail and too intelligent for this scam.
Maybe you'll remember this next time. Now put
your pants on and get out.

"Yes Daddy!" she snarled, grabbed her bikini, was
in it and out the door in seconds, "Keep your filthy
hands to yourself." Was shouted over her shoulder.

I locked the door, looked over the important stuff
which all seemed to be there. It was then I lay on the
bed.

I half expected the police to show up. No one
showed. After a few minutes I stopped breathing
like an old horse.

Sitting on the bed I evaluated the whole thing and
made a simple but concise analysis.
I couldn't be this stupid. The assault laws on this
island must be dillies. I got the idea, I wouldn't hear
from the authorities.

The second part of this interaction had been my
tremendous sexual response. After 21 years of
marriage without ever breaking the rules. This was
the closest to having sex with someone other then
my wife. The physical nudity of the girl, her curved

body, ripe breasts, the smell of Tropic Tan and soft perfume, the muted smell of her private parts caused my body to lock into place. I went into the shower, turned on the cold to maximum and paid for my sins until I couldn't remember why I was there.

Staggering from the bathroom I rubbed myself with a towel to warm up and cursed the air-conditioning.

A pair of light brown shorts, an H&S open necked white shirt and out into the warm dusk. I had made a request for change of room my things had moved 18 doors down the hall and were locked up. The in room vault wasn't much but it might be a little hard for amateurs.

The Dolphins tail was the hotel's restaurant at the right end of the bow. The restaurant was fashioned as a fish's tail. The fins separated to create the restaurant and bar, made up of palm enclosures overlooking the ocean.

That night, enjoying the view were oldsters and a lot of boomers like myself.

I sat by myself and started with stuffed blue crab, followed by sailfish steak with a nippy white island sauce, veggies du jour and some pasta concoction, which was very good. My allotment of one glass of the house white wine came and was enjoyed. I don't eat desert unless I really want to go over the line. High blood pressure requires constant watch on the food input.

While eating, I looked over the Virgin Islands Daily News. The paper had been acquired from a small table at the entrance to the restaurant. It was almost a week old but the only one available so I plowed through. Eating alone is the pits but at least reading covers the time.

Story one, the kids were back in school and the new metal detectors seemed to be working well. Lord! There was an underside to paradise.

On page eight I made the acquaintance of a certain Mr. Sutton of the Bank of England. Compacted between a short but sterling depiction of a family machete fight and an ad for Pepsi. I checked the date and made a note. Mr. Sutton had conveniently died on the same day as Mr. Lacy.

I finished my food and paid, just as my little blond friend came in for dinner looking pretty in a pink tube dress. She went crimson and I went into the bar. So she actually was staying here.

The barman was Jacob, a talkative sort from Bermuda.

"Tell me my fine friend, do you know what a Blue Hawaiian is?"

"I'll bite man", Said Jacob.

"Water,' with a little lemon in it. Keep it coming," I passed him twenty dollars. I now looked like I was drinking, without the nasty side effects.

"No problem mon "

" I like bars and the music,' I said, just as the Toppers, a threesome of Caribbean steel drums, guitar and base started 'Yellow Bird', on the bar's small stage. 'On the other hand I got high blood pressure you see." Jacob listened with one ear as he cleaned up behind the bar said.

"Sure". Not really caring one way or another.

"So this is good, 'I indicated the band,' but where's the real people?"

Jacob smiled.

"A man who likes to jump. In Red Hook there is 'HI's', a little further on there is 'Temptation,' lots of dancin. Women if you're high blood pressure isn't too high " Jacob suggested.

" I like to dance but I been married a long time and want it to stay that way."

"You have a good time dere." He smiled

"Lots of oldsters here." I indicated the couples at dinner.

" Yes, most of dem own the condos on the second floor.' Jacob said ' The younger ones are looking, extra rooms rented out to travelers like you, till they all sold." There was only Jacob, an elderly couple and myself were populating the bar.

"The little blond girl doesn't look like a traveler". I said. Indicating my thief at her table working hard at ignoring me.

"Miss Cindy! No! Too many people at The Reef, dey all full up, sent her and her girl friends down here yesterday, She from Ohio."

"Pretty girl."

"A little short but dat a matter of choice." Jacob confided.

"Cindy Lou Who, from Ohio?" I said thinking out loud.

"Cindy Connors.' Jacob corrected, 'How is your high blood pressure, man?" I joined him in a chuckle.

"Fine, just enjoying the view."

At that point something happened that you remember. Beautiful women are not
unique, there are quite a few. Really beautiful women, say the top15%, are special. They transcend the daily in thing; they also transcend Playboy's best photo upgrade. They are purely beautiful in themselves and don't require additions.

The vision only lasts so long. Those are the rules in this world but for that moment it is like a flower at its pique. They should be photographed for posterity.

This fox was not a brunet, her hair was pure jet black with white almost marble skin, which was lit by a flush of scarlet, very Irish. Her face was almost perfectly proportioned only a slightly upturned nose effected the picture. Violet eyes caressed you with their gaze. A sensual mouth carried blood red lipstick well. She walked with poise, a real lady . Her demeanor spoke of the best schools. Long and full legs seemed to make her
flow across the floor. Her waist was thin and petite. She walked across to the bar and presented her best aspect to Jacob. Some women have large breasts and some have good breasts. This lady had a great full bodice, that filled the top of her low cut gossamer white frock, to perfection. It was satin and clung to her but not enough to make one suspect she was a lady of the evening.

She smiled at Jacob. A soft fresh voice said, 'Planters Punch please."

'Yes Madam," Jacob fawned.

I noted she even sat with poise, her back straight und perfect. From her long raven hair that hung in a

halo about that angelic face, to the slightly tanned
pedicured feet, in light deerskin coloured sandals,
she was without fault.

"Well, this is a lively place," she said to Jacob.

"It starts to jump later," he assured.

"I was told this was one of the places you could
have a good time and this is going to be a week of
good times." It was obvious that Jacob would have
given her a good time without reservation. He mig
have a chance, I thought. Maybe that was the ladie
preference.

It was then she turned to me and smiled

'Lord, this is your day for trials' of the soul, isn't
it?' I said to myself.

" Hello!" she said conversationally.

" I am sure you've heard this before but you are th
most beautiful woman I have ever had the audacity
to look at." I raised my glass of water and bitters in
salute.

"Well, thank you." the voice was New York but
where? I wasn't sure. She seemed to weigh the
compliment a moment, found it acceptable and
smiled with more warmth.

"You know!' I continued, 'I read some where that
beautiful people waste hundreds of hours over a

lifetime thanking other people for compliments. Hope I'm forgiven? ' she nodded with a smile, 'Do you ever get bored with being beautiful? "I asked, then caught myself, 'I mean the side bar stuff, not the actual fact."

"You know it's not a bad question but I never thought too much about it."' She actually seemed to consider the question then smiled again. 'No! Also I am not always like this. First thing in the morning you probably couldn't figure out what it was you were looking at."

"Madame, you could be spectacular in a gunny sack."

"Are they in? I' ll have to get one." We both laughed and it felt good. .

"Oh, my name is Mike McFurson."

"Well, Mike my name is Saundra Winter." I offered my hand and we clasped. Her skin was soft but there was strength hidden there.

"You've got to be Canadian?" That one got me. "Oh?"

"Only Canadians and Englishmen shake hands."

"Got me, eh'!" She smiled pleased with her guess;

"Also you don't have an accent."

"My turn." Her eyes came up but there was less play in them.

"New York but the city or Long Island or maybe Washington?

"New York, you're right! I'm a stockbroker." No!
my mind screamed, I don't think so.

"What do you do?" She asked.

"Oh marketing. " I said off handedly,

"Here! Where can I sign on?"

"Well no, just once in a while, on an as needed
basis. It's nice though. Two days down and back,
maybe three if I'm lucky."

"So you know the place. What should I do to have
a good time?" The proper answer, of course, was
come with me and I'll take you around the island
and if someone didn't beat me to the punch and you
bless me with your favour we can make carnal,
animal, love, naked in the air-conditioning. What I
said was.

"Well, Coral World is nice, it's just up the road
.The parrots are beautiful and there are interesting
things to see through the underwater observation
station. The submarine reef tours are good but
expensive. If you're into history, the Danes built
Fort Christian in 1682, I think? If you're looking
into a fun time, I'm informed on very good
authority, "I nodded at Jacob. 'HI's and Temptation
in Red Hook are good."

"I'd offer to show you around but I have to work
and I've been married for a long time."

That caught her. Very few people would give up
what I had just given up. She didn't look for my

ring, knowing it was there. Her smile disappeared she was seldom refused but it came back just a moment later, after she considered the matter.

"OK!" She said leaving the Planters Punch unfinished.

She paid with a credit card and got up to leave, thanking Jacob. Then turned to me.

"A truly proficient man does not make love to a different beautiful women every night. He satisfies one woman for a lifetime. "

"Thank you." I said

"That wasn't a compliment, just a statement. I don't know how proficient you are." She turned on her heel and left.

"Man, If you don't mind me saying so. I would have given up my priest clothes for that." condemned Jacob.

"This is my day for stupid, Jacob. Tell you what give me a bottle of Baileys Irish Cream."

"Sure, Jacob left for the back room for a full bottle. I leaned over and disengaged the winder on my watch and extended the wire that follow it over to the credit card machine, which Jacob had slid Saundra's card through and attached its magnetic head to the computerized cash register's side. I then pushed two of the metal elevations around the face of my watch. A small green light showed under the date box on its face and I had the credit card numbers that had been sent through in the past ten minutes. With a quick look around I removed the attachment and let it retract.

On Jacob's return, I paid cash for the bottle in US dollars and made my way to the front desk.

The night manager was friendly. I mentioned that I heard there was a Connors here from Cleveland and I wondered if I knew them. No one from Cleveland the party was from Findlay Ohio. Thanks, wrong town.

The new room looked back at me with depressingly bright comfort, as if inquiring in a mocking manner, if I'd be alone tonight.

Tapping away on my laptop, the film was transferred from my wristband camera into the scanner, which was a special attachment to the computer. The information concerning my meetings of the day including Cindy Lou and Saundra followed in a short E-mail format message to Brit line.

Overnight at Epsylon, Granny's minions would sift the information and send the results to Harry Breakleaf. By tomorrow at Harry's small bungalow we would have answers and maybe some direction on this case. As I changed for bed, donning conservative gray Sears pajamas with burgundy trim.

Certain things were clear. One, Lacy was killed. I knew it. Why was the question? What, was being hidden by the killing? I had no idea. Two beautiful women in a day were two too many from the standpoint of this situation. Just, too easy and too simple. Saundra was more then what she seemed. Maybe she liked slumming but well, we would see. Downing my high blood pressure pill, I went to sleep.

Chapter Four - 8:35 A.m., The Dolphins near Red
Hook, US Virgin Islands.

Meetings

The phone broke up a sweet dream of legs, arms
and sex. A pleasant wake up call to paradise
followed. At least sunlight shone in. I walked to the
window and figured the trip to Tortola would be
reasonably risk free. The sea was almost flat.

Dressed in khaki pants and a white polo shirt I
went down to the restaurant and ate two sunny side
up eggs and bacon. Tea and plenty of toast heaped
with the local Marmalade followed. To hell with my
high blood pressure.

I then sauntered out to the rented VW Golf,
removed my Panama Jack straw hat and drove down
to Charlotte Amalie's hydrofoil dock for passage to
British Territory.

Purchasing my ticket I was reasonably sure there
were no followers, having toured around the various
streets or gades, as the old Danish owners had called
them.

We waited for the hydrofoil to lift off, there was a
delay, as there had been a breakdown. Requests for
times of departure were met with Caribbean smiles

somewhat malicious in nature. 'Don't worry man, soon come.' sort of tropics vernacular. Being a seasoned traveler you expect this sort of thing.

Finally, with a roar, we rose majestically up to glide over the ocean, for the one-hour tour to Road Town in the British Virgins.

This is a magnificent trip. As you pass St. Johns, the sky is a flawless robin's egg blue. Flying fish jump in schools, frightened by your passing over an azure sea. Finally, after a stop at West End you slant out into the sea then slowly slide to port until you dock at Road Town. The sky was pure blue and the waves small. In my Navy days this would have been a milk run. I watched the puffs of cloud rain in fifty-foot diameter patches, immediately beneath themselves while the sun shone down with disregard.

The total population of the British Virgin Islands is about 17,000. Road Town houses almost seven thousand of them. The town is full of traffic, a huge volume for a Caribbean city. An old Renault Taxi took me toward the Airport at East End and finally pulled off before a three storey Tudor structure that is Sidingham's Clubhouse.

I paid the driver and walked up the steps to the main entrance. Rudy the porter, come desk operations person, smiled in recognition.

"He's in his office.' he motioned to the stairs and I mounted them with a thanks. The interior was in British Racing Green and polished Oak. Shields had been mounted on one wall to show the golf names who had played here. Each was captured in oil and had two clubs presented below like a trophy from some dead warrior..

I felt that I might be in King Arthur's Court if Bing Crosby showed up. The fifty-ounce carpet was like walking on air. At the second floor before me, out a great bay window, was pictured a good part of the eighteen perfect greens, which comprised the course, with the sea as a backdrop. This was a golfer's dream in reality. After a moment, I went through a door, which might have hidden the cleaning supplies.

Ester's office was immaculate and simple with only a single display of children's pictures on her desk, all away at university or now living in England. She smiled her sixties something smile and amiably passed me into the royal presence.

Walley Sidingham was a self made man and has no time for small talk .His walrus like crimson face rears up and fixes on me with distemper or distaste

"I need this brochure for the Australian market in three weeks." Diamond-hard blue eyes stared out aggressively from under shaggy, red rust eyebrows over a vent-like nose and a huge walrus mustache that covered most of his fat face.

"Good Morning Walley" I smiled

"You may think so now."

Two hours followed in which we discussed and fought over the market share. Evaluated target market segments and what might be said in the copy to achieve Walley's goals.

At the end I asked to use one of the club's cars. Walley grunted that there was a mini just behind the kitchen and provided the keys. Walley felt I was somewhat less then de riggure, as I was not a line agent.

I went through the complex and came out at the back exit next to a light blue mini. It fired first time. I drove along toward Road Town then pulled off and watched to see who might pass. Never be sure of anything. I went further down the road and stopped a second time, with same result. Nothing! I had placed a computerized scrambler in the car and on my person before leaving. If my visitor left any small transmitters in my personal belongings they would be nullified.

Finally, I slid off the main road and by a circular route into the front yard of Harry's tan bungalow with its view of the ocean cooled by the continuous cleansing winds of the islands. Overhung by huge trees for shade, completely surrounded by flowering plants, the place smelled sweet and reflected a comfort of living that is seldom found. At this moment it seemed like the last homely house.

I wandered up to the front door of the screened porch

"Lovely day." I said remembering the phrase of the day.

"Yes!' said Harry, "If we don't have thunder." We of the Service will not give up these little word of the day games. Why? God knows. "But that still might not mean rain." I finished.

. He unlimbered himself from the chair in his slow easy way and opened the door offering his paw, which I took. The grasp was firm, strength and personal humanity were conveyed. I would trust my life to Harry Breakleaf without a second thought.

"Come in." Harry led me into a little bit of Empire, which had survived somehow. Harry was an officer with the Gurkhas and a number of other regiments. Souvenirs covered the walls. Pictures of men in uniform from different parts of a lost Empire. Given the teak walls you could be in a Malaysian officer's lounge. One expected a twan servant to come in and provide a drink. However, Harry would have Kim, his personal valet, in Road Town for the day.

I inserted myself in an over padded rattan chair and accepted an ice tea from Harry, who sat opposite with a pile of papers.

Harry was about forty-one and built like a truck. He had powerful arms, legs and a large head covered with well-cut thick black hair. His face could have been chiseled from a rough red rock. Pleasant, analytical brown eyes peered out from under bushy black brows. The nose was hawk-like and the black brush mustache covered his upper lip like a carpet. He had a large centered mouth, which held a pipe at all times. Harry was a soldier and a man, tough, skilled but intelligent and flexible in thought.

I enjoyed our conversations but today wasn't going to be fun.

"So what have we got?" I started.

"All of it" Harry checked a pile of papers to make sure.

"Good let's get started. They killed Lacy!"

"The question of course is they, who?" added Harry

"Mona Horror and company." My anger showed.

"What?" Harry queried, lost for the moment"

"The guy from the photo, the one that looks like they just dug him back up."

"That could have been a stakeout for drugs". Harry removed the enlarged picture of Mona and placed it on the table before me.

"What a beaut,' I scanned the picture, ' Do we know who he is?" I indicated Mona's bloodless face.

"No. But he's obviously military." Harry speculated

"Yeah!' he hates those clothes. Rather be out in the bush leading a squad. He's a merc or I'm Gumby."

"Gumby?" Harry questioned again.

"Kids show up in Canada, sorry."

"He's not a pro, he may be good at combat but no ability in spying'. Harry suggested, 'Far too obvious.' Harry continued, 'By the way sent one of my men over to pick up some things at the USVI airport this morning our friends were still there but packed up around lunch."

"Same deal, yellow handkerchief and so on?" I queried

"Yes!"

"What about the license plate? "

"Ah, yes, very interesting." Harry fished a second paper out and covered Mona for the moment. 'A David Peterson owns the car. He works for the Deville Brigade.

Maxwell Deville came down here five or six generations ago and made lots of money from sugar. The family was from Alabama. Southern leanings. The present owner, a grand nephew, can't make money from sugar. Most of the land is too far from the sea for development. So he rents out the two properties, one on TU-TU Bay and the other on the other side of the island to various militias. Sort of KKK Caribbean.

The chaps come down from the States with Mum and the kids, do some tactical stuff and have a good time while supporting the cause. The Deville Brigade are the local territorials."

"Package Hate Tours, just when you thought you've seen it all." I finished my iced tea.

"What we have here isn't militias. Not on this scale, Mona Horror isn't militia not in a million years."

"I quite agree,' said Harry, so I made a call to a realtor friend who told me the present renter at TU TU Bay is a company called Darius Corporation. They're based in Dallas. Legal, I would suspect."

"Is Darius still running people through the courses and do they use live ammunition?" I asked.

"About thirty men each week for the last two

months. No families. As to ammunition, they have a lot of noisemakers, blanks and thunderflashes. Only live ammunition for target practice. But who knows what could be brought in by boat."

"So what we have is 300 armed mercs, well trained for something. Something that they will kill for! Maybe they're going to take over St Thomas." I offered.

"Not a chance Old Thing. The Yanks would do them over in five minutes. They keep a close eye on that place. Anyway, the men were rotated out just like the militias. I am sure we could get names and so on but I'll wager they don't exist. A lot of Smiths and Jones and so forth"

"OK, so whatever is going to happen, it isn't going to happen here or maybe only part of it is." I conceded. 'How about Cindy Lou?

"You mean the Conners Girl. Did you actually spank her bare bottom?"

"Yes, full Monty."

"I say, I'd be willing to give a good word at the trial"

"Great, with a reference from you I'll have free room and board for the next forty years just on principal.' We both laughed, I continued, 'At forty eight you get a little touchy about being set up as some toothless old git, who's so sex starved he will jump through hoops for a bit. Also, she was lining me up for a knee in the goolies. What am I going to do, punch her in the teeth? Have a two-hour parley with the police? Mind you, her fingerprints were all over the place, but we could be having sex. She would be out before I finished the report.' I said in frustration, 'The local constabulary might get the idea to toss my stuff as well. Wouldn't that be fun? Anyway it worked."

"Granny is not pleased." Harry stated with emphasis.

"Jeez, my heart bleeds. Don't worry, this is the first time in fifteen years I spanked anyone. I think he's OK."

"The Conners girl comes from Findlay, Ohio works for a tire company, as a clerk. She seems real enough". Harry examined another paper.

"What about Saundra?"

"Ms. Winter isn't Ms. Winter. Her credit card says Carma Dietra - Fitzgiven, Washington. Ms. Dietra is a licensed
Lobbyist. By the way, that is confirmed, she didn't steal the card.

"Who does she work for?" I asked.

"Varies, Central African countries, some large

corporations U.S. and European and some Middle East."

"Middle east!" That didn't sound good.

"Nothing specific, maybe she is slumming. Some men get scared by big offices and titles. Also Lobbyists have a bad reputation." suggested Harry.

"Wonderful! That is just magic. She changes her name to slum. I wonder if Darius Inc. is one of those companies she represents?"
Harry made a note.

"How about these explosions?" I asked

"They stopped right after Lacy died. No more dead turtles." Harry shrugged.

"Alright let's play 'what if'. The turtles eat something that you can find near or in TuTu Bay. Mona Horror and his lot are blowing up something. Lacy finds out or maybe he calls local Government to see who makes explosions and they follow it back to him. They are really sensitive and get the wind up, exit Lacy. You have a picture of the corpse?"
Harry placed a black and white horror story on the table. I looked at it and felt like throwing up.

"Sharks didn't do in Mr. Lacy unless they have serrated teeth. Look at the slash marks."

"By God! You might be right." Harry half agreed.

"Next there is this" I handed Harry the local newspaper with the short note on Mr. Sutton. "What is Threadneedle street doing here and why?"

"Sutton was certainly part of their security group, poor sod.' There was real emotion in Harry's voice. 'He was visiting his father who has cancer. The old chap lives in Charlotte. There is no association with us or anything else, what so ever, I checked. " Harry was really upset, which wasn't Harry.

"Wrong! I bet you any money you want to name, Sutton had an accident because they were afraid he might know something. "

"That is a little stiff." said Harry

"I wonder if banks have anything to do with this? No! that's a mugs game." I considered more to myself then Harry.

"My turn." Harry changed position in the chair "Shoot!"

"The only real clue we have is that the Brigade is involved. The mansion on Tu Tu Bay is a possible location for Lacy to enter the water. It is possible that our, friends at the airport might be FBI or DEA for that matter, remember Ruby Ridge, they don't want trouble with the militias."

"Harry, if they pulled that crap on the FBI down here they'd be hanging by their balls."

"It could be drugs," said Harry.

"Yes I'll go for that but why be there for two days, probably more. Not drugs. The cartels work differently to average thugs.

This is financed. If this Darius outfit has money and it should, then it could be setting up a takeover some African country. Maybe one of the other islands, for mineral rights or something. Also the Corporate name sounds familiar."

"There are the emerald mines." Harry said helpfully.

"Oh yea! I'd like to see them go for the Colombians and God bless. That would take care of our problem real quick." I said knowing our South American friends.

"Look, Harry, I don't give a damn what it is. Lacy died for it, Sutton died for it and they were our people. That is the point."

"What will the plan of operations be?" Harry filled his pipe and lit it; Dutch amphora filled .the room.

"Well, we could get the Yanks to search the place, but I get the idea whatever there was to find is gone or very well hidden. We don't know what we're looking for.

A second move would be to send a diver or a team into the Bay. Infiltrate the place.

The answer is at TU TU Bay and we have to move soon. I figure probably by the weekend if they hold to schedule. ".

"At least they don't know about you." offered Harry.

"What about our Carma. Nothing that good throws herself at a forty eight year old guy with a gut" I said.

"You may not have noticed, Old Boy but you were all there was" Harry's sarcasm was not appreciated even if it was true.

"I kept throwing barriers and she kept coming, I'm not that hot."

"Some women want what is not on the market." Harry suggested.

"Alright I'll accept that, no one knows where I am or who I am. If not, I think the cover is too good for them to move against me unless they're sure."

"Action to be taken, eh! The Darius connection, what kind of money, where does it come from, if our friend Carma is tied in'. Harry summarized.

"I'll go swimming on Friday night if I have to but I'll want some back up. I'm way out of shape." I said Harry nodded.

"One of our Marines, Rutledge, has taken the SAS training".

"Tonight and tomorrow I'll try to get into the place standing up".

"How will you do that? If I might ask?" Harry cocked a eyebrow.

"Would your realtor friend help me to find some spots for a swimsuit photo shoot?"

"Yes, I think so." Harry agreed, ' but he won't know why and he'll be deep in it."

"Alright, some locations then and I need a gun".

"A gun, are you sure?" Harry looked worried.

" A little too much competition, old buddy."

Harry went over to a teak cabinet and removed a Webley Scott .44. This cannon was unwrapped like an artifact, which it was and handed over.

"That, Old Fellow, 'Harry pointed at the circa 1915 revolver with the six inch barrel, 'will stop anything you shoot at."

"It will work out great if I have to go over the top."

"The revolver has been rebored' Harry ignored my sarcasm,' it fires a Black Knight cartridge. One of those fellows will go through kevilar like butter".

"Great! Thanks Harry."

"Not to worry old boy. Whiskey?" We drank our Seagram's VO silently, looked out his front window, watching the sun bake the small cays on the horizon in silence."

Chapter five -12:32 P.m., Sidingham's Golf Course, Tortola, British Virgin Islands

Rest And Relaxation With A Twist.

The Mini burbled up to the back entrance of the club. I entered through the kitchens taking an apple from one of the dishes. This I munched down sucking the sweet juice. By the time I had reached the front entrance the remains of my lunch were deposited in the trash and I was ready.

Walley met me at the top of the stairs, waddling in from the Bar, which was on the seaside of the club. Walley knew where everyone was on his property instinctively, a neat trick. Behind my host were three Middle Eastern types.

The central character, dressed in a pink T-shirt and white designer slacks was a fine boned man with a creamy coloured skin. Bright eyes evaluated McFurson like a CAT scan. The face was small with almost feminine features. The nose was a slight bump and extended above a large wide slash mouth that smiled through a well trimmed beard. The smile was almost constant, like that of a good used car salesman and about as genuine.

"Got everything you need then?" inquired Walley

"Yes all set, I'll have the material to you in a week."

"Good, Oh, by the by, I'd like you to meet Mohammed Tisani.

I offered my hand and got an aggressive shake. The hand, while moist, was firm and betrayed no softness in the owner. I was not introduced to the two gorillas that offered shade for their leader.

"Mohammed would like to start up a couple of courses in the Middle East and thought you might help out flogging them. Well, I have to be away". Walley curtly made his leave.

"I was impressed with the literature you did for Walley and I felt it might be a good investment in time to speak to you." Opined Mohammed.

A good investment, hum, now here was a real business type.

"Where have you decided to put in these courses?"

We moved over to a comfortable set of deck furniture with a huge blue umbrella and sat down. The brain trust moved away a little and made like statues.

"Kuwait, perhaps in the Emirates" Mohammed confided in a soft and pleasant voice as if it really didn't matter. Lots of money here or a front that said it.

" So you're not in construction as of now?"

Always qualify the customer.

" No! Not as yet but within a few months.'
Mohammed made one of those 'as Allah gives'
hand movements, palms up.

That could mean anything from three days to the
shifting sands would turn to gold before one hand
was put to the project. I decided to play along. I
smelled something else like a test. It might be
important to pass.

"Of course you'll want to have a huge amount of
water or access to it". I didn't think money was a
problem.

" No water, no grass, no course. 'He nodded in
agreement 'I would suggest a name design course. It
draws a larger international market."'

"Please?" he interrupted, and I elaborated.

"A designer course, is designed by a name, Palmer
or someone with a rep." I continued and he nodded
his understanding.

"A Tiger Woods designed eighteen hole for
instance, would be a real draw but I don't know if he
would do it. Then there is the money to pay his fee.
There are a lot of other good golfers and some better
at developing your kind of course. Given the
location is right. The question, is will your
production be western or based on the rules of
Allah? Can women play? Will there be booze and
so on. If there are too many controls placed on the

final product you can harm its international usage
but it would be fine for local players." I looked
beyond Mohammed's head and watched a squadron
of pelicans against a clear blue-sky motor out to sea
in search of fish.

Mohammed seemed to be a little more impressed
and perhaps a little deflated, as if he was expecting
a less knowledgeable response, why?

"You seem to have a wide information base. A
man of many talents. Some less visible than others".
Mohammed asked.

"I'm just a marketer. I'm good at it but that is all."

"But to make those decisions with so little ground
work you haven't worked in the Middle East?" He
prodded

"Anyone can get background right off the Internet,
if you know how." I continued to smile but this was
going somewhere." I know about the businesses I
handle."

"You represent specifically British interests?" He
smiled it was darker now and cold.

"I'll represent you or anyone else who has the
money and the flexibility of mind to listen." It was a
statement and the truth. When the customer started
to control the game they didn't need you and I was
no 'yes man'.

"I still believe, you must become depressed

representing the old empire like this." He motioned around like the B.V.I. was a garbage dump." A poorly organized part of a non-existent Raj. I find it surprising. " This was a declaration of war without saying so. Mohammed wanted some kind of personal reaction, 'How dare you speak that way of the Empire?' Or was he just anti British? If so why was he here? Why me if I am too concerned with the old stiff upper lip?

"Walley has money and he listens. He fits the criteria" I said smiling. I changed the subject

"You of course are staying here?" I fanned my hand at Walley's Castle.

" No!' Tisani said, 'as if I might have insulted him, 'on the U.S.V.I.' That was interesting. Lots of hate there. I wondered if I should try just one little jab.

"TU TU Bay.' I paused, while picking up my brief case,' is beautiful.' I finished," Tisani's face went blank, then white for a moment. . I continued as if nothing had happened. 'I'm up the other side of Red Hook. Walley makes more on one of these digs in a night, then I make in a year. So he has me set up over there with some friend of his. There are many spectacular places though."

"Yes, the Island offers many interesting things." He eyed me like something he had not expected to find having kicked over my rock.

"Well gentlemen I have a photo shoot to set up." I gave him my card and advised he get in touch with me about six months before construction began on his courses.

He thanked me and became much more personable. Maybe he was just looking for the old boy network, which favoured the British and sometimes didn't produce the best end results.

One of the club limos was picking up people in Road Town so I hitched a ride, just in time to catch the afternoon Hydrofoil back to St. Thomas.

I needed to think and the trip provided the time. Mohammed was either peeved that I would insult him by placing him in a poor part of St. Thomas or I had got to him. If you play what if, he had come over to check out the bumbling British spy in person.

Some men crave danger and this was a dare that Tisani couldn't refuse. To laugh in the face of the enemy. My paranoia could be getting the better of me. At least my cover had held. I had given him the right answers, no bull wash and he knew it.

Either it meant nothing or I had a real lead. Would he own Darius?

I watched Frenchman's Cay come up on our

portside and pass away.

This afternoon I was going to do some touristing. First, because I deserved it and secondly, because I could do very little right now to change the situation.

Having deposited my brief case with its antique artillery piece in my car. Customs passed me through as I expected. I spent an hour shopping for little things in the warren of side streets that make up the tourist downtown core of Charlotte Amalie. I wandered down Post Office Alley, Hibiscus Alley and Drake's Passage. Most of these were cut off as dead end streets and allowed me to wonder through caves of stores with a huge variety of products. I pick up a small Emerald pendent for the princess and a nice bottle of Red Door for the wife. A brightly coloured toy steel drum from Antigua, made out of the bottom of a large coffee tin, for the middle one who was a musician.

The eldest got a watch for Christmas. I wondered how I was going to get it all back given the customs duty but I would worry about that later. For a moment the stone walled town still reverberated with the songs of the buccaneers who had walked these same cobblestones. Those good old boys would have a field day if they came back now.

I then went to the rental agency and with a minimum of difficulty, upgraded my Golf to a Mercedes. Presentation is everything when you want to get into different places to set up a shoot. I would pick the car up tomorrow. Tonight the VW would do much better.

The Golf hummed along the highway to the Dolphins I was left with a few precious hours before dinner and an evening of very pleasant but dangerous work, to enjoy the beach.

My little patch of sea by the sand was about the same. A few older couples lay out in the sun or swam. There were no kids. I love children but every once and a while you could do without their joyous voices.

I found three small palms and set up under the shade with a thick towel to lay out on and a half chair to support my back. I tilted my Panama Jack over my eyes and stretched luxuriously allowing the heat and breeze to take turns messaging my body. After a while I would swim and maybe take a walk.

For a half an hour my life was perfect. The water toward St. Johns was a swarm of sailing boats like multicolored butterflies mating.

I envied good old Breakleaf, not too much to do,

lovely house, lots of tourists ladies to enjoy. He deserved it after the divorce. His wife of seven years left for a football player. I smiled thinking of the nasty accident that had over come that poor sportsman. Harry wasn't one to fiddle with. I wonder whom he had to kill to get his little niche of heaven. Good on you Harry, I toasted the big bear with a Planter's Punch.

Carma strolled by to the right carrying her sun things. So she was staying here too. Athena stood on the shore the wind caught her hair and spread it out like wings. A see through black and white Aqua Sun swimsuit covered her spectacular breasts. She made a big deal about getting ready to sunbathe. The male population of the beach drooled along as she moved about and finally bent full over to show off her bum. What a joy to watch.

All at once my view was partially blocked by a shadow that turned into a left hip and buttock clad in a red and white checkerboard.

"Great ass, huh?" Asked Cindy Lou, observing Carma with folded arms.

"Yours is nicer," I said being a gentleman

"Great" said Cindy. I knew it wasn't great. She continued watching the white bottom of Carma's suit, then said with a little Ohio twang, " If she bends over much farther you can compare our assholes."

There was nothing funny in it but I smiled anyway. Someone wasn't happy and I better watch myself.

Cindy knelt in the sand next to me still looking out to sea. Her bottom rested on her heals, which I always find sexy. She was wearing dark glasses and a cute little straw hat, you might put on a draw horse, with holes for the ears. On Cindy it looked great.

Turning her face partially toward me she said in a very sincere voice.

"Just for the record, I'm not a thief."

"Ok!" I said noncommittally.

"I mean it" she said more vehemently, 'I'm not messing you." She was willing me to believe.

"Fine I believe you. Does it matter? Its finished."

"Yes! It matters, I wandered into your room and I was looking around. It gives you sort of butterflies. It's a funny, really lonely, hide and seek feeling. I mean someone might find you but its exciting. That's the thrill. You know what I mean?"

"Sure, I guess so but its stupid. Say someone else had walked in. Someone with a nastier personality then mine. Offering your body is nuts. There is AIDS out there and God knows what. Not to mention the male animal and its wide variety of diversions. What happens if someone calls the cops? Imagine your parents going nuts somewhere up north."

"My parents aren't there anymore.' and then in a
little girl voice, 'Why do people who never hurt
anyone and love a lot die?" her fingers brushed the
sand off suntanned knees. This one was new and it
caught me square in the heart because it was
genuine.

"I don't have an answer for that. Love never goes
away. You know, it's always there. Hold on to it.
You'll find the faces fade after a while. I think
nature kind of takes care of us that way, makes it
easier. But hold on to the love." I ran out of words
and she changed the subject.

"She's really beautiful, isn't she? Ten times better
then me. You'd sleep with her?" Hmm, so that was
it. I had not accepted her offer and she wanted to
know why.

"No, I wouldn't, just like I wouldn't sleep with you
or make love to you. I like that phrase better.

"Are you gay?", her face came around sharply.

"No, I'm terminally married". The impish features
questioned the meaning. Her even blue eyes were
almost metallic.

"See twenty one years ago I met this lady and I
married her. Made a pledge I wouldn't sleep with
anyone else but her, for the rest of my life, unless of
course, God called her. So for twenty-one years I
kept my word."

"You're shitting me right?" her face could be ugly especially when her local American roots showed.

"No!" I said shaking my head.

"You haven't slept with anyone else in all that tim

"Yup!" This made her pensive for a moment and she looked out to sea.

"Then why did you spank me? You know how embarrassing that is, how ashamed I was?"

"No one asked you into my room. No one asked you to go through my stuff. No one asked you to take your clothes off and you were getting ready to knee me in the family jewels?"

She quickly looked away to smile but she obviously had planed just that.

"Well what did you expect,' she would now use bombast to cover the truth. 'You're three times bigger then me. Everyone always pushes me aroun cause I'm small but I get even. I always get even. Remember I said it"

The next moment her cute little feet were making tracks over to her friends who had been watching from across the beach. I considered the fact that more and more each day people were blaming things on others. We have turned into a society of whiners. Redirecting blame, living happily with our failures. This one though meant what she said.

Oh perfect, now I had more to worry about. A

Napoleon complex with a straw hat. I had done
what I had done. I accepted responsibility for the
spanking and would take care of it when the
problem arose. Her fingerprints were still on the
items she had touched. I had made sure of that.

I had just hunkered down for a short sleep when
Carma's voice asked me the question of the
moment.

"Sleeping?"

"I opened my eyes to see two soft sculptures that
were her legs. She started off with,
"I see you've found someone more to your
temperament. I'll bet she liked the parrots, she
should, what is she, all of ten?" Oh, that was catty
but why was it important if I knew Cindy? Women!
She couldn't be jealous?

"Firstly, the young lady's over the age of consent.
Secondly, I met her by chance and no we haven't
seen the parrots. Thirdly, why do you care? After all
you aren't sure if I'm proficient." She really laughed
and I liked it. In full mirth Carma sounded like a
barking seal. This made her human with me and in
concert with the rest of the world in general. Carma
had a small failing, she wasn't perfect.

Venus sat down in the shade on the edge of my
towel and I made room for her.

"I thought you were working?"

"I did some this morning and I have to set up a photo shoot tomorrow. "

"Fab, can I be in it?" As if, you haven't done any modeling before. I'll just bet you were Miss South Lakes or something?

"Just finding sights. The shoot won't be for a month or two."

"That would be interesting."

"Please do not tell me you cannot find some guy to have a good time with. Everyone on the island must be blind and stupid. "

"Maybe it's only you who sees me as beautiful and seductive." she quipped.

"Oh right, all seeing, all knowing me. Lady you're not in my class. If you were or if you were willing to grace me with your favour I would be endlessly happy."

"God, you sound like Prince Valiant. You'd love to screw me."

"Yes, like to, no cannot do."

"Well if you prefer children, I guess I can't compete." She said nastily.

"I have a lady back home that I gave my word to twenty-one years ago, I've always kept it." While it was said frankly, even I was getting a little worried that I was a throw back to the dinosaurs.

This made her think a little, she looked out across the beach and back.

"Bull shit!". You've been drooling over me from the first time we met. You even ogle little miss table cloth over there."

" I like to look. Playboy gets to my house. The wife gives me hell for that but every man needs to look around. I am faithful not dead.

My lady and I are like two old shoes we match. We got a lot of scuff marks but for it all we are one set. We've been through a lot of bad times but so far we've made it."

" You got to be Catholic." she grimaced.

"Yup!". How come, everyone thinks I'm nuts? Being faithful works for me. Nobody says you have to do what I do."

"You are from another time zone. Fifties pure love, rock and true romance. It doesn't exist anymore. You want us to use your morality. We all want more for ourselves, sex is just easy, something you do, without ties and for the joy of it.

You're a martyr to some lost belief. If I'm good I'll go to heaven. You've got to believe in that. Enjoying different bodies is exciting and it frees the life lines.

What if your lady slept with someone else. All your virgin pride would be lost wouldn't it?"

"I have to trust her, she has to trust me." I said

"You wouldn't want to know would you?"

"I can't honestly say but I believe there isn't anything to know." I was lying I would like to know, then what? I didn't have an answer to that question? I figured it wouldn't come up.

"No! I don't want to know." I said candidly.

She just laughed at that. Then she looked right at me.

"I have sand all over me. Mind if I use your shower?" she was up and in my room before I could say anything. I had left the slider open this time.

Over her arm she had a small bag with some clothes and cosmetics I suspected. I got up and followed, reaching the slider just as the bathroom door closed. I took a chair across from the entrance, made a mental evaluation of my equipment and decided that it was covered from prying eyes.

The toilet flushed and the shower exploded into action. I sat waiting and placed a magazine in my lap to make it look like I wasn't waiting. I also left the sliding door open. Once burned, twice warned. .

At this point I was cold angry. I had tried to

explain what I was. She either didn't believe me or was after something else. Either way the game stopped here.

Finally the shower stopped and she moved around drying herself, I figured. The door opened, she stood naked like a centerfold. Carma's wet hair hung down allowing drops of water to role over her pointed breasts with their cherry coloured nipples. The body was beautiful, like a photograph with all the imperfections removed rather then a real human being. Here, by God, was paradise waiting. I could not breathe at first.

"You'd better put some clothes on or you'll catch cold."

She laughed and walked toward me standing casually between my knees, her soft tummy only inches away. She completely ignored the open door.

"Put your pants on." I said in an even, almost cold voice. I knew if she touched me, I would hump her over the first solid object we came in contact with.

She gave a little shrug and turned her huge breasts away showing me a thin but perfect behind.

At the doorway of the bathroom she stopped and began drying herself making her muscled body move like an athlete's, rippling sensually. I got up and walked over to the door with the intent of closing it.

As I put out my hand she stepped back and there was contact with the small of her back. My hand sliding down over her full buttock as if the appendage was under its own control. Carma tried to turn into me so that her chest would press mine. I turned away from her fresh soft flesh and went to the door. A moment later she was dressed, past me and out.

The shower and I became friends once more. Cold water is a wonderful salve for, 'I should have done it. I'll never have that kind chance again. What a complete idiot.'

I left the shower pretty well chasten. I sat on the bed in my shorts and thought it over.

I was making a lot of nothing. I touched her but that wasn't my fault, bullshit. Most men would have had her in a second and remembered it for the rest of their lives.

The conquest would have been nothing. In fact, it would have destroyed me. The center of my stupid life, all the mistakes the victories, was based on that promise and my family. This was the base of my strength. The reason I put my life on the line for the service. I joined so the enemy would never drop that bomb that I grew up fearing. So my children didn't have to fear it.

The basic problem of course was that sex is for reproduction. Like every species, we want our seed in the best looking female, to produce children that would survive and reproduce. That need for rape, like selection, was lost in moralist history caused by the Christian fear of damnation and the family unit. All of which were slowly dying, it seemed, from the birth controlled life style we had developed. Marriage was important when pregnancy was an uncontrollable extension of sex. Now with the pill and contraceptives that wasn't important. Today of course they could produce a child with some sperm, an egg and a test tube.

Maybe the girl was right. Sex didn't matter. It was just a necessity. A bodily function, like going to the bathroom. I could not accept this concept. There has to be humanity in it, love perhaps. The difference was that when I made love to my wife there was something, a feeling, a purity, a sweet sharing. Perhaps life was too short or perhaps at the end of it that single human bond matters more than that last statement of virility.

Carma's little test had been to prove a point. Women always have to be right, have to make sure to have what they cannot have. This, however, was too much. The lady spy was projecting an intense need to be near me and that was false.

Chapter Six - 530 P.m., Wednesday, The Dolphins, American Virgin Islands.

Music and Secrets Told.

I limbered up and dressed. Typical tourist, flowered shirt and Bermudas. I left out the black socks and leather shoes, for sandals. A trip to Red Hook provided three Jamaican pies at the 'You Come Inn,' a little place that looked clean and offered wine. The food is savory and good but I would feel it later.

My first destination was 'HI's', a small club where the music was sweet. I sat for about a half an hour in the dusty, little corner bar, enjoying the beat and the people .The band was small, a threesome that did Yellow Bird and Jump In The Line, to perfection. No one showed up of importance. The general population of the bar, being local, with a few wary tourists.

Temptation was a great place. Jacob was right, dancing was the fete. I enjoyed the sweet music. Dancing a few was fine but this was too fast for me. The warmth of the bodies, the soft and loud conversations, eye contact and body contact stimulated my senses more than needed. Still none

of the special individuals I was looking for.
Perhaps it would be better if I didn't find them.
The bartender suggested Tom's down by Tu Tu Bay.
  "The music is real nice and they got women up de
stairs." He confided.

  Tom's is a long, two-storied, wood rectangle with a
large porch. A bar made of old mahogany fills one
side of the place and a long staircase the other. The
doors of the various girls were on the second floor
across the way. The patrons sit drinking and listing
to the music, keeping an eye on their selected
partner's room coming open.
  The music was some of the best I had heard. Their
rendition of Bahama Mama got the whole place up.
There was a lot of sweat and stale beer smell along
with good laughing conversation. Sitting with my
back to the wall at the end of the bar closest to the
door, I studied my target. The individuals at the bar
and climbing the steep stairs for release were from
TU TU Bay. They were mercs and some even
carried guns, hidden but obvious to anyone looking.
A big blond man in jeans and a plaid short-sleeve
shirt, jumped down the stairs two at a time, finally
swung around the end post of the stair, making the
whole case shudder. Weighing in at two hundred

and fifty pounds and moving along like a big Kodiak. He continued along the bar until he reache me and the only open space.

With a nod and one foot on the rail he ordered a Bush and slugged back most of it at one go.

The band offered six players with drums; a clarinet, guitars and base swept up into Yellow Bird.

"I love that sweet music". I said to start off

"Yeah! It's OK, a little slow." he suggested.

"Its laughin music,' I said, 'Up north it's Cryin music, the Blues."

"Yeah! So what's the difference?" He asked interest

"Well, this guy lost his love see but he puts the pain off to the Yellow bird, let's it carry his pain away. I kind of think it's a little better than. 'I lost my job, my wife lost her lock jaw, and the Coca Cola Machine just fell on my ass, Blues.' He laughed and nodded.

"The blues can be sweet though, if you're in the mood." The merc said.

"You mean you get so low down the music is higher up." I suggested

"Right, that's it."

"So how do you think the Steelers will do?" I changed the subject feeling a little stupid.

He was a Baltimore fan because he came from

Maryland. The 1970 grad ring made him my age. As a matter of fact most of the mercs were my age. For about half an hour we talked about life.

Jimmy Collee had a wife, three kids and a good job but it left for Mexico without him. He figured he'd be in better shape soon. I said good but didn't ask how.

We were disagreeing about Lynn Swan versus someone when Mona Horror was there. No noise just those porthole eyes looking right at me. I ignored them but gritted my teeth.

"Looks like someone wants your ass." I said to Jimmy

He grunted and looked over his shoulder. There was instant recognition.

"Only to kick it." Jimmy commented.

"See you." I nodded and Jimmy went through the door, Mona still tried to nail me to the wall with his eyes. He knew me, which meant one of the young ladies or someone at the hotel had me pegged. The other mercenaries left quickly. One man who had to be roused from his companion's room on the second floor, made a big deal of it until he saw Mona. He instantly became quiet and meek at that point. There was only the sound of his boots on the old wood floor as he left. Mona turned and was gone.

The question was simple, would I get to my car twenty feet from the front door?

The bartender was the owner. Tom was six foot
five of pure muscle, compacted into a coal black
skin.

"So you closing up?" I asked a little flippantly.

"We open for a good time, better with dem gone.

"Seemed all right." I said.

"This bunch ,' Tom admitted 'ain't so bad. Its dem
black haters we had down before. They got no
respect for a respectable place.' Tom polished
glasses as we talked. 'Dey find out real fast we got
no respect for dem." The sentence ended with a
grunt.

I had a real good idea how the island's
multicultural personality would react. I bet those
Oki's got out of here with most of their skin and a
clear understanding of life under a different sky.

I took a chance.

"These guys into construction?"

"No dey ain't builden nothin, unless it has a trigger.
Girls say they all going to get rich soon." Tom
raised his eyebrows to indicate he'd believe it when
it was in his hand.

I thanked Tom for the music and wandered onto
the front porch, which was cool after the bar. A
mixed group of men chatted in the night wind. One
bid me good night. The soft night breeze ruffled my
hair as I walked cautiously over to the Golf

clutching the Webley Scott, hidden in my nylon sport bag. I made the car and unlocked it. Well at least there was no explosion. Wonder if I could actually hit anything with my cannon if it came to that? In my mind there were too many witnesses for an attack.

Grabbing my flashlight, I looked under the bonnet. There was nothing around the electric starter or the gas pedal. I got back in, said a prayer and turned the key. The car roared into action and I pulled out on to the dark road for the longest, short ride in my life.

The Dolphins and my room were quiet.
I sat down and typed the facts I had obtained on to the net.

a) The mercs were Americans but older more controllable men.

b) The senior mercs like Mona Horror were in hard command. The reason I had made the car was simple. Controlled troops do nothing without direction from the senior powers that be, which Mona was not.

c) The mercs were going to get wealthy. That seems like a large scale robbery but the cash seemed to be more than a lure it was a new life for a bunch of guys who didn't have a lot of options. This was their shot at the brass ring.

d) There was too much money behind this deal for a robbery. I believed a medium size secret service was behind it, maybe Middle Eastern?

I had plans A and B for tomorrow and then Granny could get a real line agent in here to clean up the mess. One thing was clear True Love was the target.

I sent the new pictures of Mona Horror and Jimmy along via computer, signed off, checked the Webley, put it under my pillow and slept.

Chapter Seven -8:30 A.m. Thursday, The Dolphins, Near Red Hook, U.S.V.I.

The Great Charade

It was light and it had been for sometime. I lay in my comfortable bed balancing the results of the new day. Granny had no one to come in and take over. This left me on the line with limited resources .I had two options to acquire some information but it wasn't going to be easy and might end up with me dead.

Dead, nothing, oblivion, no more angel's kisses from my little girl. No more house on Saturdays, lying in bed in the late morning, listening to the lawn mowers making their way across adjoining lawns.

Would death be worth it? Would my little part of the planet be any safer that I had been there one last time? Mona Horror would kill me without thinking. No one had given the order up to now, which is how I had survived the confrontation at Tom's house of pleasure.

If I went out today he would be looking for that order? Would he find it?

Plan A was slim. I would get into TU TU Bay and look around using the photo shoot as a cover. The pictures I took would allow our mini assault team t plan for later tonight when we would scuba in and get what information was there or die.

Plan B was worse. Failing the photo shoot ploy; it was arranged that I fly over the target in a small plane. Photos of the location would provide relevar information but going too close, would give it away. Whatever pilot chosen would have to be the right one, certainly a quiet one. The information obtained would be flawed anyway. However, it would provide a rough outlay. The details would be lost and in the dark that would be fatal.

I went into the shower cringing with fear, picturing my potential end, but somewhere inside me was one question. Who would speak for Lacy or Sutton? Knowing neither, they were still on my team. Someone had to do up that bastard Mona Horror. McFurson, was he the balance or maybe just another body? Well, we would see.

Donning my now clean gray suit, the Webley Scot

was secreted down the back of my pants, covered by
the jacket. I grimaced, thinking about the endless
humour that blowing my ass off would create.

I changed into a more comfortable white island
shirt and Khaki pants the Webley Scott transferred
to it's small canvas sports bag. Only an idiot or
someone hiding a gun wore a suit in the tropics.

The Panama Jack and sunglasses were only props
now. My Mercedes hummed along to the local
realtor. Here I made a day of it asking to shoot
different parts of the island, three of these would
just be drive ins, a simple look see unless something
was interesting.

Mr. Arrnie Letly, the owner of TU TU Bay, was a
short, fat man who wiped sweat from his balding
forehead with a white hankie. He had a round face,
a small nose over a pudgy mouth and a weak chin.
His nasal voice was pleasant and rather soothing . A
ten-minute discussion of the property, my
customer's need for privacy and the amount they
might be willing to pay made Mr. Letly's calculating
mind evaluate the total potential profit. This in turn
instigated a ten-minute telephone call where the
initial stiff resistance was slowly broken. The
potential renter was only here for a day or so, the
contract stipulated he could show the property

and so on. Finally, there was grudging acceptance.
Arrnie and I would turn up at the main gate at 2
P.m. and be let in. We could look around certain
areas, others were out of bounds. That was fine with
me, I just wanted the beach and the house.

At the appointed time we reached TU TU Bay in
the Mercedes. True Love, an antique, very
weathered sign said. The original owner had
pretensions of a happy home life. I wondered if he
had found it? The main gate was topped by the old
bonnie blue flag of Dixie, the Stars and Bars, the
Confederacy's honour still upheld. I wonder how
Robert E. Lee would view its use now and its
significance as a symbol of hate. How would that
thoroughly honourable man accept the reality? I
believe the old weathercd, bearded face would be
clouded with anger.

The fence was ten feet high and topped with razor
wire. Arrchie pointed out the security of the
location, which included video cameras, and other
monitoring devices, all of which were of interest to
me. We drove round a snake like drive, which
allowed a treed area to cover the house from the
main road. The mansion, which in its time must
have been the belle of the island, was set like a
white diamond in this leafy green setting. On the
right of the

mansion was a group of makeshift buildings, which seemed to be in fairly constant use, given the lack of grass in and around them. There was no one visible. A set of three air-conditioned, single story barracks stood quietly to the left of the main house. These were divided into individual motel like rooms. This must be where the vacationing clansmen and others tied to the militias, stayed. Painted white, with red tile roofs, they seemed new and well kept. The mercs must be laying out there or on some other part of the property.

We stopped by the house. It was built long ago and had the elegance of the old south. A large central stair case in the middle of the pillared facade which was freshly painted white, lead to French style lead glass doors. I took out the Minolta, taking various pictures of the building outline, the stairs and then followed the line of the old house to the back. A slight hill bibed the stone base of the house, then faded toward the back, where a door allowed entrance on the corner closest to the dock .To the left of the house was the beach.

Three Zodiacs were tied up to a redwood deck like jetty. Fitted with single 200 Mercury engines they looked aggressive and fast. Each boat had what I imagined was a kevalar-based windshield, metal being too heavy.

There were two 50-foot Starward cruisers a little off the dock anchored and ready.

A quick walk to the beach found it unguarded. I walked around taking photos that might interest my semi-existent customer. Terry Bell at Dextra Fashion in Toronto had used my services in the past and was always interested in anything I came up with. She would cover me if Arrnie called.

I got the distinct feeling I was walking on man made objects. Mines or sensors could be secreted under the sand, either of which could be operated electrically from the house. When I asked Arrnie, he said there was nothing he knew about.

When I suggested I liked the beach, Arrnie rubbed his fat hands together. We talked dates and options. During a slow walk back to the house he explained the potential of a historic sight that dated to the 1850's. I faced its two floors of colonial splendor. I presumed if one went inside one would find a large rounded staircase in the grand entrance. However, the building for all its pillars was only facade and didn't go back more then 40 feet. Like the South Carolina slave Mansions, this was a working or seasonal home with a larger and better one in Charlotte Amalie, strategically close to the Governor's residence.

We didn't get a chance to go inside. Mona Horror
stepped out of the front door. I thought I saw a
woman and a man behind him but he closed the
door too quickly. Dressed in camouflaged fatigues
he strutted down the stairs to the bottom. Here, he
faced me with rough arrogance.

"See everything Boy?" he clipped off, Arrnie
blanched.

"Mr. Jug may I introduce Mr. McFurson." I nodded
coldly.

"Mr. McFurson is setting up a photo shoot, bikinis
and swimsuits. Of course that will be after you leave
Mr. Jug." Jug didn't like me knowing his name. His
scowl deepened.

"I'm not your Boy," I said evenly

"You might be surprised." Mona said in a nasal hiss.

"I personally have never had homosexual interests
but with your wide military experience, well, I guess
you pick stuff up? It was obvious orders for my
accident had been given. His body tensed to spring,
the eyes white hot with anger. Only Arrnie's
presence saved me from dying right there.

"Mr. Jug, please, we will be leaving right now."
whined Arrnie.

"There will be another time." Jug threatened.

"I don't think so but sometimes bills need paying,"
It was said with such soft vehemence I surprised

myself. Mona 's face changed he got very thoughtful, then he nodded.

"Until then." But the tone was more guarded. He turned and was gone.

Arrnie's gaze moved from one to the other of us in financial horror. As we turned away, he asked, "Is there something wrong? I have to apologize for Mr. Jug, I do hope this won't effect the shoot."

"No Arrnie, everything's right out in the open, I like it that way." He seemed to accept that as a compliment to the sight and was visibly relieved. We left then.

I lay on the bed and relaxed as best I could. I had the Webley's cold metal handle in my hand under the pillow. If they came here it would be through one of the doors. Of course they could always lob some kind of grenade through the window.

I had moved upstairs into an empty two-bedroom suite and left the old room as bait. Jacob had set the whole thing up. A couple of bucks in the right place will do wonders. Rutledge would come into the point on Coki Bay with his equipment. We would then take on the sea side of True Love. One way or the other I was out of here with the old SAS man tonight. Tomorrow I would be laying on a beach in B.V.I.. or dead somewhere.

I considered the day's events. I should have never confronted Mona. That was juvenile and I already knew he was gunning for me. I guess I didn't want him to think he or his people intimidated me.

Realistically, Mona Jug was just a competent soldier, doing what he was told, His skills paid for in advance. There would be nothing personal, in him causing my death, until I made it so.

I had sent Jug's name off as soon as I got back, including the photos care of computer processing. Rutledge would be looking at the pictures right now.

I considered the situation clinically. We had no proof and without it neither Breakleaf nor Granny would call in the American armed forces to flush the place.

Darius Corp. was a computer firm owned by a Lionel Lincoln Adams. Mr. Adams was a brilliant, if somewhat self-possessed individual. As Mr. Adams was black, it seemed strange that he would finance the TU TU Bay operation, if there were white extremists involved. Headquarters felt the corporate name had been borrowed.

The rent money was being paid up front for True Love, negating the need for a credit check, Arrnie confided. The use of the Darius name was someone's idea of a sick joke. The information w s not passed on to Darius for the present, just in case there was some tie in.

  Mr. Adams was interesting. Based on the profile sent to me, he had been a gang banger in an earlier incarnation, had grown up on the very hard streets of South Chicago. Shot twice, on different occasions, he had been arrested for the shooting death of a rival banger by seventeen. As he was young and had not pulled the trigger himself, he ha done five years. In prison he had found computers and fallen in love. Leon was brilliant. Some men have special gifts. Lionel had found his. Computer were a wonderful toy and tool. He took as many courses as possible and became a good, if not, model prisoner .He was released early.

  Back in the hood, Lionel started a small compute repair business to support himself. He was able to create a new program that controlled heavy industrial equipment and patented it. By thirty- thr he was a millionaire. He was a powerful man and a follower of Mohammed. His conversion in prison was real and a shield against the more unpleasant aspects of that life. While this point was not lost on Granny, there was no direct line of intent between Darius and TU TU Bay. The man running the show from Alabama was Sayleen Lieless a white racist and ex clansman. Nothing in this thing made sense.

Mohammed Tisani existed and was from somewhere in the Middle East, traveling on a Jordanian Passport. He was wealthy, reportedly from the import export trade, and seemed harmless. Although he had some interesting dealings in Lebanon related to high tech weapons, his background was very fuzzy beyond that.

Carma was what? Bait maybe but if so why the second time?

I summarized what I knew. Someone with money had brought 300 odd mercs to the island, to train them for some kind of mission, which they believed, would make them rich.

Given the investment so far the return would have to be spectacular. A simple business reality was that investment should produce a substantial profit. At least that was the normal end product.

Terrorism was another possibility but the men recruited were older, seasoned veterans, all good Americans with families. Their dying for some vague dead communist life style or some Middle

Eastern religious revolution was not in the cards. It was possible this was all a cover for something else. Then why so many gunmen? Armed men in the heat of battle were hard to control. The best laid plans go wrong, then what? I shuddered to think of three hundred heavily armed men or any part of that group, in a major city facing the local police force after a botched bank job say and the slaughter that would follow.

Herman Jug was everything I expected. Jug was born in Bowen Kentucky to a father who beat his wife and three children regularly. The elder Jug drank what money he earned. Herman's loveless life was spent slaving on his father's semi-productive patch of land.

At sixteen Jug left the farm and his father's drunken abuse for the Marines, some trade. He survived three tours in Vietnam, all up country and rose to the rank of Sargent. Not the easiest trick. After the war he had stayed on but the need to see combat demanded he find it. Abandoning the Corps, he had participated in wars all over the world. He trained Afghans against the Russians and Tutsi warriors against the Bujumbura Government in Burundi. He was a soldier for hire without too much definition of right or wrong. He had lived in the jungle and was a trained killer.

The phone rang, interrupting my troubled thoughts.
No one knew I was here but Jacob. I picked up the
receiver .It was his voice. He didn't seem under
pressure, just excited.

"Miss Cindy she's hurt." He started.

"How bad, where is she?"

"Dey took her to de Hospital at Red Hook, I guess
one of dem mini buses hit her, her friends are out
somewhere. You the only one here, maybe you want
to pass I understand, just thought you want to know.

"You sure ", I said working out the time before: I
met Rutledge.

" I got the call from the hospital, just now. You
want me ta go?"

"No, I'll go."

It took me five minutes to get to the car and
another fifteen to find the two story white building,
cursing all the way. What did the girl matter? The
father in me wouldn't leave her all by herself in a
mess like this.

Parking the Mercedes as close as possible, I went
through the front door of the clapboard building.
Facing me, right across from the entrance behind a
low counter was a rather plain, young woman
dressed in hospital whites. This wasn't a real
hospital, just the local Doctor's office with a few
beds available upstairs. The paint was peeling and

the smell of old wood impacted on my nose.

"Excuse me, I 'm looking for Cindy Conners. I believe she was hurt?"

"Oh! Yes, Miss Connors she was here but she was only a little cut up in a skateboard accident, she is fine now ". The girl was scared stiff. That should have been my first clue.

"Thanks," I said, questioning how stupid I could be. I turned to my left to leave, and there was Mona Horror and a second man in a blue, quilted sleeveless jacket. Both men had Uzi's or Macs. They must have been waiting for the girl to push a buzzer in an office down the hall.

They were only a few feet away. I turned the other way and there were two more. The door was out of the question. I took two steps along the hall to my right. There was a green, wood door that lead into a corridor to the rear of the building. I went through the door hoping to block it. That was impossible as there was nothing to place against it and no lock. As to going upstairs this was firmly blocked with a thick fire door and a padlock. I got the terrible feeling this was a mousetrap and yours truly, was the mouse. There were five stairs that descended into a concrete tunnel. At the bottom to my left was a concrete room, which extended perhaps twelve feet by five across. A bare light bulb lit the

green fire door at the other end. There was a half
wall inset to the right side of the tunnel like room,
which was probably used during hurricanes.

Going through the door was an invitation to death.
I heard the steps of the followers coming down
behind me. In two movements, I smashed the bulb
then opened and closed the fire door. Now hunkered
down behind the half wall, I balanced my Webley
on the cinder block and waited. The old, 'will they
find me?' feeling struck me right in the crotch.
Crouching there my teeth were clinched so hard the
gums ached. I had never killed a man before.
Could I do it?

Jug and friend turned the corner slightly crouched
but not too worried. They should have been, I drew
a bead on Mona's chest about mid point. I felt
nothing for this animal. He represented a bill to
collect. There were two lives he owed on and I was
going to reconcile them.

I steadied the gun with the two-hand police grip,
my thumbs crossed solidly and squeezed the trigger.
The Webley exploded into the small area like a field
gun.

Mona's mouth made a perfect "O" and he went
backward. The other man fired his Uzi at me but the
bullets sprayed above me. Everyone knows a
submachine gun lifts upward to the right as it fires

in a steady burst. The man compensated but too late, small chunks of concrete showered down on me, cement dust filled the air. The noise was deafening. My Webley Scott blazed twice more. Black Knight charges ripped through the Kevalar and the big body. Huge patches of blood sprayed the wall behind him and he went down in a heap.

I now had to decided to go past the two downed men who still might be very effective, plus the reserves who would be following down the stairs any minute. They would not make the same mistake as Jug. The other option was to go out the green fire door.

I placed my hands on the green metal and listened nothing. I opened the door slightly and listened again. Behind me I could hear the pursuit moving down the stairs. In my memory, an old combat instructor told me always go to the left. I went to the left and slid along the stonefaced wall which edged five stone steps coming up to ground level.

The man lurking behind the top of the tunnel brought his Uzi down on my head with the force of a sledge, pain exploded in white light and then inky blackness.

Chapter Eight - 7:30 P.m. Thursday, True Love – TU TU Bay U.S.V.I.

Rude Awakenings!

I came up a long way to the light and my first impressions were bad, as if the dream hadn't ended. The pain in my head was outrageous to say the least. I could not seem to move either. My eyes opened to bright, overhead lights focused on my face. I looked down and away to find my hands tied with chain on either side of a metal table with a slightly lifted edge as if to keep fluids in. The chain between my hands stretched across my chest. At either end the links then looped around the wrist and were padlocked. I was naked, my white body stretched down the table. I could barely see my feet from this position but they too, were well tied down. It felt as if they were fastened together so that the two soles were evenly situated over the edge of the table.

Terror! The first wave of it hit me and my body reacted immediately. The heartbeat rose and the skin tingled and I began to sweat. Fear robbed me of my very existence and my breath was like that of a trapped animal. Shaking, I raised myself against the bonds with all my force and fell back.

At that point two things kicked in. One, I knew in my soul I was going to die. My mind seemed to accept that. Secondly, the mental molding which had been implanted under deep hypnosis so long ago, back, in the early eighties, clicked in. My body relaxed, not completely, but substantially. I was blanking on specific information, my home address, anything to do with the firm. Torture, at this point, on a physical level, would have little effect. Even Pentothal would have limited results. Only long periods of stronger drugs , along with a suitable regimen of pain and lack of sleep, would allow the enemy into the limited information I possessed.

On the other hand, my mind cleared. There was an acute interest in everything around me, which included any means of escape. I was not impervious to pain but the limited time available would make me useless to the enemy. Unless they decided to take me along when they left, my secrets were safe.

I did a mental check of my body, with the exception of a huge headache, it seemed in good shape. Not being shot was something. I had no illusions. This was going to be heavy handed and very bad.

I had killed. Was this just retribution? I had not wanted to kill the second man. Not knowing him, his death was pure self-defense. Mona Horror was different perhaps, also in self-defense but with no remorse. So I would pay for the dual sins of dealing death and stupidity. Anyone else would have left the girl to her fate, the father in me had reacted to her supposed fear, her unchampioned aloneness in a foreign land. If it had been my kid would I have done less? No!

The minds behind the lamps were tactile and very competent. They had not expected me to be armed, if they had there would have been a different direction taken. The trap was superb, well-defined, simple and inescapable, once entered. These people were pro's but with very little finesse. The table and the attachments indicated they were not aware of my mind definition. The whole presentation was staged to create fear and to break down the defenses of the captive. The end effect was to do the exact opposite. Rutledge would look for me then, he should get back to Breakleaf but that would take time. I just had to hold on and pray someone had seen something. With any luck the opposition had thought I was working alone and had taken me back to TU TU Bay.

"Good evening Mr. McFurson", a silky Middle Eastern voice said from behind the lights.

"If, you're the police I want to see the Canadian Consul." I returned in a reasonably even voice. The pain in my head made movement impossible so I lay still, closing my eyes against the lights.

"The police,' the voice actually allowed a short laugh. 'no not the police."

"Oh,' as if this was a new thought to me. 'Well if it's ransom, I guess my company will pay."

"You work for yourself Mr. McFurson." He said with bored finality.

"I work with a company down here. They will probably back me if the amount was reasonable." I offered. In my mind's eye I could see Walley barbecued before he'd pay five cents for me. The firm would pay, of course but this was just fluff, they would not contact Walley. These were the preliminaries.

"You killed one of my people," he said. Ignoring the side bar. I hoped it was Mona Horror.

My mind screamed 'No kidding and what happened to Lacy and Sutton?' To him I said,

"Your people were armed with submachine guns what the hell would you have done?"

The fist crashed into my abdomen slightly off center so I didn't vomit but hard enough to remind me of my manners.

This brought the voice into the space between th
lights and my eyes. He was bearded ,lean and tall
perhaps 6 '2". The voice had an Arab's face with ;
large nose and runny brown eyes that understood
hate.. A small hard mouth formed words but I wa:
in too much pain to answer. I twisted slightly. The
was no escape. He spoke again. This time I
understood.

"I will ask the questions and you will answer
them." he repeated in a low venomous voice. The
tone change was a warning and I took it.

"What do you want to know?" Came my gasped
reply. I listened as his footsteps moved away.

"You are a member of the British Secret Service.
I laughed hoping to hell that it seemed genuine.

"I'm a Marketing Consultant." Ask at Sidingham'
on the British Virgin Islands. I do brochures."

"You are very well armed for that." he countered.

"After some grotesque threatened me earlier
today, I went out and got a gun." Let's see what yo
do with that?

"A little large perhaps?" I saw him heft my Weble
Scott just to the right of the lights

"I told the guy I wanted a big gun. I didn't want to
miss."

"With armor piercing bullets?" Sarcasm!
"It had six bullets and the guy said it would work,
it did, that was enough for me."
"Perhaps his name was Sidingham? " No, you aren't
going there.
"No! Walley wouldn't give you the time of day
without making a profit but he doesn't sell guns.
This was a local guy, Black. He didn't give me his
name and I didn't ask."
"Why not a gun shop?" Was he buying this stuff?
"You know how long it takes to get a gun if you're
an alien?"
"Oh, I see.' He said. 'But, then again there is the
watch, very interesting. The little packet of acid
inside .We have another just like it. Mr. Bailey was
much more forth coming." No he wasn't buying, he
knew and was being thorough. It would start soon.
"I bought mine in Toronto at the Eaton Center."
He gave a crocodile sigh, as if he could do nothing.
There was a sharp swish in the dark and razor sharp
wand of pure white-hot venom hit my soles. The
pain shot through my body like a flash of lightening
burning out the nerve endings in the spinal column
as it tore through to the brain. My body arched like
a bow against the chains. I heard someone scream
like a dying animal and then

realized it was me. I continued to scream as each cu
eviscerated my soul. I took five perhaps as many as
eight before the blackness captured me.

I came to but did not move. Perhaps my body did
move but had been twitching and the initial
movement was missed. I had not fouled myself.
Strange what comes to mind . I kept my eyes closed.
The pain was horrendous. I almost vomited. I hadn't
eaten tonight and I was glad of it.
Through the mist of pain came two voices. I
concentrated. The first was Mohammed's that I was
sure of.

"This is stupid, Hedi " they are hypnotized they
can't remember anything once the hypnosis comes
into place.

"God gives, sometimes hypnosis does not work. I
had to find out." Said Hedi. I presumed that he was
the lean, tall one.

"Try the Pentothal. I think they sent us some other
drugs as well. Ask for Dr. Adaman. He is in Red
Hook . Pay him well. We may need him again.'
Mohammed paused. 'Get what you can then kill
him and I don't want a body this time. We would
have been gone tomorrow. This was unnecessary."

"He was far too close." said Hedi with a growl.

"You answer to me,' said Mohammed vehemently. 'If you had left the first one alone we would not have had this one." He paused again and thought. 'You are a good man Hedi but this is not home and you cannot act without thought. Do as I have said." He finished as if he were speaking to a wayward son.

"As you command." said Hedi with a little sarcasm.

"Has the other one been taken care of?" Asked Mohammed with impatience.

"Not yet. Jug's injuries disallowed him from taking action, however, it will be done when I finish here."

"Good, no more untied camels." Mohammed laughed.

"No!" agreed Hedi,' Not with billions at stake." Joining in the small joke.

As they left, the overhead lights were turned off. I opened my eyes only a little. There was a guard at the end of the table. He lounged against a large filling cabinet bored and disinterested. Dressed in fatigues the guard had an open face with a small mustache and a pursed mouth under a fine nose and intelligent looking eyes. The hair was full and well combed.

His upper arms were huge. It would have been him to use the whip or whatever instrument was selected on my feet. This was evident from the blood on the jacket. He was Arab as well, keeping things in the family.

Blood had trickled down the table toward me. They had bound my feet so I would not bleed to death. Some had seeped through and was drying on the table. The physical pain was over. I figured they would kill me fast. The drugs would probably leave me unfeeling to the end, whatever it was, that helped a little.

The room was set out as a medical ward or hospital. The walls were sound proofed. Originally it had been used as a root cellar. The room was small and had only one entrance.

It was through that door Jim Collee entered. He had a white porcelain mug of coffee in one hand. I could smell the rich aroma. This he offered the guard who took it hesitantly. Obviously there was little love between the Arabs and Yanks.

"They told me to drop this off." Jim said in a flat voice.

"Thank you" the guard, said formally. Collee made to leave then his body shifted. He pivoted with fluidity that would have made a marshal arts expert blush. Collee's left arm wrapped around the guard's neck, the ten-inch knife in his right hand was

serrated and very large .In an instant it was buried in
the guards lower chest up under the rib cage into the
heart. The man collapsed in Jim's arms, the cup
exploded on the floor and the door closed. There
was no sound. The guard's look of disbelief could
have been humorous but wasn't. Collee didn't look
at him. The big American stepped over the corpse
and was beside me.

"You dead?' he said with a harsh edge. He could
find out easily and he might help me.

"No." I said intently.

"Listen! They're going to kill me cause I talked to
you, just cause I talked to you. I ought to tear your
heart out." He stopped, then went on. 'Here's the
deal. I get you out of here, you get your outfit to
take care of my wife and kids."

"Yes! I think I can do that, if Tisani's people don't
get to them too soon." Collee considered this for a
moment.

"I guess I don't have a whole lot of choice."

He took a forty-five Colt automatic from his hip
holster and shot the locks off. The noise was
deafening but the soundproofing would hold. He
had the chain off and was working on my feet in a
moment.

"Looks like they done you real good.' He
commented.

Sitting up was an effort. I felt the blood flow back into my legs and feet. The pain intensified and I grunted with it.

"That prick Jug was going to whack me. One of the boys from the Gulf heard them and he told me, would have helped too, but he's got kids." They had wrapped the ankles with silk and placed the chains over them. I saw the blood flow out a little but it had clotted. It took all my willpower to shift my legs over the side of the autopsy table, which I lay on. I had lost my revulsion of this metal, final place of humiliation of the body. Escape was sweet.   I prayed I could remember something about my people before this Jimmy individual blew my brains out.

Collee stripped the clothes from the corpse. The pants he compacted and put over my feet. The contact almost put me out again but I fought it. I wasn't staying here. I dragged the pants up and lifted my butt to get them on. He tossed me the fatigues jacket. This I also put on although it was covered with blood. I was suffering from shock and would need the warmth. The boots were a size eleven and my size nine feet went in with a little help. The contact with the floor was awe-inspiring. I took the weight with a scream. Then, with pure force of will, said to the cold face that moved hazily before me.

"I'll be fine." My memory was coming back.

"Anything for the pain?" I asked.

"He handed me a bottle of extra strength Tylenol.
placed five, ten or twelve in my mouth and began t
chew them. Jim went and got me water from the ta
in a paper cup. I downed the mushy mouthful.

"Let's go." I said between clenched teeth.

"You got big balls and all horse, but you ain't
walking. I'll carry you."

"You got bigger balls, You superman?" I asked
trying to focus.

"Hell no, I just got to get you to the boats. It ain't
that far."

"Give me my gun and that portable phone on the
counter." The request had an instant result. He
looked up hard fixed expression. His face went co
calculating the potential of having me on his back
with a loaded gun was not to his liking.

"You going to carry me and shoot at the same tin
you are superman." he hesitated then smiled.

"Ok!" He went around the table and got the items.
Collee wedged the door open.

"Gitty up." he said and I jumped up as best I coul
as he took me piggyback. We went through the do
and closed it. He jogged to the end of the hall,
which was lit. I worried about video monitoring bu

Jimmy had already fixed the problem, the camera was out of commission. The ground to cover was thirty feet of the cream coloured hallway. After an eternity we made the door and I turned the handle while Collee pushed.

"Sentries " I queried, as we moved out into the velvet night. Its warm wind was a tonic. My memory was coming back fast as I perceived escape. Sweet freedom! How can I describe the sensation.

"That prick Jug ran things, now he's shot up and we are leaving tomorrow. Its' just the rug merchants. Everybody else is holed up with some beer."

We had exited through the lower door on the seaside rear of True Love, we were at TU TU Bay. Collee's boots crashed on the wood planks that lead down to the boats. Each step seemed to target us for the opposition but there were no shots. Jim stumbled under the almost four hundred and fifty pounds he was transporting. I divided my time watching every bush for a possible enemy, hoping I didn't miss. There were only three shots left in the Scott. The real trick was staying conscious. With about ten feet to go Collee went down hard on his left knee, my feet contacted the wood with the same force. I gave out an animal howl, low and short. We had just about made it, he blew like a winded workhorse and I watched for any movement. There was none.

"I hate being forty five. Everything is falling apart." he grunted between breaths.

"Tell me about it" I drew myself up and placed my feet on the deck. I used his prone body to lift myself to my feet. The pain cannot be explained.

"Help me and we'll get there." He rose and placed his shoulder under mine, half carrying me. We hobbled to the Zodiacs. He dumped me in unceremoniously. I dragged myself up a second time allowing my lacerated feet to hit the salt water in the bottom of the boat. I stifled my cry of agony with my tongue and almost bit through it. The animal noise seemed to get Collee back from his sitting position on the pier where he seemed to be set in place, never to move again. He dragged himself into the boat and stumbled across to start the single Mercury engine. The other Zodiacs rested at strange angles from their moorings around the wood terrace. It was obvious they were going no where, Jim had been busy.

I got one rope, he the other. The boat shot out across the small lagoon made by the reef. In a moment we were out past the two Starward cruisers over the passage, which was lit under the water by some kind of neon lighting which snaked across the reef.

"That's deep!" I said indicating the chasm in the reef.

"They blasted it bigger, a little at a time. Probably for the Starwards," said Collee concentrating on his navigation.

The spray hit my face and pure joy of survival lifted me. I cried, great tears rolled down my face and I wanted to laugh out loud.

I would live and go home, I said a private thanks to God for this huge chunk of luck. Life lost and then found, how precious the silky night was, how wonderful the water, how glorious the stars. Thank you God.

The roar of a twenty-caliber machine gun is unique and as frightening. A bullet whisked past and I swear my hair was ruffled by it.

"That will be the patrol boat." roared Collee over the engine. The spotlight that had missed us on the first pass now had us captive.

Collee turned hard to starboard and let fly with the Mach he had secreted in the boat. I raised myself against the movement of the boat and the Webley spoke twice with a solid roar. I had one bullet left. We were now parallel to the enemy, a second blast from Collee got the light. I heard it audibly smash like a crystal punch bowel hitting hardwood.

Without the light the machine-gun fire became a lot less accurate. Their larger engines allowed them to follow our wake. The sea around us became a fairyland of stalagmites as the bullets churned the water missing but coming closer.

"I think we're screwed." Said Collee over the sound.

"Not yet, give me your grenades." Jim had two attached to his webbing and passed them over. Throwing them was out of the question. The distance was too far but maybe we could get the opposition to come to us.

I took the bailers from the bottom of the boat. We had four or five bouncing about. The four that fit together best were chosen. I sat for a moment and figured distances in my head, then pulled the pin, counted to four and placed it between the two plastic half jugs, so it was airtight and would float. This I let go into our wake followed by the second. We waited, counting well beyond the correct period for demolition. Bullets sliced past us on the right, they were gaining. The grenades must have sunk.

The explosion was closer then I had imagined. Shrapnel whistled over my head.

Our pursuers were shoved to their right by the force of the blast. The second grenade in its white cover was almost under their bow. I ducked. The Zodiac rose from the surface with the force of the explosion, like a water skier starting a jump and then hammered on its back in a delicate ark its nose shredded. I could see the fire start to eat into the patrol boat's body as the larger Zodiac settled. The occupants tumbled out and then the flames became smaller and smaller as we made away.

I sat back and relaxed for a moment.

Collee slowed the boat down as we shot across the black ocean with only the lights of St. John and St. Thomas to direct us.

"So what do we do now?" He asked over the slowly turning engine.

"I can navigate. We head for the British Virgins."

"That's an hour across black water horse. "Collee made the statement and emphasized it by spiting over the side.

"Listen you need help maybe we go to the police here."

"No,' I said 'We land anywhere on the island and they will be looking for us. All we have to do is get to the medicine line. Once we're in British waters we get picked up. First, you got to call your wife and tell her to get to somewhere safe, then I'll call my people and get them clear."

I opened the phone and asked the operator to give me Baltimore. I was then required to give a bell call card number, that was memorized. I handed the phone to Jimmy.

He dialed the number and spoke to his wife in short sentences. He was Ok. She had to take the kids to Dave's. Yes, Dave's. The FBI would be there to get her and the kids."

He had done his part and passed the phone back. I rang the Governor's mansion in the British Virgins. From here I was transferred to Breakleaf who was on H.M.S. Dove . They were waiting for me just off Frenchman's Cay.

"Hi!" My mouth was dry.

"How are you?" Breakleaf started.

"I'm fine, one of the opposition got me out. He has a family, which is in danger in the States. We will have to help them."

"Lovely, I'm glad its you who will ask." said Harry.

"Just make sure we can scramble as soon as I get there. You about where we discussed?"

"Yes!"

"You got a doctor?"

"Yes. Are you hurt?" The concern was there.

"Ya, I'm in pretty bad shape."

"Want us to come for you?" Harry would carry the ship on his back.

"No." But make sure the Army, Navy and Marines show up at True Love. The opposition is Middle East but I couldn't tell where. The Middle Easterner

I spoke to you about, he's in charge. Should you find a tall thin prick with a soft voice, I'd like to have a talk with him. "

"I'll see what I can do." said Harry.

"I'll see you Harry. If I have a another problem I'll call."

"Right, take care we will be expecting you. "

" So now what?" asked Jimmy.

"See that center light there. Sail just to the right of it and keep as straight as possible."

Jim got the boat going and we shot across the sea. Fortunately it was a quiet night. There were no big waves and no ships. I read about a tanker that sailed into Brisbane one morning with a good size yacht plastered to its bow. The tanker captain had never seen them.

The one thing I didn't want was to run into trouble because we only had so much gas and the Zodiac was not made for major sea voyages .We were no match for a large fishing boat let alone some 10,000 thousand ton merchant ship.

The miles passed. I was growing sleepy and dosed off periodically. With the exception of waking me up for course confirmation, Jimmy sat like a rock at the engine. The depth of Collee's strength amazed me; they build them tough in Maryland.

The darkness was an enemy now. Reefs, rocks and other obstacles were out there in plenty.

A small spotlight on the sideboard helped on two occasions, keeping us from running into a hazard. About an hour and a half later we came upon the Dove about where Breakleaf said they would be.

Jimmy brought the Zodiac in. Harry's worried face showed over the side. Two Royal marines hauled me aboard and off to the cabin. Another got down and disarmed Jim and placed him in the back of the ship where he was given hot chocolate and was made as comfortable as possible but watched closely.

Harry followed Dickey Talbot, the local doctor, into the cabin. Dickey started by removing the boots. The pain was excruciating and I screamed.

"My God!" Was his only comment .He cut away the bandage. Mumbling "I do hope we can save the feet."

"Harry he is not cutting off my feet." I said weakly through a fever that had started to grab me on the trip.

"Of course not old boy." said Harry and I knew if it were in the realm of the possible that would not happen. Harry, for his failings was as loyal a friend as is possible.

"I need a phone." Harry blanched he knew I was going to talk to Granny and he was glad it was going to be me. On my part the call had to be made before the darkness overcame me.

. I took the cellphone and attached scrambler.

"Hello Granny."

"Yes." he said with exasperation

"Jim Collee has helped me escape from the opposition. They're Middle East and professional home team people."

"Do you know from where?"

"No.' I was rolling along the edge of sleep. 'Some of their associates had accidents."

"Really, how sad." Said the cool voice.

"Yes, they were terminal."

"How many?"

"I think up to five or six all in. It was a big accident spread across quite allot of space."

"I see, " he said coldly.

"We have sent our local friends in to see what we can catch. "

"Do you think they will get the bulk of the remainder?" Granny's voice remained even but he was seething.

"No I think they will have already disappeared.' I told the truth, 'I would appreciate if you could get on to the mainland powers that be and take care of Jim's family."

"I want them picked up from the following address. I gave the street and house number. He will need asylum too. He saved my life and should be a useful information source. Harry will talk to him now."

"You realize what kind of negative position a request like this puts us in with our friends." Granny queried in an icy voice.

"This is good for them too and I want it done. I never asked for anything before but this, I want it done."

"Agreed." He wasn't happy.

"Twenty minutes later one Major Amhurst, the British Military Attaché from Washington and two associates gently took Jim's family into custody from Dave's. The FBI got two local Middle Eastern men, who showed up at Jim's house about an hour earlier and were waiting outside.

Chapter Nine – Midnight, HMS Dove, British Virgin Islands Waters

Shots in the Dark

The Dove was built as part of a group of armed launches which had been destined for Hong Kong. The Communist Chinese takeover, however, had caused the Admiralty to reconsider the disposition of war ships and Dove had come to the Caribbean. Sporting twenty-millimeter cannon and a crew of twenty, she was a formidable patrol boat with a shallow draft and some hitting power.

The return to Road Town was smooth at almost twenty knots. A military ambulance whisked me to the local hospital where a group of doctors looked at the damage. The whip used on the soles of my feet had had a slender blade inserted into its fine but iron hard structure of rhinoceros hide. The blade had slashed the skin so that the cuts opened out like canals, destroying a large part of the nerve system. The local medicos took one look and decided I would have a better chance at a hospital in the American Virgins.

The U.S. Navy helicopter that flew in from the Charlotte Amalie, was well equipped and the personnel seemed to know what they were doing. I was of course, under heavy sedation. Loaded with antibiotics for my high temperature. This sickness was created by the infection in the lacerated areas. I could feel the drugs kicking in by the time I was comfortably installed at the hospital.

Len Burie was a newly graduated Harvard podiatrist just in from the mainland .He smiled down at me, looking like my eighteen year old, assuring me I would be fine. "Good enough for me", I croaked from my misty world. I almost said kid but saved myself from that disaster.

It took two days for the infection to clear up, enough for Len to graft skin from my thigh, onto my lacerated flesh. The left foot wasn't as bad, he said in passing. The seawater seemed to have helped quite a lot with the infection, which really hadn't set in. My temperature dropped proportionately.

I lay in a private room and looked at the ceiling. Dozy from drugs but still awake enough to talk with Harry, who had dropped in, with the traditional bag of grapes and a pad.

The debriefing covered everything that happened. The deaths of U.S. citizens took precedence during the conversation.

"Did they catch anyone at the house?" I asked

"No, done a bunk, I'm afraid, still we were expecting that."

"Yeah! How they get away?" I asked.

"The Starward cruisers in the reef. The U.S. Coast Guard went out that night but didn't find anything. The next morning there was wreckage off St. Martin. It seems there was quite the explosion. Only bits and pieces left, but we figure the blast killed all twenty- two men on board."

"You mean they wiped out their whole team." I said in astonishment. Harry nodded.

"Of course, the loss of yourself and Collee prejudiced their operation .If Collee had identified the other men in his unit it might have lead us back to the principals.

"Jesus, these people don't wait for much." I said.

"No." Harry agreed.

"Still leaves about three hundred men 'I said' Did we get Jug?"

"Fraid not! He was shot through the upper lung. With the exception of that he seemed to be in reasonably good shape, but he was flown to the States for surgery. Once he got to Miami he was moved and we lost him." Harry concluded, he seemed very uncomfortable.

"Hmm," was my grunted reply. It wasn't Harry's

fault. However, you sort of wondered how
somebody that badly wounded could be lost.

"They find any bodies at True Love?" was my next
question?

"No, you're in the clear there They seemed to
clean up their own mess.

"I wonder why, but then the Yanks would love to
find two dead potential terrorists. This way we look
like we gave them a bad lead. That must help you
no end with the locals.

"Not to worry,' Harry pushed it aside.' I expect our
friends made for St. Johns or one of the Cays.
Probably sank the boat and went to a prearranged
escape route. I would suspect they were off to
Puerto Rico. More likely Cuba on second thought.
Anyway, gone."

"Another interesting fact is that the hill behind
True Love was a rabbit warren of tunnels.

" That's interesting, what did they have in there?"

"Oh, equipment, old and new, food, spare parts.
The Yanks confiscated the lot but there wasn't
much of any real interest."

"Was it well hidden?" I asked.

"Not particularly, the majority was garbage after
all."

"Where did the tunnels lead?"

"Oh, escape hatches, spots that were well camouflaged to cover movement. Some had boats nearby or cars hidden on the hill. I'm told this is pretty well what they found in like places where these militias have their bases."

"Great!' I snarled 'All the comforts of home. What happens to the property?"

"The owners through our Arrnie are screaming for it back. One suspects they have another group of people coming."

"What more mercs?" I demanded.

"No, just a group of your, fun seeking, gun toting, pathological types." Harry's sentences always seemed clipped as if one extra word might offend.

"We found out, our Arrnie doesn't own the real-estate. A company purchased it three years ago from Atlanta. He just fronts for them with a commission ratio you'd ransom your mother for."

"Do we know who owns it?"

"Oh, that's where it gets interesting, the ownership passes through the dummy Corporation to Liechtenstein . You know how hard it is to get anything out of that lot. After the European stop you need a shovel to sort it out." Harry smiled at his own joke.

"This thing stinks to high heavens." I added.

"You say these chaps were Middle Eastern. Was i P.L.O. or Iranian backed?"

"I couldn't tell you.' I said 'Did the names I gave you help out at all?"

"Hedi is fairly common. One would guess Mohammed has disappeared into a new cover. We think he is Iranian or Iraqi controlled certainly not Jordanian as his passport indicates." finished Harry

"I'm a Canadian, eh? My passport will hold up, th : Israelis make a great copy, I hear."

"I realize that' agreed Harry, ' not the Israelis surely. I would be very surprised."

"They might know who we are dealing with and they owe us at least one."

"True", Harry ruminated.

"How's Jimmy, he get away all right?"

"Yes, off to the wilds of your country with his wife and family. Asked me to pass on his condolences 'Horse". Harry smiled.

I remembered Jimmy's stoic face like something cut out of granite in the gloom taking us home and his easy smile of gratitude at the end.

"Good' I said ' What he give us?"

"Well', Harry referred to some papers' these men

were all recruited in threes, all dependent, as
friends, on each other. That is the old Soviet system.
Three times ten created thirty. The offer was some
money up front and of course, the big return at the
end of the day. The deal was made by an agent at
some hotel or other safe place it was described as a
bank style job outside the U.S. Millions of dollars
are the prize. Actually one million per man. The
house had a cut of 25%.

"That's way too low". I insisted 'with the amount
of money tied up in this deal."

"Exactly, something on this scale would have at
least made the house 60%, if not more. The real
question is what or better who, is the house. In most
major cities there are local gangs that get a piece of
the action or unfortunate problems develop for the
organizers. One would assume they would bypass
that problem." Harry said knowingly.

"So then what?" I prompted.

"Each man agreed. There were those who did not.
These I suspect were disposed of. All the people
chosen were down on their luck or deeply in dept.
They all required money to start over or to find the
their dream. The bottom line though was as follows,
no drugs, no booze and no outside connections like
say, a brother in the police.

experience. They all had families. One would suspect that gentle hints were made as to what might happen to the little ones if anyone got out of line and so forth.

All the men were pre vetted and kept under surveillance until their group came down here. Some of this is surmise but it seems correct.

Charter planes left from one place and returned to a second near by. In cases where the distance was excessive rent-a-cars were laid on. All of this was financed." Harry stopped to let it set in.

"Harry, no Middle East budget covers this kind of operation, anyway the C.I.A. would be all over them. The funding alone would lead them right to the source.

"Perhaps,' Harry once again agreeing, 'however', the but was coming. "The money could be obtained. There are a lot of Muslim sympathizers in the U.S. who could be funneling money into the kitty."

"The Middle East is tied up with the Israelis, neighboring countries. The rest is in Europe. What do they want here? Money fine, but money isn't it. Twenty-five points is way too low."

Both of us thought for a moment like hunters, who had followed a track and returned to the place they started.

"Why here in U.S. territory?" I asked first.

"You usually train men in the environment they will fight." Harry suggested.

" Could be the southern states?"

"No, Jim said off shore." Harry corrected

"Caymans, Mediterranean, Brunei, could be anywhere at all." I shook my head", what else did we learn?"

"Well the training was intensive everyone's actions were choreographed, timing was very important, seven minutes and out. They used the wall parts you saw going in to True Love to change the basic format of the bank. Each scenario was thought out minutely. One group would do the robbery the rest would play the customers and staff. They know where the guards will be and how to control them."

"The money expended on this deal couldn't be recouped in a million years from a bank job. Look Harry, a bank job,' I started slowly, 'is a mugs game, unless the payroll is just in. or all the deposits come in just at the same time. The amount of money on an average day is what $50,000 cash, maybe less. In a large or central bank maybe a million or two, tops. Just to get the information about the target you're talking a major payoff. Everyone would know. We are talking cash, markable, numbered cash, easily traceable and in large enough amounts that a fence would have a coronary. Even if you fence to Mother Teresa you get maybe 25 points.

Collee and his boys thought they were going to walk out with a mill each. They'd have to knock off the Mint or the Bank of England."

"Oh! Quite if chaps are ready to take on the Coldstream, S.A.S. and every other military unit in a hundred miles.' Harry said in defense of Britannia. I ignored him.

"So the ten men loaded with four or five fourty-pound bags, if anyone remembers to bring bags, right smack into the Royal Marines and you've got World War Three.

Or worse the local police turn up to be massacred. Remember those two half-wits who screwed up the bank job in L..A.., it took half the police force to kill them. Even then it was the SWAT team who finally finished the job. Imagine if they turned thirty teams loose on a city and timed it right, you could rape the town." I finished.

"I see what you mean the first two teams draw the police the rest pilfer at will."

"Not in a really big town.' I said, 'Not Detroit or New York, something smaller. But then you have no money."

"Right' said the tired Governor's assistant. "If we can figure all this out in twenty minutes then the average merc is going to see through any plan to drop thirty teams in thirty cities. It would make a great spin though. 'U.S. ex military in roaring gun battles', no one would feel safe and just imagine the publicity value to our Middle Eastern friends but Jim isn't that stupid. Any road, the getaways were to be orchestrated." Harry sighed.

There was silence for a moment then Harry looked out the window to the sea and said.

"I believe this is finished, we stopped them. We know too much, the major centers and Banks will be warned, certainly in Britain at any rate. They lost what four teams. No, I think, we can safely say they are stopped or at least stymied for a good long time."

After Harry's pronouncement the silence closed in again while I watched the dust particles float in the rays of sunlight. It would be easy to stay here forever but outside the world still went on and I would have to rejoin it soon. I could feel my jaw harden.

"Harry, I think you're dead wrong. I looked into that bastard Hedi's eyes. He's not some big time crook who is stymied, he's a fanatic. Torture came easy to him. The men that died mean nothing to someone like him and the mind behind this one is on the same wavelength. There's way too much invested in this deal for them to back up and let it go down the tube now. Something a lot bigger than a few million and hatred of jolly old England are behind this. We can warn everyone but of what, maybe you'll get hit. No, it's too loose. The powers that be will forget ten minutes after it's issued. We got a big problem with no handle."

Harry considered what I said, but I knew he did not agree. His concern was British interests and those were covered.

"A huge cover up for something else?" Harry suggested.

"Yes, I thought of that too, but what? Maybe Granny can figure this one out"

"Anyway, I've told you everything I can remember Harry. They did blow up the reef so Lacy was on the right track after all. Cold comfort that."

"Well, no bodies, no murder, no problem. I believe you're out of the woods,' Harry said standing, 'Granny wants you in London as soon as possible."

"Ok."

"I'll be in touch. Lots of rest that's an order. See you later." Harry's patented firm handshake followed.

"Thanks, Harry."

The room was quiet again and I slept.

Chapter Ten - 3:15 P.m., The Hospital, Charlotte Amalie, U.S.V.I.

SWEET PAIN

The rain had just started. Only moments before the windows were pristine. Small pearl like drops, developed quickly into huge water bullets that threatened to blast through the thin glass, into the quiet cool hospital room. Drops that battered the windows, until the very flow of water, eye patched the view. Cutting me off from the exterior world, making me alone and restive.

Some tourist was swearing up and down because he had spent all that money and now was equally trapped in his hotel room. He was not getting the tar that would make him the envy of the office back in Texas or Wisconsin.

The rain delivered by great black thunderheads, darken my clean antiseptic room. The rain was created by the tail end of a tropical depression. This is the marketing term for the hurricane, that was beating up on Cuba, far to the north.

The rain surrounded me. I had always loved the sound of it rattling on the roof. Often escaping into a long, quiet walk during a downpour when a major problem

needed real consideration. The rain had always been
my liberty and my security blanket. Today it helped
a little.

I remembered the nights so long ago as a child, I
had huddled warm beneath the covers knowing, the
security of my childhood room as the drops pattered
above. Knowing in my heart of hearts that I was
safe, that the rain and its accomplices the lightening
and rolling thunder were banished by the inborn
power of my father's home. The rain softened the
depression I felt from screwing up everything from
start to end.

So far I had solved no mystery. I had killed, but
not Mona Horror the one person who really needed
killing. The men I had killed were just shlubs like
me, in a sense, forty on the outs, too little money,
not enough dreams. They were old, but not old
enough to collect a pension, if it existed. Having
been fired from rock solid jobs, in many cases with
companies who had fraudulently made a promise
for the future. Christmas was tight and bare. Wives
became enemies sensing the horrible truth of the
downward fall. Just when the last reserves of
humanity, shame and strength were almost gone,
Salvation? One job doing what they had been
trained to do so long ago

in the desert or the dripping jungle. To use abilities that came to hand again as if they were never lost. A million dollars, enough so that you would never have to worry again. A little ranch in Montana, that condo in Florida, the happy family and life style, instant American Dream. The name True Love was chosen with an enlightened mind's razor edged brilliance, with multiple meanings and mean hearted humour.

The great raindrops became teardrops. Twenty-two of these men would never have their dream because of my actions. I had to stop this. I was becoming maudlin. These men were mercenaries. They knew the score, had gambled and lost. So that I could go home to my family. In the house I owned, on the street that was so familiar, that it was almost painful to remember.

Only Collee had lucked out. I hoped the ex Marylander liked snow. The Canadian West was cold as hell during the winter and hot as the bottom of a frying pan in summer. Good on him if that was where they had sent him?

The rain continued to hammer the window. I had chosen Cindy Conners over duty, or better, in spite of it. It was a stupid and poorly defined action. The

question was, had I run down to the Red Hook
hospital because of fatherly better sense? Or more
realistically because of the girl's honey white skin,
perfect breasts and peach coloured nipples? Was it
to save her or have her? To play white knight so
that her lush body would open to me.

 At my age you dream of that happening. Some
men buy it outright or others find a mistress, in
some cases by luck, given the opportunity. Others,
the vast majority, simply lived in their mind's eye.
There seems to be so little time left. At forty-eight
you want it now before it's too late. Had she been
ugly, would I have gone? Yes!

 My thoughts drifted back to my long-suffering
wife, with her home-coloured blond hair. It was
kept long because I liked it that way. Her body,
which though a little heavier like my own, was
given to me with a pure trust and love. I had never
broken my word, never slept with another woman
during our marriage.

 I had called home on the scrambler through a cut
off in Cleveland. Happy voices poured down the
line to me. Her concerns, the boy's good humour,
my little daughter's fear and joy at my regained
health, and they were waiting for me. In a week or

so I would start to walk on crutches. My feet would be numb but usable. I would be back to my world and all of this would be behind me.

For the moment I was laid out flat on my back. My newly soled feet strung up in small hammock like slings, which kept them off the bed and away from contact with anything that might cause anymore pain. At this point sneezing was enough to cause that.

The sensitivity level was high as the stitching took effect. Tubes for saline and other more powerful agents extended from a harpoon in my right arm. This appendage was attached to the raised metal side of the bed with a combination of tape and cloth so that I was comfortable, without inhibiting the flow of those important substances into my blood stream.

The local cable network on the room's TV was my only outlet. As everyone knows if you have 30 channels there is never anything on. My present state disallowed the use of my computer. Concentration was a problem with the amount of painkiller in me.

There was of course a second source of entertainment. People from the CIA and US Navel Intelligence wandered in periodically to ask the same questions Breakleaf had. Of course my answers were more controlled, telling them what they needed to know without disclosing anything that might hurt the Firm's interests. I got the nasty feeling, from their bored reactions, that they knew everything already, which was very annoying.

The door opened with a definite creak. Every wooden door it seemed creaked in the tropics. I turned my head to my left, my eyes made me wonder for a moment if I wasn't dreaming. It was Cindy Connors standing there by the door. Her ghostly apparition made more surreal by the darkness of the day and the fact that the thin candy striper dress cast in shadow gave the impression of a mirage in the dusk.

It was her, blond hair hallowing that face, the same pinched, pixy features but set and hard as if sculpted. She moved toward the bed slowly slipping out of her brown leather sandals so her petite feet patted over the tiles. Coming to rest about five feet away, she undid her dress, the buttons opened like the buds of a flower commanded by the sun. Only there was no sun and Cindy should be in Ohio.

What do you do? You watch as the dress slips off to the floor, she steps out of the circle of cloth.

The beautifully muscled legs flex, the hips move alluringly, breasts press like ripe fruit against the cloth looking for escape. Beneath the almost white hair in the rainy dark, cold, blue eyes, almost crystalline, watch with amusement.

Somewhere between fear, curiosity and drugged uncertainty, you watch disjointedly like the kaw of an ancient magician, having exited your body and hovering from a neutral perspective. You watch the unfolding panorama with increasingly quickened breathing and the proscribed sexual reaction.

One tiny hand looses the white globes, now free they stand out firm moving slightly hypnotically, with the flow of her body, the nipples hard with passion. Cindy slips her panties off and is beside the bed naked. Her scent hits me like a bulldozer. It is clean, mischievous, powerful, alive! I want her more then life, all else flushes from my brain.

There is no love, allure or even softness in the eyes. They accuse and there is anger. Or perhaps I misread them in my groggy state. I am engulfed with the perfection of the nubile, honey-coloured body. The golden eye that covers her mons vagina beckons. The sweet luscious lines of flesh that send out the message no reasonably sane man could miss for what it was.

She lowers the side bar to the bed in one competent movement. Her hand then draws back the sheet and lifts the hospital gown. She touches me and I gasp, I am completely aroused. With both hands she guides the contraceptive down slowly to the base each movement causes such intense sensation that it can only be described as sweet pain. On the knife-edge between pleasure and destruction.

Cindy places one knee on the bed and straddles me. She leans back until I feel her moist life source envelope me partially. Now in position she simply sits down slowly.

The pain from my feet is blunted by the drug and the passion but still is there like a blade in my soul. I cry out, my free arm grabs her upper arm. She gyrates up and down slowly as if calculating the proper speed, setting the metronome in her body, now faster as she closes her eyes, straightens her body and with majestic power hammers down on me.

Forgotten by her I snarl from sensual bliss to the shock of searing pain of each downward stroke on my stationary feet. My body keels like a ship in a point five gale. I grab her breast with my free hand and pinch her nipple unmercifully for what she is inflicting. Cindy rises up to the height of her stroke, snarls at the pain, lost in her passion and crashes down shaking with the force of her orgasm .She stops momentarily to weather a second and third.

She breathes deep and moans like childbirth, the depth of the explosions tensing every inch of her body. The powerful mussels of birthing envelop me inside her. The feeling is unique, indescribably sweet. Poised on the edge of the cliff. My hand now clamps on her buttock with all my power leaving fingerprints, she cries out. I reach for the ring and grasp it as I join her, explode, vent, empty myself, shake in my turn with the magnitude of the relieved tension.

She continues for a few seconds but the pain is less as the serenity in golden waves of post sexual lassitude take over. She is still having orgasms smaller now. The red blotches like small, blood fed lakes appear on her breast tops telling me the secret, that the orgasms are real. Short barks of pleasure bespeak her slow coming down, finally tightening her frame for a last explosion. She shakily dismounts and reaches the floor with a thud on one foot.

Without a word her feet pat back to her panties like a crumpled butterfly on the floor. These she pulls up with a snap giving me a last glimpse of her full bum.

Cindy turned and moved back to the bed with solid, forced steps. Reaching over she takes my testicles softly in her hand.

Her voice is as hard and cold as her face is inches from mine.

"I could have cut your balls off." she says with a vengeance and a hate that only women are capable of. The hair on the back of my neck rose as her grip tightened.

"You didn't really hurt me that much." She hissed, 'But you took from me."

"I said I would get even, so today I took your 21 years of virginity. You didn't scream rape and you could have told me to stop. Now your old lady can't trust you, because the first time is the easiest. What are you going to tell her?" With this she tightened her grip on me and twisted vigorously.

While I rolled into a fetal ball of pain, Cindy put her bra and dress on, in another minute she had retrieved her sandals and was at the door. She stopped there.

"Now we are even, maybe next time you take advantage of someone you won't. Asshole!" She was gone.

It took time for the pain to leave my middle. I didn't think she had done permanent harm. It took time for my breathing to come back to normal.

I was bleeding from the heal of one foot. I called the nurse while cleaning myself up. Finally I lay back and watched the rain.

Chapter Eleven -Near Hull Bay, 9:00 A.m., Monday, U.S. Virgin Islands

Questions and Answers

I was able to walk again. Gingerly at best, with a cane for the next little while, although I left it in the Jeep. It had taken hours slowly dragging my feet between rail supports, gaining strength. Finally standing on my own. The soles of my feet had healed. Today the doctor had let me leave the hospital by myself and drive over lush green hills, pimpled with small bungalows and shanties, to Hull Bay in the North West Corner of St. Thomas. I had cut off onto the dirt track where the doctor had said it would be. The foliage had closed in until a small white villa came into sight. I parked just before the drive and made my way through the light brush to the beach. Trees separated me from the house. My sandaled feet left clean prints on the edge of the virgin expanse of creamy white sand. Suffering my weight, the soles hurt with a dull throb but I was becoming used to this static pain. The Webley Scott weighted on my shoulder, still in its light sports bag. The bag also contained a thick, body length, white towel, suntan oil and a book, one which I didn't expect to read.

No one thought I really needed the gun but I
wasn't taking any chances. There had been no tail
from the hospital. Of course, following someone on
the island with its twisting mountain roads, that
seemed to offer only single lane capacity, was
almost impossible without immediate recognition
on the part of the target.

A smile crossed my face as I remembered a
Canadian Tourist looking up one of those almost
90-degree grades and saying, 'Imagine taking a car
up that with snow on it, eh?' Only a Canadian
would think it, only a Canadian would say it. Only a
Canadian would come to a tropical paradise and see
snow. It was good to know that I could still smile.

I found a place that was partially shaded and sat
with my back to a tree looking out toward the low
green humps of Inner and Outer Brass Islands.
Pelicans squadron out to fish, small delicate birds
captured minute living prey along the edge of the
surf. Chasing the out going sea, running from the
incoming waves. It was close to 90 already but the
grayish-black clouds on the horizon carried more
rain, marching like a hazy army toward me. They
massed on the far horizon giving me time before
they struck. I lay back against the twenty-foot tall

palm and watched a living post card. The view of a never ending royal blue sea, constant waves and the empty perfection of the beach.

Home tomorrow, landing at Toronto, returning to Niagara, not by way of the QEW but a more round about route just in case. The wife, the kids, the house, all of it would be the same. I would be different.

To add to my other accomplishments, I had completely miscatagorised Cindy. She had to be US Navel Intelligence or CIA, probably Naval Intelligence, she wasn't tough enough for CIA and they didn't run much of a show down here to begin with. I had not seen her after our afternoon in the rain. However, Cindy would have to be connected, to know what hospital room contained her quarry and when it would be safe to get to me.

It was time to resign. When you couldn't keep up with the players you pulled the plug. I had a blind side to women or maybe my male metaphase was clouding the vision. Fourteen years was enough.

I could make more money in my own business. The travel would be missed, the escapes from my mundane side. On the other hand if death swallowed me up who would take care of my family.

With the Russians there were rules. Now, here, there was only survival. The face of Hedi was engraved on my mind with a red, hot brand. His hate was the rule that controlled all the rest. He was a zealot, which made him unafraid of death, nerveless to it. His own death would take him to his God's Garden of Wonders. Mine would what? Bring me face to face with whom? Did I know my God? Maybe that was the difference. Perhaps Hedi's belief was the strength I didn't have. We didn't have.

The Arabs who had been considered as lesser beings for so long were learning. The power of Mohammed and Mecca was growing; the west was at its apex. If one Mohammedan leader a sultan evolved to mold the weapon, the world might understand the reality. For the moment the west was on top but for how long.

My joining the firm was not by accident, by referral or recruitment in some bar by a bewhiskered major of the old regiment. I had submitted my resume to the British Trade Commission with a covering letter offering my services.

I made only two provisions, one the job be non-line. A line agent was on the battlefront in direct action with the opposition. With a family I could be a risk. Secondly, I would not work in or against the interests of Canada. The decision to join MI 6 over the CIA and RCMP was made for a number of reasons.

CIA was the largest of the western services but in many ways the least effective, the least scrupulous and the most brutal.

Moles and a Federal Government that made Canada a sieve for information hindered the RCMP. The fact that Americans didn't tell Canada about Granada before going in, was a clear indication of the US Government's take on the matter. Of course I saw things differently then. Now, from hindsight, perhaps the Yanks were manufacturing a war, a movie-like news event that the Prime Minister of the day could not have stomached. You can't look glorious from a make believe war when someone questions its reality.

That was another reason I should resign. I knew far too much. My vision of the world was too jaded, too jaundice. In the end it was a young man's game.

My grandparents were Scots. The tie to the old - country, as we called it then, was still strong. When I was born Britain had owned most of the world. The Queen was revered. Being, part of the Empire was still a thing of value.

The decision to work for the service was also financial. I expected and received reasonable compensation for my work.

The daring do was only of partial interest. The most important reason of all was to do something in the war against Communism. Vietnam had been an option of course but it was a stupid and unwinable war.

The Americans, without a predominant colonial history. The ownership of occupied territory and its maintenance to preserve the glory of the father, land, were at a loss against a determined enemy. The Vietnamese had been freedom fighting for over 500 years.

Of course I know now that Vietnam had a major part in the destruction of the financial stays that supported Soviet Russia. The huge investment in arms for the Vietnamese, with no hope of repayment, had destroyed the ruble.

Afghanistan had been the final straw, an affair that the CIA provided to teach the Russians a real lesson in military 'Hard ball'. In the end the strain was too much and although the Soviet financial structure

stumbled along for a while, every American who
died in Vietnam made the demise of the Evil
Empire possible.

Finally capitalism, the almighty dollar was its own
sword to kill the beast. Without hard currency the
Soviet system could not continue. It had imploded.

Eight months passed, I had almost forgotten about
my resume, with a new baby and a new house in the
works. Then early one Monday morning a letter
arrived. This missive requesting I show up at a
British owned company in Toronto, at such and
such a time for. a posting interview.

In a quiet, clean boardroom, I was interviewed by
the then Captain Theodore Boothby-Staters. Good
couriers, with established covers, were hard to come
by. We discussed the RCMP as an option; however
the purely defensive nature of the organization plus
the limited needs for personnel not from the
Mounties curtailed that direction.

In the end I was hired after successfully
completing hours of tests and a wholesale vetting by
a number of agencies. A trip to London was laid on
where a month's training was provided. The cover
for my stay was provided by my involvement in a

major, marketing campaign for a process food manufacturer.

Code, weapons, and hand to hand combat were offered, along with a clear definition of the enemy. Some of this I had taken during a stint in the Royal Canadian Navy. Brain molding is standard issue but only to increase the reserves and to strengthen the individual for survival. The Firm never wanted automatons.

Our class graduated, signed the forms, which bound us to the Service Secrets Act and was sent out to do the Queen's bidding.

Having been acclimatized, I was provided with a series of fairly simple assignments, which eventually lead me to an expanded roll all over the United States, Central America and the Caribbean. Over the years I became a prime courier. This allowed me to carry large amounts of money and very valuable consignments. At one point, trips took me away as much as twice a month. The tremendous advances in computer technology made the service less important. As the wall tumbled, the rules changed. The targets of international espionage became far more industrial and this changed the job once more. A Cleveland check off had become necessary. Check offs are a telephone Gordian knot through which there was no passage. Information was taken in different world locations and fed back to the agent, after evaluation.

There had been some talk about me joining CISIS, the new Canadian Spy agency, but I had been MI6 too long to change now. What CISIS knew about my movements and me was hard to define. As my trips were outside the country they seemed to turn a blind eye to my comings and goings. If I believed myself to be a threat to them my resignation would have been turned in long ago. .

Years of meetings in dark places had toughened me, but drained my reserves. Normally retirement is early for on line agents. Sometimes forty is the cut off, either out or inside for promotion. For me the rules were bent. My time was extended. This decision was based on the consideration that, I was less in danger and suffered less stress. Both conclusions were questionable.

Lacey's death and the follow up were way out of my league. Even with the help of Breakleaf, I had not completed the assignment. The end results of my labours were more questions than answers. On the positive side, we knew a lot more than we had started with and done some damage to a plot, which had the potential for far reaching negative consequences.

The sea remained aqua blue. It always was here. It was a part of me.

A larger part of me, wanted to stay. Just stay, to hell with everything else. Fish on the beach, live in a grass hut, find a Cindy Conners for my own. Swim everyday in the aqua blue waves, laugh, love, and enjoy the little time I had left.

But no! I would be on the plane tomorrow. As if on cue, a jet from the airport appeared over the trees and circled out, over the ocean toward Central America, leaving a vague rumble in its wake. Home, tomorrow my car would run up the drive to my wife and children. I would be confronted once more by the problems of survival in the real world.

What would I tell my wife about Cindy and our time in the rain? Nothing! Cindy for all her vengeance had been a 15-minute blip in twenty-one years of trust.

If I had instigated the act then it would have been my sin. A fair argument could be made for my taking some kind of action to stop the process. In fairness, there had been no viable defense put up. No strong terminating words. The drugs pumped into me were part of it but that was an excuse. I had just survived an ordeal. No one can understand the experience of near death in battle if one has not lived it. The need for a strong vital life force was beyond my capacity to stop once the act was underway. At that moment I needed the raw sex Cindy gave. The power of the act had made me more whole than all the doctors on earth. If I had sinned, then I would be responsible for the act. I would live with the stain and sin no more. Anyway, the wife would never believe me even if the truth were forthcoming.

Another reason for retirement was the fact that the 90's reality was completely out of sync with my 50's morality. What girl back then would have taken the action Cindy had? My spanking her was the result of an on the spot situation and in hindsight, wrong. However, I believe I would do it again.   Cindy had gotten even in her way and saved me in the process. The wrongs and rights seemed to cancel each other out. So be it.

I still had to face Granny but I didn't fear that. I could also let him pass judgement on many things not just my retirement, thereby shifting the burden of all this off my own shoulders. We would see where that led.

Finally, the problems were flushed out of my mind because nothing could be done about any of it, either way, at the moment.

The soft wind, which preceded the storm, ruffled my hair, as if God's hand were there. In the religious pictures on the wall in my third grade class, Jesus meets the little children, his hand on a worried boy's head telling him things were bad, but not that bad. I would let God carry the load for a while.

It was cool in the shade, but the burning globe of the sun still warmed the air. Time stood still for a while, as it does sometimes in paradise and I slept, until the raindrops forced me back to reality and into the Jeep.

Chapter Twelve - Niagara Falls, Ontario Canada.
2:00 P.m., Tuesday

Home

The Civic climbed our drive and I got out. Home
was what? Where you returned to, perhaps? Today
the house was beautiful beyond words. Every brick,
every peel of paint was important to me. I had
thought of my family, my wife and the kids.
Strangely the most important thing after hello's and
touching was just to sit in a private secure place and
quietly watch some television.

Men dream of the far horizon. We would live there
if it were not for the anchors that tie us to one place
A woman who loves us and children who we must
be there for. If simple sex was all of it, why stay? In
our world, where there was no fear of pregnancy, if
proper precautions were taken, men should be in
constant rut. Some were, but the vast majority only
wanted the security of a woman and a home.
Married men became fat because we did not want to
attract the members of the softer sex. We made the
statement, we were off the market. Wives made the
mistake that we are slobs. Perhaps they were right
because we also forget sometimes that

our ability to please women kept our anchors in place, secured the seat before the fire or television set. Somewhere between completely tuning out and bringing home flowers everyday, lay harmony. Those who have found it, good luck to you, for the rest of us, well we try.

The kids were at school. It would be sometime before the troops got home. I walked to the door and opened it with my key. Our fur ball of a dog came over to say his greeting and I petted him as he whined a little, as if to say "it's good you're back."

The Wife came in from the kitchen sporting a white blouse, jeans and slippers, no socks. A pink kerchief held her hair from falling forward while she worked. Her bright wide face exploded in a smile. The same smile I married her for all those years before. She had been cleaning something, her hands covered by yellow rubber gloves.

"Hi" she said with real joy." You didn't call." Now she was mock angry," Don't go off like that again without telling me." I took two paces and kissed her as hard as I could, locking her body to mine in a bear hug of joy and passion.

"What's with you." She gasped as we came up for air. I just looked at her with the sappy smile I save for moments like this. With practiced movements I

unzipped her jeans and pulled down her pants
before she could react.

"Are you nuts?" she howled, as I flipped her over
my shoulder, closed the door with my foot and
carried her up the stairs her bare bum bobbed over
my shoulder. 'Put me down, someone's going to
see' she protested giggling.

I carried her into the bedroom and dumped her on
the bed, dragged off her pants and pulled down
mine. I swear I didn't even take off my overcoat.
The two of us made love like animals in a pit.

Finally, we lay naked on the bed, Clothes strewn
everywhere, a single sheet covered our sweat
drenched bodies. I petted her hair and kissed her
again. The wife nuzzled into my shoulder and made
a contented cat sound somewhere between a purr
and a yawn.

"That was really great," she said finally, 'but
why?"

"I almost got killed" It came out blunter then I had
planned but how do you say it? "I needed you bad."

"Well you had me bad." We both laughed at this. I
realized how beautiful she was in the depths of the
laugh and the fear she was masking.

"How bad was it?"

"Bad." I said simply. "If you give me five minutes

I'll have you again, bad."

"What, are you nuts?" My mouth covered hers, my hand held her ample breast and our bodies came together again. Sex was slower this time; I touched and felt, doing the things I knew she liked. At the apex she had an orgasm, her body shivered with its onset. Nails dug deep into my back but this was her way and I didn't mind.

We lay still again like two people who had survived a marathon. I ran my hand over her soft behind. Her muscle tightened slightly as she gave a little internal stretch. Her head rested on my chest, wet hair spread like a dirty blond sun.

"Don't get killed but need me like this more often." she said with a hug. I smiled and she became more serious. I could not see her face but I felt her body tense.

"What happened?"

"The opposition got me, they hurt me but I got away. I'm fine now." Was I? I weighed the next words "I think I'm going to resign."

There was silence like she might be saying a silent prayer.

"OK, I was going to say something about it but I wanted you to make the decision. I'd rather have you home. It's never been like this before. Things are all right, I guess, if you call being scared all the time all right. The kids are older now. They need you. They don't listen to me anymore. Forget all that. Are you sure?" In the end she didn't cry. She had let me have my way.

"I screwed up. Fortunately, the only one who got hurt was me but it could have been worse, lots worse. You can't make mistakes out there. Being a courier is one thing, they put me on line. I figured I'd make a name for myself, it was stupid. Hell, I could have been killed! I drew her to me as if unsure of how long I had in that darkened room which smelled so intensely of our bodies and lovemaking, how long my would my string last.

I could smell the fear again of the torture room and heard the soft swish of the whip. My soles hurt involuntarily and my body stiffened.

"Are you alright?" she cried.

"Yes, I love this room and you and us. You don't know what you have until you come that close to losing it. We'll have to tell the kids I fell on glass and hurt my feet. They had to resole them."

"They tortured you,' her voice caught in her throat and she hugged me.

"It wasn't that bad, I lied." She knew I was lying but simply hugged me more tightly.

"Christ, how small we all are and irrelevant. You always think you're going to live forever. I love you, I should have said it more often."

"Don't die." The Wife said with tears on her face.

"I won't, too much to do. Five minutes to blast off."

"Are you nuts?"

Chapter Thirteen – 8:30 A.m., Port of Hampton
Roads, US Naval Base, Norfolk VA.

A Slight of Hand.

Yan Van Pallon was a Dutchman. A Netherlander
of the old school. An Amsterdamer of the Old
Church and the red light district beyond it. For
twenty-eight years man and boy, he had given his
life to the sea and the ocean going tug boat fleet. In
every sort of weather he had sailed Holland's Pride
to every size port across the world.

Today entering the huge U.S Naval Base at
Norfolk, Virginia, he stood on the flying bridge
and allowed the pilot, a talky little Yank, to bring
the Jan Van Klu, his huge ocean going tug, through
the busy shipyard. They past great new nuclear
carriers, fast frigates and missile studded cruisers,
waiting to leave or refitting from voyages to far off
places.

Yan spoke to a deckhand as they passed a huge
carrier and her screen of war ships leaving harbour.
The salute was given, as tradition required, by a
merchantman to a man-of-war. The Dutch flag
lowered to half-mast. To Yan's surprise and
pleasure the carrier responded. Her great Stars and
Stripes dipped to recognize the smaller vessel.

Here was another man of the sea or perhaps a woman? Things were changing but as long as this way of life remained until he retired Yan would be pleased to let younger men handle a world of women on ships.

Van Pallon, being a seaman, could appreciate the quality of the ships he passed. He also knew to the Guilder the salvage value of each, if he could get a towrope on them. He smiled into his beard.

Finally, the tug passed on to where less used ships, were docked. Until they entered the graveyard of the US Navy. To be fair, there were used ships docked all over the U.S. but this was one of the largest sites.

Yan was not a morbid man and this was just steel and rust, yet the hairs at the back of his neck rose slightly at the sight of such a battalion of fine ships waiting for a call that would never come. It was eerie. Some might be sold but he knew the Russians were selling their fleet like a man brushing lint from a suit and at such low prices. These fine ships would finally go to the nacker's yard. The great tug, with its short powerful body, driven by two huge Hanza and Loyd Diesel Engines, carefully bypassed a partially stripped landing craft attack ship and an LST, finally coming into view of his tow, four ships, a small minesweeper and two old oil burning submarines stripped of everything of technical value, tightly

boxed together so they would move as one. About
100 yards behind was a third submarine. Van
Pallon's face clouded as he did some quick
estimating of its value. The ship was a diesel unit,
long and lank, an "S" type or a later model. Her
paint was almost perfect, there were no broken
railings or deck sprouts. The sub was in beautiful
condition. Someone in Costa Rica was going to get
a reward if he got that for scrap. He checked the
manifest but the numbers were correct. The ships
were going to August Soto of Limon, Costa Rica.
This gentleman was starting small, stripping ships
for the growing steel refinery he had in the city.

Much like Bangladesh, the system was based on
strong backs and lots of available unskilled labour.
In Bangladesh the ships, huge hulks, were warped
up on the beach and thousands of people descended
on them like ants on the corpse of a whale. In
hours, the ship was stripped of furniture, fittings,
anything of value. In less then a week the steel was
cut and ready for reuse. The money paid to the
workers was small but in a place like Bangladesh,
it was a fortune. In Costa Rica the same plan was
slowly evolving. Starting with small ships like
these and moving up to larger vessels as the
equipment

became available. Soto was making a living for ten villages with a few tools and a beach, not to mention huge profits for himself.

This submarine would be a blessing. If Soto were smart he would resell it to one of the local Central American countries to be re-commissioned into service with one of their navies. He would mention it to August when he saw him. Yan felt better for not being the mortician for all of his tow.

The Assistant Administrative Harbour Manager for Norfolk Navel Base was Bill Dratton. Now old Bill was, on the surface, an honest and fair man. He was just about next to God with respect to the harbour, the ships in it and the support systems required for a ship to go to sea. Big, bluff, with sandy hair, a square seaman's face and a winning smile most people liked him right off.

Unfortunately Bill had this little problem. See Bill liked the ponies. Well, not just the ponies, he also liked casinos and football betting, well gambling in general. As a matter of fact, old Bill was into the local loan sharks for a half a million dollars. This provided the opportunity for the local organization to suggest that he help them, which meant obtaining material from the base including some pretty sophisticated weapons.

Bill did have other options. His creditors could give him a gravel nap or he could go to the Feds and wear a wire. Of course, the local mob knew where his family lived and were keeping a close eye on him. Should something go wrong and the boys found out, his kids meant more than his life. He didn't want to have his family on the run forever either. The other options were to run or kill himself.

While Bill was pondering this dilemma, the clouds separated and the light shone. His savior didn't look angelic. A man named Lieless, a rotund hard-faced individual with a smile about as real as a four-dollar bill. At least he was Southern. Someone a Virginian could trust. Mr. Lieless wanted something far less terrible than the sharks. A single shipment, a certain submarine was going to Costa Rica. Lieless wanted it loaded with supplies from the Navel Stores on the base. For this he would offer old Bill enough to cover his debts. The only part of the deal that bothered Bill was the request for twin Fifty-mm Gattling Machine Guns stored at the base for use on attack helicopters. The rest, food, K rations, clothing, bottled water, some light weapons, rope and a lot of small stuff including blowtorches and other dismembering tools was nothing. All of it would be easy to provide. The payment would be in cash. The submarine would be broken down to scrap and the job would be done. Why this specific submarine, not that it mattered, they were all being scrapped or sold off? This one was newer, pick of the litter, better founded, which meant a little more profit for the end receiver. The heavy machine tools, cutters and drills would help the operation in Costa Rica and increase the profitability.

A simple swindle, Bill in his fevered brain could live with a simple swindle. The man he would work with was Terry Bains. Bains, who clerked in supply, had control of the movement of the items required. This all checked out. Bill had made immediate inquiries on the sly. Bains was black but reliable, having worked at the yard for years. What his end was, Bill figured, had to be money, although Bains wasn't a gambler.

The submarine Sand Darter was exchanged for the older "S" class ship originally selected. In return, a suitcase filled with $250,000 in used currency covering the first part of the agreed amount, was provided to Dratton. Bill thanked God as his financial associates called the same day. He gave them the money and told them the rest would be available at the end of the week, as that was the due date set by the boys for payment. The sharks were forced to back off. Breaking their word would be inexcusable. They might snap legs, but loaned out the correct amount and when paid, they let the pigeon walk. These were the rules. They lived by them. However, they immediately looked into the why and where the money had come from, as it hampered some very lucrative plans. There was no word on the street and even their people in the shipyard were surprised.

The Sand Darter was kind of special too. You see the Hollywood people wanted to make a movie with, an "S" type submarine and well, seeing the script espoused the Navy point of view, the old Sand Darter was dragged out, spruced up and re-engined. In fact, the Sand Darter had sailed up and down off the coast for a month during the filming reaching speeds of up to 18 knots. Sand Darter had finished her movie career and had been placed back into the fold. This was by pure clerical error and two years before Bill's little problem, but it didn't go unnoticed.

Bains filled late trucks with shipments for the active fleet ships down the line. For two weeks each shipment carried extras and a new helper each night. Bains would work a little on the minesweeper, removing a list of parts required by his department, undersigned by himself. The parts were useless but while he worked, other hands filled the Sand Darter with Lieless's list of supplies. Only Bains returned in the truck each night.

Asian Eleiani had a good business. He sold meat to the base. His company was well known and the meat was of the highest quality. His trucks came to the base every day.

As they were refrigerated, they were less well looked at and tended to pass into the zone without too much trouble. Terry Bains met each truck directing it to a little-used rear docking area. He made sure he was first in and a local worker helped with the meat. The man, of course, was already in the truck as it docked. Afterward the extra worker was hidden in an unused bathroom until night when he became the next helper on the late truck. Eleiani knew nothing of this.

That dull, windy morning, as the gray clouds scuttled across a frigid November sky, Yan Van Pallon looked at the old Sand Darter with a critical eye. Twelve men crouched inside the hull of the submarine waiting for the remainder of their plan to proceed. For a week they had slept in an airless coffin, coming out only at night, to pass boxes in the November cold. Here they sat for a few moments in the luxurious night air, chilled to the bone, hidden by the windbreak of the conning tower.

Each new man was a story in himself. Especially picked for the job. They entered the United States through major airports, on fishing boats or across the Canadian Border. Carrying fake documents and speaking little English they proceeded to their goal, a large red brick house on a residential street in Norfolk. All were sailors. Most had submarine experience. They were veterans with years at sea. One was a cook, one was an engineer and one was an acrobat.

The cold was the worst part for the stowaways because the temperatures in their own countries were so much warmer. The hull gave some respite, streaming with condensed moisture. They wrapped themselves in mounds of blankets. They also had and thermo-sleeping bags the best the US Navy could offer. They ate K rations, smelling their own stink and prayed to be warm again.

The sound of chattering teeth welled up to Abdullha Kindaani as he peered through the fixed periscope. This had been left partially up so that the would be members of the Sand Darter crew might know if they should set off the charges which would sink the ship, kill themselves and a wide range of people in the immediate area.

Abdullha's grave broad face with its shovel beard, was affixed to the eyepiece. Shivering with the cold, he prayed to his God and watched the Dutchman survey the cables and other lines linking the tow.

Van Pallon checked the hatches on the subs personally. He moved from one to another to make sure they were water tight. If the submarines turned turtle he could right them again. The air inside would keep them on the surface, but a loose hatch was death and Yan had never lost a tow. The tow, overall, was ungainly and would be a problem. He did not like the boat trailing, for a number of reasons. However, the eight-inch Lancaster steel mesh hawser that tied the Sand Darter to the thick stern pylon of the minesweeper seemed to make him more comfortable. The North Atlantic was known for its November storms and the Caribbean

for its late autumn hurricanes. Yan would take no
chances. He almost had the fourth ship tied to the
outside of the other three but decided this would
make the tow more ungainly. A hardened hand
caressed his beard. The tow was as ready as it
would ever be. He snorted at the something, he
could not put his finger on. His weathered hands
wrenched at the hatch cover on the Sand Darter's
conning tower. A foot away Abdullha held the
electric detonator that would kill them both.
Abdullha watched with horror as the hatch gave
slightly then held. The would-be skipper, placed
more pressure on the red button in the face of the
detonator. The plastic was slippery in his hand,
then the upward pressure to lift the hatch stopped.
Yan looked at the hatch and made a mental
calculation accepted the cover was strong enough
and turned away.

  Back on board the Van Klu, Yan asked the pilot to
take her out. The Yank nodded. His name was
Knowlen and he whistled, 'Blow the Man Down',
as he pulled away from the dock taking the tow in
line. He knew his stuff this talky Yank; Yan nodded
to himself and hummed along under his breath with
Knowlen's nautical tune. The five ships moved
across the rough harbour water like pearls on a
string.

Kindaani relaxed for the first time in months. He wore the slouch cap of his navy without an emblem. Beneath the plastic visor his sharp brown eyes fixed on the future. His nose was Arabic straight, over a pursed and pensive mouth.

Abdullha feared and looked forward to taking over this ship. Would the engines work? Would the tanks blow? Allah alone knew. But he had faith in his God and American machinery. The plan would work, he reassured himself. One trembling hand, pried the detonator from the clutched fingers of the other.

Kindaani was flabbergasted at the amount of supplies he had received. The heavy cutting tools were never unloaded but then, the cutters were only a cover. On the other hand bedding, televisions, microwaves the list seemed never ending. Each day more and more, as if someone had opened the great horn of plenty and aimed it at the Sand Darter.

In his navy, supplies were always short. The food eatable but limited, this was like heaven.

He feared that the fuel tanks, being half filled, would give them away. They had waited day after day in fear of discovery. No one came. It appeared no one cared. Abdullha was not surprised. The west had so much. They discarded things that in his land would be highly valuable even in a used condition. They had so much, what matter an old sub soon to become scrap.

Entering Canada on a visitor's visa. Abdullha had simply disappeared one dark, night down a small, seldom-used road, on the Quebec border into Vermont. A quiet thin faced man in glasses who, had met Kindaani at the airport, now drove the great four-lane highway that spread south allowing 'for the flow of thousands of new cars, shining in the sun of late autumn, on the road to Miami.

Grocery stores here in the United States were filled with food, piled on all the shelves, so much. The helper took him to the great red house in Norfolk and said a soft goodbye in Syrian French.

Abdullha spoke to the people because he had a few words in English. There was no hatred, no cast down, he was not spat upon. In America he was treated with the same practiced indifference as everyone else.

In a land of infidels there were mosques well appointed and modern. The word was here, what made the hatred between governments did not make the hatred between people. Christians, Jews and others lived side by side, on the same street and yet there was no warfare. Kindaani could find no anger for these people, still he was a sailor and he had to follow his orders.

On the Jan Van Klu, Yan and his men made ready for sea, out past Fort Monroe and the mouth of the Chesapeake Bay to the open Atlantic. The Dutchman would stay close to land and a safe port incase he needed it.

Night found the little string of ships off the Carolinas. The dark surrounded them like a raven's wing. There was no moon. Running lights defined Van Klu's flock on the dark rollers, twinkling across the waves.

Abdullha waited before sending Ali forward. Ali was small and smiled a great deal. He was the joker that made them all laugh with his antics but he was as strong as steel and brave as a bull in heat. Finally the captain nodded and with a grin the fine formed Ali was gone forward, up the hatch and to the towline that stretched to the other ship. He attached a ring style safety clamp around the cable. A line that wrapped around his waist now attached him to the heavy hawser. Now with the superstructure of

the minesweeper as a blind, he nimbly stepped up
onto the cable. His practiced grace showed him to
be a trained acrobat. Like a squirrel he navigated the
wet rope, velcrowed shoes giving him extra traction.
He reached the minesweeper in minutes.   Ali
crouched behind the steel pylon and removed the
flask from his belt. He made a small hole in the
cable and placed a few drops of the specially
formulated sulfuric acid, into the cable. He could
not see it eat its way into the nylon and steel but the
strands were weakening as he crouched there.
Having placed the flask back in his belt, Ali was
back up on the rope. With miraculous dexterity he
was on his way back to the submarine. He slipped
once but caught himself, balanced like a monkey on
a string, then like a jack in a box righted himself
and returned to the Sand Darter. Each night he
would perform this feat. The rope must look like it
broke of its own accord. Every possible subterfuge
must be made to cover the sub's disappearance. It
must be as real as possible, right down to the rust-
like stains created by the acid and the slow
implosion of the cable. Patience was their greatest
weapon. .

Slowly, day by day, the little procession moved
along. Only one weak storm tossed the trailing sub.
The hidden seamen suffered seasickness, even with
the small pink pills that were handed out in
bunches. The heat in the hull became unbearable
until night, when the hatches could be opened.

Car lights from Florida's A1A highway, which
followed the coast, glittered in the distance. The
small amount of acid from Ali's bottle was slowly
eating away the strength at the center of the cable.
Once a day, a small motor launch sailed back from
the Van Klu to check the tow and make sure no
damage had occurred the night before. All seemed
well but Van Pallon was still uncomfortable with
the rear most submarine he could do little more then
check it. Yan would not lose a tow. His brand of
seaman ship did not allow for big mistakes or small
ones for that matter. The elder Van Pallon, his
father had been happy to restate almost daily "The
difference between a good carpenter and a poor
carpenter, was that a good carpenter could fix his
mistakes." Yan knew his mistakes could kill him
before he could correct them. Like an itch he could
not scratch, he watched the Sand Darter.

The sea remained calm around the tip of Florida.

Miami passed a glittering display of multi coloured
lights. The keys stretched away to starboard. Cuba
rose up on Van Klu's portside. The Cuba deep
separated the two.

The barometer fell about midnight and the sea took
on the gray oily surface that heralded a blow. Yan
battened down his hatches, closed his sea doors and
made for the safety of Mexico across the deep.

The wind rose and the rain rattled down, then
washed the ships in sheets. Visibility was poor,
Abdullha decided the time was now, before the
opportunity passed. Ali opened the hatch and stood
up into the storm. The little acrobat knew he must
die this night because no man that lived could walk
the curling snake that the cable had become. Yet he
moved to the rope and placed his ring safety piece
on it. If he got to the other side he must cut the rope.
Unless of course it was ready to give and then hide
on the minesweeper if he could, until he could get
away at Cancun. Ali placed one foot on the cable
and froze the snap of the tearing cable came to him
like a riffle shot carried on the wind over the storm.
His mind had just realized he did not need to make
the crossing. He was mentally thanking his God,
when the eight-inch cable now freed of the
tremendous tension snaked back

across the space between the two ships like a giant whip and literally cut Ali's fragile body in two. He was there and then gone. The man behind moved out and pulled the ring of the cable from the submarine's towing capstan, allowing its weight to carry the remaining cord overboard. It would stay on the surface being lighter then water initially.

The sailor raced back and slammed down the hatch, spinning the wheel to lock, just as Abdullha flooded the tanks and the submarine sank like a stone. With no momentum, it simply sank like a breached hull. He let her fall 100 feet, 150, 200 at 250 the hull clanked and moaned at three hundred, the old metal almost twanged with the tension of the water pressure at that depth. Abdullha balanced the bubble and demanded power.

Sumaraai's father had been a camel driver. The boy, wanting more had taken work on an old coastal steamer shoveling coal. In thirty years he had risen to Chief Warrant officer and an engineer. The only residue of the desert left in Sumaraai was a tongue with a lash in it that made strong men pale. The foul language, now disposed on the engines of the Sand Darter, his crewman and this cursed pig bladder he was in, was like a symphony of anger. The men laughed behind their hands inspite of the terrible danger, for they knew if Sumaraai could swear the problem, could be fixed. It was the silence they feared.

"Start, thrice cursed son of a whore's plagued backside." The engine coughed rheumatic and died. "Start you floating indignity to a turd's leavings." Snarled Sumaraai. The engines whimpered almost caught and died again. " Start you pus filled, misabuse of space, accused whelping of a rabid camel and the lowest blighted scum wadded male syphilitic in the gutter." The engine coughed again, sighed as if considering the matter, then roared into life. The cheer of triumph went up all over the ship. "Quiet fools!' Abdullha bellowed over the air-conditioner that had also come on. 'They will hear us." In a second only the air conditioner could be heard.

The breaking of the towline woke Van Pallon. Van Klu accelerated with the loss of pulling weight. This drove him from his bunk behind the bridge like a screaming whistle. He was on the bridge in seconds. The tug was already turning to see what had happened.

The submarine was almost under water when it came into view from abaft the minesweeper. She must have hit something, was the first thing that entered Yan's mind. Then he knew, with a bitter reality, that he had been taken. How, he did not know but he knew. The Darter settled down, down, down as if she had been holed but he knew she wasn't, couldn't be. There was no wreckage. The storm was hammering the rest of his tow. Yan had to make the Mexican coast, dropping into Castro's Cuba trailing American warships, was out of the question. As the sub passed below three hundred feet and beyond the range of his radar the bitter Dutchman turned away and gave the SOS signal that a ship was down. They dropped a buoy. Thinking better of the storm Van Pallon turned North to the safety of Florida. The Van Klu chugged out of sight followed by the three sisters. Both the Cuban and the US Coastguard sent out ships but found nothing.

South between Cuba and Jamaica deep beneath the storm men cried and ate and drank and praised God. Few of Sand Darter's new crew laughed and then it was weak. They remembered Ali.

Chapter Fourteen – 10:00 P.m. London, United Kingdom

Face to Face.

Heathrow was busy as usual. The security was about the same or slightly lighter given the IRA wasn't blowing things up, at that exact moment.

One of London's pleasant and easily the politest cabbies in the world took me to the Selby Regent. The room was expensive, small but well appointed. The trip was exhausting and I was still suffering from jet lag. I sat on the orange brown bedspread and removed my shoes. I had not been followed from the airport. In absolute honesty, I really didn't care. Tomorrow my life as a spy would be over. In one more day Air Canada would carry me back ove the Atlantic and home. After that someone else could take the weight of the world on his or her shoulders. Someone else could face the opposition and defend me for a while.

I changed into conservative light blue pajamas and ordered a meat pie, mashed potatoes and vegetables I also asked for a bottle of Blue Parrot a good sweet Mosel wine. This was delivered while I watched the tube. There was a range of comedies. I recognized Roland Atkinson, surely one the three funniest

comedians on the planet and some game shows. I half watched until my eyes would not stay open any more. I would face the music tomorrow. One of my blood pressure pills and I would be asleep. One more check of my laptop. There was a message from Road Town with Breakleaf's call sign. A quick translation and the information appeared from a mass of cover material. Well I will be damned, wait till Granny got this bit of juice.
Thank you Harry for the help.

Nine A.m. sharp, showered, dressed and on my taxi tour up passed the Parliament buildings, the Guildhall and the New Bank of England Building. Touristing, of course, was only a visible part of the package. No tail showed, had it I would have returned to the hotel and called for instructions. I got out at Nelson's Column and walked across to take a look, having observed the monument erected to one of England's greatest hero pigeon droppings and all. I walked to the nearest point where I could take a Double Decker bus. Four stops and off. Buses are the hardest things imaginable to tail. No one was there I thought? Now a new cab, for a further tour to St. Paul and so on.
 Finally after being sure I had no tail I took a third

cab to a point two blocks from the headquarters court and walked the remainder of the way.

The November wind cut into the heavy, black wool, overcoat I was wearing over a blue Henley wool suit. The scarf at my neck was wine coloured, black calf leather gloves made in China protected my hands. It seemed that everything was made in China nowadays. The coat was British made, but purchased in the US. My black Florsheim Oxfords clicked over the cobbles past Granny's sleeping oak. The bright, aqua, blue door was flanked by a brass plate that stated Epsylon Computer did business at this address.

I entered and met Hammond the concierge. The ex-Royal Marine appeared from his glass-fronted booth. He was poured into a nondescript, vaguely police like uniform. Constructed of 250 lbs. of solid muscle, he probably knew more ways of killing you than you could count. He produced a good-natured Midland's smile and nodded.

"May I see what you've got then, sir?" he indicated my brief case.

I passed it over and with one quick motion he looked into its battered interior.

"All right then, the top of the stairs to the right." He said helpfully.

I had never been in headquarters before or at least

this one. The old head office had been near White
Hall before they had departmentalized it by regions.

I made the top of the stairs passed through the
defensive door and got a smile from a proper
looking thiry-ish secretary. Large dark rimmed
glasses sat on the bridge of her nose and short dark
hair almost touched her shoulder. Her face had once
been beautiful and still held its ground against time.
Small wrinkles showed around the corners of the
mouth, which was large and sensuous. They
continued around pleasant brown eyes and made
telltale inroads at the base of the nose.. This would
be Ascot, Granny's secretary. It was said in meaner
quarters she was the real Director of the North
American Bureau.

"Good morning, I hope you had a good trip?" She
said smiling again.

I nodded and she directed me to a boardroom. I felt
uncomfortable and wasn't in the mood for small
talk. She left me there having relieved me of my
coat. I sat on the near side of the oak conference
table in a comfortable tilt-back, light blue chair. My
report looked lonely on the table's dark surface. Its
twelve pages had already been dissected, I was sure
but you never took the chance something wasn't
clear. Eleven other plush chairs surrounded the

table. The walls were light gray and bare.
Phosphorescent lighting left the room in a
comfortable glow, not overly bright but easy on the
eyes. The room was obviously sound proof.

I figured there might be a wait but no, Granny
came in about two minutes later.

Standing up, I offered my hand and he took it
firmly.

"Well almost lost you that time." He said but not
callously, simply stating a fact. Granny looked
trendy in a soft gray wool suit with its matching
blue silk shirt and tie. His walk was relaxed but the
back was ramrod straight.

"It's good to see you too." I quipped. Granny
laughed.

"Touché. How's your wife?"

"Well, thank you."

"Your children must be getting on?"

"Yeah! The oldest is starting university next year."

"Ye gods, don't give you much of a chance do
they? Grow up before you can appreciate them,
gone before you know it."

"Tell me about it." I said in agreement.

He sat on the other side of the table. Looked at his
watch and right at me.

"Business I'm afraid, sorry." He was I could tell.

"No problem boss." I said leaning forward in my

chair. He smiled again. No one else addressed him
in that manner. He didn't mind or didn't seem to.
We were friends or as close as you got to it in this
business.

"Right!" He said, sitting back in his chair and
taking out a cigarette from a gold case. I said
nothing. He would not ask my permission to smoke
and I didn't expect it. He lit the Players with a gold
Zippo and sucked the smoke deep. This was going
to be short and to the point, I knew Granny. He had
other things on his mind.

"I thought you did rather well, until the hospital in
Red Hook." He started.

"Thanks, but I know I screwed it up pretty badly."
My attention was fixed on my hands.

"No, you didn't,' He said flatly with some
irritation. 'If you are alive you did bloody well, so
let's get past self-recrimination, shall we? Why did
you go back for the girl?" This was an excellent
question.

"Not some sort of sexual thing I hope?" he added,
his eyes x-rayed from under arched brows. That was
a fair question too. I didn't like it. The way it was
asked indicated Granny knew something. I had an
answer rehearsed and ready, best of all it was the
truth.

"No, I got a kid her age. At least I thought was her

age. Couldn't leave her there all by herself hurt and
so on." I trailed off then looked up perhaps fearing
he wouldn't believe me. "I missed her completely. I
should have known she was U.S. Naval Intelligence
right off. I'm getting too old for this stuff Granny. I
was playing daddy and she was covering me."
I spoke looking him in the eye. The golden brow
arched.

"Piffle." He snorted.

"Sometime when I get good and drunk I'll tell you
about Singapore and a certain Russian Agent.' We
both knew that would never happen but it was a
nice gesture. 'Did she set you up?"

"No!' I said honestly. "I have to believe Jacob took
some money from the opposition.

"Right, I agree, they can't find him. His clothes
were in his room. I suspect that he was introduced
to the shark population off St. Thomas."

"Brilliant!" I said, out loud. I liked Jacob. He
might have been forced to pass me that message but
I suspect he was simply greedy and had been dealt
with to remove loose ends. I felt no ill will. I had
bribed him too. Anyway he had already lost his
chips.

"That prick Hedi was behind it or Jug.' I now

quietly played the cards Harry had given me.
'Breakleaf sent me a message. They killed Lacy for
nothing."

"What!" Granny had strict rules about information
flow and it should have come direct to him. A storm
was brewing behind his white, bloodless, rage filled
face.

"It's not important now,' I said trying to make it
less a problem.' But they got the guys who were
killing the turtles. It's in a report from the Colonial
office. I guess two islanders an Amos Fleet and
Taffy Hands from Tortola, found a box of grenades
off a wreck. The grenades are new so I figure they
stumbled on some drug stash. They have been doing
some dynamite fishing. Throw in a grenade, collect
whatever comes up. The turtles must have been in
the same area. After a blast the sharks just go nuts
all that blood and dead fish. The Leather Backs that
weren't eaten outright made it to the beach and died
there."

"Good God!" said Granny with real vengeance. '
Why kill Lacy then?"

" He was good at his job that's all.' I shook my
head, 'He checked out the Colony, didn't find
anything and decided to be thorough. He called the
local government in Charlotte Amalie to see if

anyone had been blasting. Someone passed it on that he called. Hedi was left in charge for some reason. The opposition of course had widened the entrance in the reef by blowing it up in small parts. Collee told me that. Hedi put two and two together and got a hundred and five, scratch Lacy."

"And our fishermen?" Asked Granny, his face was dark and foreboding.

"They took their profits and went on a bender. That was why the turtles stopped dying. After the money ran out they went back to work, nearly blew themselves to pieces. They're in the hospital at East End, had no part in anything at all."

I had just taken the torch for Breakleaf who would catch it for missing the grenade angle. Good friends did that. However, there was no blast. Granny got real thoughtful and I figured this was as good a time, as any.

"Listen Boss, I think it's time I retire. For a lot of reasons, the American girl, Jacob, getting captured, not getting the proper information myself. I'm getting old.' I sighed 'I was too old for this kind of thing from the start. I should be home with the family. They're getting big and.... " That is as far as I got.

"Save you're self pity and your resignation will you. We have a problem here." Granny's face presented a wintry expression and he was right of course.

"What do you want to know?" I said with equal frost.

'Tell me about the opposition." He tilted his chair away from me.

"Mohammed is the brains, at least on the ground. He runs the show and he has a good working knowledge of the rules of engagement. He's either Russian or US trained."

"U.S.?" Granny queried.

"Yeah! The CIA's been training the Palestinians for the last five years, part of the Palestinian land deal. That's one of the reasons the Mossat has been getting kicked around lately. The Arabs are learning. Mohammed might be part of that, he sure as God made little green apples, isn't Jordanian." Granny nodded and I continued.

"He didn't dream up this deal. That's from somewhere else, he's a journeyman spy not an operator."

"Any idea who?" Granny asked. He of course knew about the CIA and the Middle East land deal, but was probably surprised I knew.

"No! This whole thing stinks, nothing fits. However, one, there is going to be one hell of a robbery. Two,' I counted on my fingers, 'someone trained 300 odd mercs and they are armed to the teeth. Three, there are billions of dollars involved. Four, the target is tied to us somewhere down the line, I mean Great Britain. Finally, there is a ton of money and manpower behind this operation." I finished and sat back.

"Hum" Granny stated while leaning back in his chair until he finally was almost lying there staring at the ceiling.

"Why a robbery? What is the money for? That is the question. Getting it is simply the prelude.' Granny spoke slowly gesturing with the shrinking cigarette.

"Waste Not, Want Not, Covet Not, Spy Not, hey." This was Granny's favorite saying. 'Also, I think your man will use pick of the litter, so I don't believe you're facing 300 men, perhaps 60 at most. It gets too unwieldy after that. I further believe this is a one of a kind situation.

As to us, I can't see the connection. Hedi thought there was a threat. He was a little over zealous but he removed the threat. Simple mathematics there." Cold logic came with the Director's job. "You're absolutely right about the power behind it. The Arab tie in is very important. The American Mercenaries really bother me. Defining the connection between all these items is the most important aspect."

"Do you think it's Iraqis?" He continued in a moment. "They killed one of our people in Chile hanged him in his closet when he tied into arms shipments to Saddam."

"I really don't know, " I said, not knowing much of anything but it would be nice to put the blame on old Saddam.

"Something else," Granny lit a second Players. "True Love isn't owned by your friend Arrnie. He sold the place two years ago. The new owners are American through a bunch of cut offs. CIA perhaps?" Granny suggested.

"Not in a million years, Hedi is a believer. Dying for him is a one way paid trip to Valhalla. He isn't owned or operated by the CIA. He's an executioner come torturer and he likes his business but foremost he's a believer. He wouldn't last ten seconds with CIA. They kill him just for tranquility sake. Mohammed might be trained CIA but he doesn't answer to them. The, 'They', whoever they are, are from the Middle East. Jugs just a yes man with a gun.

If Langley knew about this one that girl from Naval Intelligence wouldn't have been following me. She never would have got that far. Someone in the Power Plant would have waved their magic wand and she would have been warned off."

"For some reason they don't seem to be too afraid of the Americans on home court." Granny rubbed his chin with his free hand.

"I think the True Love cover with the militias has been working real well for them. After Ruby Ridge, everybody stateside is scared stupid to start something and make a whole lot of martyrs. I think the Americans have been keeping an eye on the outside. No problems, no investment."

"This thing's big as a blimp.' I continued. ' I may not be real smart in the field, Boss, but you can feel the drive in this one. They're going at it like it's a fight that has to be won. This isn't half-baked. It's for all the marbles. There's power behind it."

"How is the Bank of England tied into it?" Granny didn't agree with my analysis.

"It all comes back to Sutton. He's the only piece of the puzzle that doesn't fit and the one thing that ties it all together."

"That does not answer my question." Granny snapped.

"Why kill Sutton?" I asked, "I give you Lacy. He's obviously a threat. Hedi is out of line, but you're right, he has to cover the potential problem. Now think how fast it happened. The action was knee jerk. Sutton was killed for the same perceived threat. He was killed wasn't he?"

"Oh, yes! His neck was broken before his car went over." Granny confirmed.

"Fine, here's a guy who has nothing to do with any part of it. If anything he's a glorified security guard, not their internal branch. His dad's dying of cancer. That is the only reason he's there. Sutton has no connection but they must have been watching him prior to Lacy's call. That's the only way it could move so quickly."

"Yes, of course. You're right." Granny was pensive, half there. "So the target is in the United Kingdom, or at least British related. One of our banks or a section of them. Channel Islands, Caymans, Montserrat before the eruption, Assumption, Turks and Cacaos. They're all bank havens of varied size, or here of course." Granny ruminated.

"I don't think it's here, but who knows? Anyway, to look at billions you'd need trucks to haul it away."

"Right, let's look at other things. What about the other girl?"

"Carma?"

"Yes, our Washington lobbyist." Granny confirmed.

"I was saving her. She is definitely opposition. She has to be. When they missed me at the airport, someone looked at the flight list and they called all the hotels to figure out where I went. They sent her down to check me out."

"I agree, which reminds me I don't like you using women and children as a divergence. It isn't sporting." Granny wagged a finger at me.

"Piffle!" I used his word and he didn't like it. "That baby vomit got me through the airport and identified Mona Horror, I mean Jug. If it hadn't been for that little ruse, I would have been dead or out of there. Blown in a day."

"If anyone ever gets killed because of that little ruse, you'll answer to me." His voice dropped to a whisper. Now that was a cold threat and one to remember.

"Fine, I resign and you can go to hell."

"Sit down,' He demanded. Then the voice became more conciliatory. He raised an elegant hand, " That didn't come out the way I wanted." I hesitated for a moment then, chastised.

"No one is going to shoot me in the middle of the airport. I've worked that fiddle a lot of times and nothing's ever happened. Do you think I could live with myself if someone died? Hell I have a family too."

"Forgive me its been a long day and it's 10:30. You were telling me about Carma." Granny was mad as hell.

"Fine, look she finds me at the hotel, maybe Jacob tags me. The first meeting was probably coincidence. She could have asked at the desk and got my description. I just happened to be in the bar. The second trip was targeted. I told her I worked on the islands. I said I'd be at Walley's and Mohammed shows up. I said I was going to run a shoot for the swimsuits, I did. Nothing screws them up like the truth or at least, half truths."

"That's why you had the latitude until you showed up for the walk about at True Love." My Director suggested.

"That and I challenged Jug, which was patently dumb." I conceded. 'The one thing we have is that we know Carma isn't Ms. Snow and we know she is tied to them."

"Yes, we've been keeping an eye on your Carma. You'll find this interesting. She has been to the

Caymans three times in the last four weeks."
Granny rolled his head toward me and smiled.

"So it's the Caymans." I sighed and concentrated
on the tabletop.

"Perhaps, or they know, we know, they know and
it's somewhere else."

"The Caymans would work on a lot of levels." I
said more to myself than to my boss.

"Absolutely, of course I'm still sparse on the
ground. You know Carma and the rest of them.
Lorning is out there, good man, but then I really
have no one to back him up and the Colonial people
poo-pooed it."

I didn't like Lorning. We had run into each other
before. He was a competent man, but was too much
book and heavy handed for my taste.

"You want me to stick around then." I said off-
handedly.

"Yes.! It would help to no end."

"Look, what I said about retiring. I'm serious."
Granny seemed to deflate somewhat.

"I was serious too. I don't have people right now
and the action will take place soon. You go to the
Caymans and if you see Mohammed, or any of his
happy band or anything, you tell Lorning and he'll
take care of it. You're only there to observe.
Period."

This was my baby. Lacy had found it by pure luck and diligence. I believed this deal was important, very important. I rung my hands and scratched my nose.

"O.K."

Chapter Fifteen – Tuesday 11:30 A.m. London,
United Kingdom.

After Thoughts

McFurson left, pensive and uncomfortable, with
his decision to stay on.

Granny watched him leave the boardroom still
almost horizontal in his chair. There had been no
handshake. Anger creased Stater's slender mouth.

So McFurson wanted to retire, damn him! How
dare he speak to his Director like that? Granny had
given the Canadian his trust and covered for him
when he fell down.

Resettling Collee had cost Granny a great deal, not
simply in favours to the US and others, which
would have to be repaid, but the vetting of Collee
and his family had taken months. Granny was
reasonably sure the man wasn't a plant but you
never knew. The potential return from Collee in
information was negligible. Then, of course, there
were the powers that be that questioned everything.
All the delicate explanation to these hard hearted
souls as well. You'd think Boothby had started a
war with the Americans rather then uncovering a
plot.

However, while Boothby could be very unpleasant if crossed as many in and outside the firm had found out to their discomfort, Granny wasn't one of the 'I'll get even with you', types, which in many cases, allowed for overkill. Perhaps that was why he and the bloody colonial got along so well?

When you boiled it down to its base point, Mike McFurson was spot on in his self-assessment. He was too old. Granny knew it. Under normal circumstances he would have asked him to go back to his family in the wilds of Canada. Granny also knew McFurson was not finished yet. Some men had more in them than they thought. Others believed they had it and did not. McFurson had made mistakes but had survived. He had proved smarter and more resilient than Granny had suspected.

In truth, Granny was less then half convinced that the Caymans were the target of Michael's Mega Robbery. If there were to be a robbery?

Granny chapeled his fingers on his chest like a penitent king laid out in Westminster. He wondered if this outward show of concern had any value on the other side? Did it accumulate some measure of goodwill versus royal sins? He decided God would not be placated in the least, Granny wouldn't be.

He would have to find people to cover the various colonies for a few days concerning the potential robbery. These would be mainly senior police people and Governor's security types like Breakleaf.

Which reminded him. Granny would have to send off a rocket to jolly old Harry about those grenade happy Islanders. West Indians were never faulted for their silence, no tomb like leanings here. Talk on the docks, on the beach or in the local pubs should have reached Handsome Harry, if he was about his business.

Breakleaf was too involved with the Governor, the social life and the wide range of female tourists visiting the British Virgins. Women hoping to take home a unique memory, which the mustached Major was more then ready to provide. If it weren't for Breakleaf's work with McFurson and his shortage of people, Granny would have transferred the khaki Valentino to a colder clime. Let us see how Harry did with Eskimos say. Granny's smile was not pleasant. The smile quickly disappeared though. Transferring Breakleaf, no matter how much joy it would give him, would of course, cause the Governor's security man to resign and leave a hole elsewhere.

Granny felt like a grand master whose pieces kept disappearing. He drew another Players from the gold cigarette case with the gothic "T" inset in its face. It was a gift from Mommy. Poor Mommy! She went to her grave thinking her son was a computer technician and after doing so well in the army too. Granny sighed and sat upright.

So McFurson wanted to resign did he? Well bugger that for a lark. Boothby needed everyone right now. That was of course why he was financing McFurson's trip to the Caymans.

Michael had his quirks; most importantly he had the policeman like need to see things through to an end. McFurson believed in the Mega Robbery, Good! Let him look around. It couldn't hurt and would do him a world of good.

Carma, Michael's big lead, had only been to the Islands once, not three times as Granny had suggested, to get McFurson to stay on. Then she was only there for a weekend to sleep with some US Senator. Lucky bloody him! Carma was a beauty. From photographs Granny had seen, the woman was spectacular, that kind of model, come super star perfection. If as the U.S. Navy said, McFurson had turned her down bare bum naked and dripping wet. 'You're a better man then me, Gunga Din.' It

was, however, somehow reassuring that kind of
virtue still existed. Mrs. McFurson must be some
woman.

On the other hand there was the U.S. Naval
Intelligence Ensign. McFurson had looked away
quickly breaking eye contact when discussing her. If
Granny had any perception at all, the old bugger
could be rogering her, good and proper. The vision
of McFurson's overweight body locked in combat
with the blond passed quickly through Granny's
mind. Boothby shook his head in a short agitated
way as if he had touched fresh offal. Lord that was
frightening!

At any rate it was McFurson's sin and McFurson's
conscience. His life was his as long as he hadn't
gone over? No! Not McFurson surely.

Granny figured the Mega Robbery if it still existed
was off the tracks for months. The amount of
planning required would be dramatic. The simple
fact that he knew anything at all meant that the
opposition would have to take time to reorganize.
None of the Friends (Information sources) around
the world had any input into this robbery. Perhaps
True Love was something else?

McFurson would go to the Caymans to get back in

the hunt. He would look for his Mega Robbery,
listen to his beloved reggae, and enjoy the sun. He
would have time to think and rationalize his future.
Michael had killed, that shakes a person to the
foundations. He had faced torture, the mind molding
had helped but it was never intended to turn a man
into an automaton. McFurson had felt the pain,
faced death and navigated a black, empty sea. By all
rights he should be drooling in some hospital.
Granny knew there was enough strength in Michael
to overcome his problem. Once McFurson had his
self-confidence back Granny would start him out
with light runs until he was back in harness, but no
more line work. If not, Michael had earned his
vacation and well Granny would find someone else.
He wasn't too worried though. You could bet on
some men, Dr.M was one of them.

   There were so many other problems out in the real
world. For instance, Canadian Helicopters were
disappearing from their warehouse. It seems these
mothballed Canadian Forces units were being
whisked away across the U.S. border and then by
devious means to the South Pacific, from there over
land to the Middle East. Fortunately for everyone,
one of his people in Canada had been informed and
with a lot of work and luck turned it over to the

Canadians and FBI, without being involved. The first helicopter got as far as Taiwan and stopped dead.

The customer was not happy, there were a lot of red faces in Canada and heads were rolling at this very moment in Langley. Of course there was some little praise for the firm. This in turn would take care of Collee and a lot more. That was on the positive side. Along with McFurson's little card trick in the U.S. Virgins the old Firm was coming back with a vengeance. Of course it was the U.S. who stopped the helicopter. With the repatriation of Hong Kong to the Red Chinese there was no British flag in the east, unless of course you counted in Pitcarin and the thirty or so stalwart souls who lived on that particle of the earth.

The Empire, England couldn't hold on to the vast crimson lands that had once populated the globe. Too expensive, too colonial, too politically incorrect. Let the native's lead their own lives. Granny realized his pieces weren't just disappearing. The chess board was being pulled out from under them. Well there would always be the Embassies and the service, more important now that the old friends were more enemies and the new friends in East Europe not yet assured. There was always something to do.

Take the submarine that had sunk off Miami for instance. The Americans had lost it. Technically it was scrap but then the Dutch tug captain was screaming blue murder and the sinking seemed unusual. Granny had requested that any information that might be of interest about the Caribbean be passed on to him because of the Virgin Island thing. Who would want to steal a submarine and one about to be scrapped at that? Of course the Colombian Cartel had used a sub for sometime to move drugs to the U.S. and other destinations nearby. Its old, oil powered, engines seemed to be hard to follow for the thousands of sensors the U.S. had laid down to follow Soviet nuclear submarines. They could hear some Russian sub commander cough in Vladivostok but the old oil burning subs sounded like fishing boats to the scanners. Absolutely nothing like technology.

Of course it was easier for the cartel to move drugs on the cruise ships that stopped all over the Caribbean. Puerto Rico was a prime location for this sort of thing. Crewmembers were threatened or

paid to carry large quantities of the drugs to Miami.
Crew personnel were overlooked, by customs and
tended to filter out of the port areas in Miami, as
their faces got to be known and therefor considered
non threatening.

The interesting part of the sub thing was that the
Americans, for some reason, had not told him about
the sinking. His man in Miami had picked it up
from the Port Authority. Granny could only suspect
that the CIA was up to something and didn't want to
share. Of course, if they did lose the sub and it had
any value, the embarrassment would be
excruciating, especially after the helicopter thing.
Another less pleasant possibility was that the scrap
sub had hit another unit, say one of their Trident
nuclear boats. At the moment the Trident Fleet was
being refitted or so the US said. Maybe, like the
pilot who had cut the ski gondola cable in Italy by
flying too low on a training run, one of the Tridents
was out and about and there was a mistake. The
possibility of a fully armed nuclear submarine on
the floor of the Cuba Deep would close down
communications between the US and everyone.
However, the Russians who usually knew about

these things five minutes after they happened had been very quiet. The submarine was someone else's problem.

Granny breathed out the last of his Players and stood up. McFurson was on his own. The Americans were too for that matter. Granny had his budget to present. If it wasn't one thing, it was the next.

Chapter Sixteen – 8:01 A.m., Monday,
Seven Mile Beach, Grand Cayman.

Unexpected Meetings

The wind swept in off the ocean from Mexico,
sweet and clean. It disturbed the palms and cooled
the morning heat. I, Michael McFurson sap! Sat in
the cool shadow of The Quest, a five, star, luxury
Hotel, that towered in pink splendor, ten stories
above the beach bordering the A1 HWY. The A1
snaked off north to the turtle farm and south to
Georgetown, through a maze of malls and hotels.
White, padded, lawn furniture surrounded the small
restaurant island, on the pool deck. I was the lone
customer.
Granny had huckstered me in but then I wanted to
fall into the trap. Being a courier gave my life
something, meaning, others couldn't understand. It
made me really alive. At the moment, when I was
closest to death at True Love, I was so alive my
heart raced with the purity of its hallo. How could
you go back to the mundane after an experience like
that? So I had to make good or no more adrenaline.

For two weeks I had wandered Grand Cayman until I knew Georgetown, the capital of the British Dependent Territory and the surrounding small towns like the back of my hand.

I had rented a car to drive the highways and back roads at first, but later I had jogged. Running killed time and allowed me to look into areas where a car was a hindrance. I had become tanned and my gut had more or less disappeared. I cut down on my food for the thirtieth time sticking to the diet finally I felt better than I had in ten years. That much was positive.

The rest, well, I found nothing, no face was familiar, nothing , no one who I could tie into the robbery.

People smiled and offered directions on how to find places. They knew nothing of the visitors I was looking for. A large group of Americans all big men. They must have thought I was fey.

If Carma had been here, she had not returned. Lorning had given grudging support. He, of course, was too much part of the team not to pitch in but it took a lot out of him. In actual fact I knew he thought I was nuts to suggest someone would try an

Island robbery. I know this because he straight out told me. His ferretie, triangular face with its calculating light brown eyes, pencil thin nose and small slash mouth seemed to gyrate so that the thinning silver hair bounced as he snapped off the information.

"Which end they hit on you, mate? We got the Royal Marines here. The security people for each of the banks are capable blokes. Your bunch of mercenaries would be decoed five minutes after they landed. Where the flaming hell is you're lot going to go if they do pull it off, sprout wings and fly? We can close the airport in five minutes and the HMS Seagull will track down anything that floats. We do things right here. I'm not Breakleaf." He finished.

Of course you're not Breakleaf, his parents were married to each other. I thought to myself.

"Listen I know what I heard. This might not be the place for the robbery but Granny thinks it is." I suggested. This finished the conversation Lorning wasn't going to upset anything Granny had put in place. It was agreed meanly, that Lorning would keep an eye on the airport and pass on all flight lists to me for verification. I would check out the passengers from the cruise ships. My job was made easier because the passengers had to come in on jolly boats, about thirty at a time, as the harbour was too shallow for the great passenger ships. This meant that everyone got off at one place, The Port Facility pier. Here they took the mandatory picture next to the 'Welcome to the Cayman Islands' sign with its crested turtle design sporting a tricorner hat. It was then mandatory to cross Harbour Drive to be dazzled by the local merchants.

This was purely going through the paces though. There were thousands of places to come ashore from a small boat at night. It was like putting your thumb on a sieve. I knew Lorning was right, barring a miracle we would only know about the robbery after the fact. Then it would be up to him, The Royal Cayman Islands Police Force and Captain Reggie Bloodworth of Third Commando Royal Marines, to hash out.

The one argument for my staying was that I was really enjoying myself. I walked from my bed and breakfast in Georgetown through peaceful streets to the pier each morning and watched the tourists come ashore, exchanging glances with the scantily clad girls and enjoying the scenery. I would then go to one of many good restaurants in Georgetown for a Crab sandwich or a nice fish salad for lunch. Afterwards I would take a quick island wide drive

just for my own sake, then a slow walk around the
banking district. This itinerary varied but in the
evening after a good seafood dinner, salmon steaks
or other freshly landed fish in special sauces. I
would either listened to some very good Island
music with some good people or sleep soundly afte
checking the lists from the airport.

Each day I woke up in paradise. Miss Andrea
Jones, my fifty something landlady at Saraphine
House, a great rambling white building with soft
beds and friendly security, would make me a light
breakfast. While doing so, she would tell me about
the day's events and things to do about the city, in
her enchanting island twang. Once a day I went to
Seven-Mile Beach to swim and look at the Hotels.
The girls swirled by in their bikinis and I lay in the
sun.

Of course it couldn't last. The Governor was
inquiring into exactly what was being learned? As
well as what the hell was going on? I suspect good
old Lorning was behind this and he had a point. I
had found out nothing, only that I loved the Islands
and wanted to stay forever. This, of course, was not
what I was here for and Granny had to be
remembered. He was a good guy but he wasn't
going to pay the bills forever. The Cayman Dollar

being worth a dollar twenty-five U.S it couldn't last.

The guy, who coined the phrase "HE HATH FOUNDED IT UPON THE SEAS" the Cayman's motto, really knew what he was talking about. However, I was going to send Granny a thank you note. I'd tell him that it looked like the Caymans were not the target and that I would be going home.

Then last night a name, a single name on an arrival list changed it all. Lionel Adams was on the Caymans. Why?

Darius might be sending its President to the islands for a little sun but then why in November. It was cooler now, less tourists. He could be here to make a deposit. Billions of untaxed dollars came here on Lear Jets, just like the one Lionel had taken, to make sure the money wasn't taxed.

North American commerce came to the Caymans to keep their money and make sure their Governments didn't know where it was. The British had made a profit from this little three island group because dollars placed in its banks, were completely secure, no one could look into who banked here or where the money came from. This of course was a godsend for the Drug Cartels who laundered obscene amounts of loot as fast as it could be gotten to the islands. The British Government was trying, to stop this practice, to be fair.

Whatever happened, I at least had a lead. I was here drinking tea waiting for Mr. Adams to come down.

This of course could simply be embarrassing. Adams might have nothing to do with it. Perhaps he was just here for a little sun and no more. Reality or fantasy I had to know. I would confront him.

If told, Lorning would want him followed. I knew from cold experience that the mind behind this whole thing was far too organized to lead us anywhere at all. Maybe our friend had a weak link. God knew what that might be, but then that was my job to find out wasn't it?

Something else was bothering me. I was being followed. I hadn't seen the person or persons but they existed in half glimpsed movements and cars that turned too smoothly away. After fourteen years you knew. They were very professional. At first I thought it was Lorning. It might have been but he didn't have that kind of finesse.

It's the little nuances. Like trailing your car from in front, very difficult! The multiple cars used in sequence. When you live or die from the watch you keep, you know when it's happening like so many times before. No action had come from the surveillance. This meant someone was watching until something happened. It could be CIA, they were good enough and the reason wasn't lost on me. The fact that I had found out about True Love after only three days, while they had been next to it for all that time was sure to make me a big hero with the Americans. After a while I put up with them. I put the Webley Scot in my sports bag and waited. Just as a precaution I told Lorning, who gave me a funny look but later said he thought I might be right. You'd think on an island this small you'd be able to find anything you wanted? Like who the hell they were? It seemed that was difficult for some people.

I found myself surrounded by Reggie Bloodworth and his crowd; Lorning was trying to be a good sport, I suspected. I still didn't like the local man but I did have more respect for him.

After a couple of nights I took Reggie aside and told him he didn't have to keep a leash on, I would be fine. He of course denied his intent at first. But

after I asked him if he had enough of laughing at
my tired jokes? He smiled and told me to watch out
for myself. If I needed anything at all I need do is
ask.

Reggie had been On the Falklands and knew his
business. The a handsome young, Royal Marine
Captain, sporting black hair, an easy smile from a
wide mouth, which was set with perfect teeth. His
nose had been broken. The word was he had gotten
it from an Argentine FN Butt driven into his face. I
had it on good authority that Reggie had killed the
enemy sergeant wielding the gun with his bare
hands. People liked to be on the right side of old
Regg. Something in the intense blue eyes under his
knit brows and the coiled movements of his 200-lb.
body told you so. I felt better for his offer.

Adams could have the answer to my questions. I
hoped so.

Chapter Seventeen - The Quest Hotel, Seven Mile
Beach, Cayman Islands, Monday: 8:05 A.m.

The Light

   The elevator had huge, bronze doors. These were
indented with a squared pattern, which seemed to
spread and then disappear into itself. I watched the
Quest's large reception area through the sliding
glass doors to the beach. Three men exited the
elevator doors as they pulled back noiselessly.
Lionel Adams was far more distinctive then his
picture indicated. At six foot he seemed to tower
over the two brothers who had graduated from street
drug peddling, to prison, to bodyguard status.
Uncomfortable in bright island clothes they prowled
along behind their master like two slightly peeved
leopards. The physical strength of the two men was
obvious. The large floral shirts hid guns. Each man
had his personal street walk. Each man would kill
without a lot of thought, if any.
   Adams walked with the ramrod-braced step of a
drill sergeant. Confidence radiated from the man.
He wore expensive Brooks Brothers sunglasses. A
flowing large sleeved white shirt that was
reminiscent of buccaneering days and beautifully

tailored light brown Tommy Halfinger Islands slacks were an excellent choice for the heat. These were worn over a pair of soft brown Gucci loafers. I liked people who understood how to dress. It not only showed character, it was a statement. There was no question Adams was powerful, fit and well muscled. This attire simply accented it without putting up a billboard.

I got up slowly and meandered over to the desk, which seemed to be his destination. There was a soft hiss as the glass deck door pulled back along its skids commanded by the electronic trip wire of the heat of my body's approach. One of the two hard-eyed companions immediately picked me up. I must have looked reasonably non-threatening as I had dressed tourist in a white polo shirt from Arrow and Crest Line white pleated pants, my Panama Jack pushed back from my face and no sunglasses.

On reaching the desk I waited politely as Adams inquired if there was any messages. He ignored me as completely as if I were one of the planted palms that lined the large pink marble reception area.

I concentrated on the desk until he started to turn away.

"Lionel Adams isn't it?" I asked. Two things happened simultaneously. The smaller of the two bodyguards stepped between Adams and myself. His dead shark eyes bore into me.

Adam's head turned slowly like a turret until his eyes rested on me like two gun barrels.

His eyes were remarkable in that the pupils were the colour of coal and as dead to light as a black hole.   The face was soft brown and mask like, at first glance. The eyes that controlled the features were broad set, intelligent and questioning. Below them the nose, which was wide and unattractive over set a mouth that wouldn't smile well. It was large but straight as a die. The cheekbones spread like the upper sides of a heart then flattened to a small pointed chin. His ears were small and the hair was short, close to the head like a mat but was real.

The eyes summed me up in a glance. The soft sneer that danced along the mouth spoke of someone who had little patience with common people and less for those who's skin was white. He didn't know me, that was obvious.

"Cuttie.' The voice was a deep baritone and very smooth. The small guard moved back but watched me no less closely. The other one, the taller moved to the far right of his boss to get a better shot , if it came to something. To me the baritone bell toned. "Yes." It was a flat offer to state my business with as little time loss as possible.

"You're Lionel Adams with Darius Computers aren't you? I read the piece in Black Exec. I was impressed with your new 560 MRS for conveyor assemblies. Really nice stuff." I smiled.

The gun barrels didn't react but the face showed a little movement, which might have been the start of a smile. Being a celebrity was not completely foreign to Adams. The profile of the company was high enough for that. To be picked out because of Black Exec, was certainly not expected especially by one of the colour challenged. The Black Exec. piece had been required reading as part of Adams dossier.

"You read Black Exec.?" He asked amused. He seemed to relax as did Cuttie and the taller man.

"On the plane, You see, I am sort of the competition and I like to keep up. I'm Michael McFurson of Epsylon Britain. I do their marketing." I offered my hand that he took in an iron grip but only momentarily.

"Epsylon,' he thought for a moment, 'Oh yes, you do a lot of small stuff, watches." He physically

stiffened as if the single word triggered the reaction.
The eyes got more intense, if that was possible.
Cuttie moved closer. His hand disappeared under
his shirt. I didn't move. Whatever happened it
wouldn't happen here.

"McFurson," he said in a less tense manner,
"Interesting." I had nothing to lose now.

"You've been doing well with Darius. Its too bad
about that matter in the US Virgins. I was reading in
the local paper about some southern clansman using
your name for a contract on a base or something for
the militias. I guess there was a real stink.?." That
caught his attention.

"There is no local paper here," Adams said with a
really hard edge.

"No! I mean in Charlotte Amalie on St. Thomas. I
think it's called the Daily Tribune or something." I
went on like I hadn't noticed.

"Interesting, I like to know what people are saying
about my company as you can understand. You had
breakfast yet?" He asked.

"No!" I lied.

"Like to have some with me?" He indicated the
deck and I nodded. We moved out onto the shaded
restaurant and took a chair.
My mind was saying, 'Well idiot you've got your
chance don't blow it.' Adams indicated his boys

should take another table. Cuttie really wanted to frisk me but that wasn't going to happen so he glowered at me from a few feet away. Adams didn't seem to see me as a threat. I ignored the muscle as it was in check and concentrated on leader.

"Tell me McFurson,' the bell tolled again ' what else do you remember from that story?"

"Well let's see, Adams." I searched my mind for the non existent story. If he was bent he would be uncomfortable, which was good and if not, it didn't matter if he checked. Also, I reminded him that he wasn't the only human at the table. While his face flatted slightly he seemed to reconsider me.

"Not much really, just that different militias had been coming down from the US for cut rate vacations at a place called True Love.' It said, 'they used Darius as a cover for the lease. I was out at True Love, looking at locations for a shoot. That's why the story caught my eye." I gave him a moment to evaluate that bit .

"It was obvious that the story had to be wrong given who you are. I couldn't see you financing package tours for a bunch of Clansmen." I laughed. There was no reaction at all as Adams absorbed the information.

The girl came over and asked for our order. Adams requested half a grapefruit, a raisin muffin, with lots of real butter and coffee. I ordered pancakes, with a side order of bacon and a large glass of orange juice. The waitress was cute, with a coffee complexion and bright eyes, she smiled but it was wasted on Adams. He was busy.

There was silence for a moment while he gathered his thoughts. He leaned forward on his elbows and looked at me over his clasped hands he had long fine surgeon's fingers. I met his gaze with the same easy going, I hopped, stupid look, I had started with. He seemed to come to a conclusion and said.

"Tell me about True Love."

"Well it's like an old plantation house. I don't know if you've gotten down to the Carolinas but there are a lot of them like that down there. A little like 'Gone With The Wind.' Lots of pillars big front staircase, big veranda of course its thin, just veneer, no back to it. Not like the great English houses with different wings and so on. They had a motel building where the tourists must have stayed. I guess one of those groups turned violent and the whole US Marine Corps went in and cleaned the place out. They didn't say anything about arrests.' I finished and waited for him to ask again. He sat there bobbing his head slowly listening the gun barrels pointed at the white metal tabletop.

"Lots of security I guess?" Adams offered. not looking up.

"Yes! The guy who showed me around pointed it all out. Barbed wire, patrol boats if you can believe, even video cameras.' Something was bothering me. Something that should be obvious and something, I should be picking up on. Perhaps something my host was gently pointing me to. Then, by God it hit me. I looked at Adams and his cold black eyes came up to mine. He actually half smiled. Like a master helping a student he seemed to expect me to take the next step. I couldn't go back now so I went forward.

"Would you mind if we played a game of 'what if'. Just for a moment?"

"No," he said watching me with interest. Enjoying the moment.

"What if, a man of colour,' I started, 'someone with the resources wanted to keep an eye on the elements of society, most likely to do damage to his people. He might want to get them into a place where he could watch them." The reality and the brilliance of the scheme hit me like a brick. It was so simple. 'He might finance their vacations, as a group, to a place they would feel was safe because it was fronted by an ex-clansman. Who he had subverted or bought." I slowed down, the smile was making headway on Adams face. His head still nodded softly.

"He might." Adams said gently.

"He might wire their rooms and the telephones. He would know everything they talked about, all their secrets. A less scrupulous man might even put cameras into the rooms." I revolted slightly thinking of little children getting ready for bed.

"He could get him some real good footage of them dumb rednecks humping their skinny assed wives or more likely, their girl friends, make an interesting Saturday night viewing. Of course you'd have to bring your own popcorn. Hell, there's a big market for pornography too" Adams finished. He was smug and it took the shine off the size of the achievement but you couldn't fault him. The operation at True Love was exquisite. Any of the major firms would be proud of it.

It passed my mind that there was a huge amount of information that was being made available to the FBI, which was why True Love was left alone, why the Americans were mad at me. The tapes of these men cheating on their wives alone could keep them quiet and behaving for a long time.

I could see the disciples of hate hatching their

plots in what they thought was perfect safety.
Walking up to the big house to be served by black
servants in white gloves and be treated like the old
South still existed. Adams fed their fantasies then
stripped them bare ass naked. This was an important
service because these people were playing with
bombs and chemical warfare. These were real
threats and deserved the type of thorough work
Adams was putting into it. The government,
controlled by the law, could never do this,

Then again Hedi; Mohammed and the boy's were
something completely different. Somewhere up the
way, Adams had moved out beyond the lines he had
set. He begun to working on something else,
something far more devious and dangerous. The gun
barrels watched as I worked this through. The face
was closed but not dangerous yet.

As my granddad used to say 'Periodically you get
what you wish for, so watch it'. Well I had the
scoop but only part of it. I measured the distance
between myself and the boys at the other table.

Our food came and Adams seemed to lose interest
in me as he attacked the grapefruit with a spoon.

"We both know you wouldn't have anything to do
with something like that but the man who did would
be both brilliant and courageous." He looked up

realizing.that I was sincere and gave a small nod.

"Was there something in that story about how they found out about the True Love thing." He asked. In fairness he had given me something and now he wanted something back. I needed more information maybe a little bit of honesty would go farther then a lie. I gambled.

"I remember it said that someone just was following up on some dead turtles asked about explosives and who might be using them, some guy just doing his job, I think it said it got him killed." Well the ball was in his court.

"Hum,' he snorted and shook his head. There was real anger for the first time the face clouded and I didn't like it one bit. Whether it was because he felt for Lacy or because his own people had screwed up was hard to say, but I figured the latter.

I started to eat my pancakes to allow things to simmer a bit before going on.

Chapter Eighteen – Monday, Three A.m., Seven Mile Beach, Grand Cayman.

A Walk on Moon Light

The powerful Branner twin diesels died to a burble. The sixty foot Sea Spear motored to a stop a mile or so off Seven Mile Beach. The Captain was a thin decisive man of the Levant. He watched as the small submarine was lowered over the seaside of the ship, on a specially designed hammock sling. His vessel moved softly on a quiet surface. Only the sluggish splashing of the waves broke the silence. Black Ocean speckled with moonlight stretched to the empty beach. Lights from the hotels and restaurants dotted the shore like the far edge of civilization in an endless quest.

The Nep Two, a long underwater sea torpedo with its manta ray like body, could pull six men with relative ease. Slowly, stripped to their bathing suits, their faces covered with diving masks, carrying small water-tight nylon bags over their shoulders, six mercs swung out into the water to grasp the mini-sub. One by one they settled into the frame. Each placed one of the oxygen mouthpieces, extending from the central tank on the specially

fitted multi source, into their mouths. With a soft
whoosh the Arab driver took the Nep Two down.
He would motor two to three miles up the beach
before turning toward shore to cut the swim time,
then dropped off three of his passengers. Further
down the beach he dropped another three. Finally
the Nep turned back to her mother ship, to be
hoisted aboard. The engines bubbled with more
force. That night's cruise around the island
continued.

Each team swam, the short distance to the beach,
in slow even strokes, undisturbed by the other
occupants of the sea. Finally they rose out of the
water, like ghosts. Strong hands removed their
masks as they immerged on to the pale moon lit
sand. Looking like late night snorkelers, they moved
between two hotels into an area of bush and small
trees. Covered from the road and beach, they
stripped off their bathing suits, changing into the
light shirts and shorts from their bags. A small
towel was also included for a dry off. The
waterproof package also carried bare identity
papers. Each man wore a hat. They moved through
the brush to the A1 and walked along it.

The truck was right on time slowly driving toward
George Town. The lead man took out a bicycle
reflector and flashed it in the lights of the minivan.

```
            COLES BOOK STORES
               CENTRE MALL
                 545-1395
          GST-FED #: 897152666

SALE    000700  0019  004  00002 05534
          02/08/16              19:37

LOCAL INTEREST  957 1 @           9.95
   07.0% GST - FED                0.70
          TOTAL SALE             10.65
       DEBIT / CHEQUING          10.65
AUTH#:228625  REF#:0553  BATCH#:0329
TERMINAL: 00556448  OPERATOR: 00000602

   00 TRANSACTION APPROVED THANK YOU

         ********************

SHOP ONLINE..INDIGO.CA

           CUSTOMER COPY
```

It stopped and the three men slipped inside.

The two lovers, who lay naked, hidden by the palms, watched quietly. Being young, they giggled at the nakedness of the men and wondered in whispers where they were going. The girl said it looked like they were walking on moonlight, as they came out of the sea. The boy was running his hand over her thigh. In a moment she forgot about the men from the sea, as the boy raised up to mount her.

Ten teams came ashore at different places all over Grand Cayman with similar pickups. Each truck carried six men and an Arab driver. There was almost no talking. These were the pick of the litter; the strongest, fastest, smartest of the three hundred trainees. The men knew each other from a two-week mission refresher course, which occurred at a small property on one of the lesser Florida Keys. They trusted each other and were ready. The trucks went to different sights, isolated rented cottages, empty garages and warehouses. Each truck was different, purchased or rented legally. In as many cases as possible, the truck was brought into the building. The men piled out and lay down on pre set camp beds to sleep after checking out their weapons and equipment for the next day. Necessities, like bags and masks were left near the

entranceways of the buildings not to be forgotten.
Leisure clothes were laid out for the next day. The
Arabs took watch, while the majority of mercs
being old sweats, dropped off to sleep. They had
learned long ago you might not get another chance.
Some sat restlessly checking clips and honing
knives. Each little precaution, they believed, was the
difference between wealth and death.

At seven A.m. sharp the men were awakened. The
Arabs served a hot breakfast, sausages, eggs and
strong coffee.

The leaders asked specific questions. The mercs
chanted in reply as they had done for two weeks.
'Number one gets out first, Number two follows,
once they're in. We all follow nice and slow.
Number three and number four cover the doors.
Two and Five pick up quick. We bag all the money
in the till, plus what is in the side rooms.' They had
been told they would find the money in suitcases
and brief cases in large denominations. 'If the vault
is open we get that too.' Times were shouted out for
each procedure. Seven minutes was the upper time
limit. The Arab seemed to have no direct
responsibilities outside of being there.

The suitcases were in the locked rooms because
some of the bank's visitors were nocturnal. Sunlight
tended to disturb their visit. A little too easy to spot

them. That wouldn't do would it? Seeing the vaults
didn't open until morning, as they were time
controlled, the suitcases were labeled and the cash
placed in the box the day after. The latter part of
November and early December was the high water
mark for these donations, with year-ends and tax
time coming up.

'If someone makes trouble?' the question was
asked. 'They're dead,' came the reply. The men
held up their silenced automatic, semi automatic
machine guns and assault rifles.

'OK, relax.' They were told.

For an hour they sweated, drank orange juice and
waited. Just as the tension became unbearable, at
eight ten Am, they started to move out. The men
with the farthest to go, those from around Rum
Point, moving first. The trucks slid into the stream
of traffic and made their careful way to George
Town and the treasure they were about to loot.

Each vehicle had to be in front of a specific bank
at exactly 9:02 A.m., opening time. Road work was
taken into this schedule and the trucks moved
around problems over pre defined paths.

The city slowly surrounded them. Each truck not
recognized by its fellows had a specific route

in. Each bank was completely different and the units would not help each other. At eight fifty-five Mohammed Tisani walked the district. All the trucks were in place, all was ready. He thanked Allah for his kindness and with a light, singing heart, went back to his Mercedes four-by-four to wait.

Chapter Nineteen - Monday 8:15 A.m., The Quest,
Seven Mile Beach, Grand Cayman.

Do You Know?

Lionel was buttering his raisin muffin and I was
just finishing my glass of orange juice. I thought for
a while there would be no more conversation. Then
the bell tolled again.

"What do you know about my people Mr.
McFurson?' The question was casual but it would
lead somewhere.

"You mean American Blacks or the Black race, the
employees of Darius Corp or Americans in
General?" I countered.

"Hmm! He snorted semi smiling. "Black
Americans."

"They didn't become Americans by choice, for the
most part." I started

"You are kind, Mr. McFurson, in chains and four
hundred to a ship living in their own excrement.
Yes, I would say you are being kind."

"Of course there were thousands of Americans
who fought to free them." I suggested. Adams
smiled.

"The Civil War, Mr. McFurson was a positive

attempt by northern industrialists to destroy the Southern Cotton Compact. Lincoln, my namesake said, he would free all the slaves to win the war or none, if that was what it required. In the end he needed the 90,000 black men he recruited, to win the war." This guy had all the answers and endless hate to go along with it. Adams stopped to eat his muffin, so I tried to move the conversation to its point.

"It seems to me that your country has provided an opportunity for you to reach the level you deserve." I suggested, hoping to sound a little pompous to see if he would come up for the bait.

The gun barrels came up from the table pinning me to my chair.

"I have a gift Mr. McFurson. I had to get shot and go to prison to find it. I had to do that while not getting AIDS or dead, in an over crowded hellhole. Do you know why I started with computers? It was the cleanest room in the crib." His eyes seemed pained

"Most of the brothers I grew up with died before they were eighteen or went to prison or both. Do you know the percentage of black men in prison relative to the 13 % of the population we constitute?"

"No, I have no idea." I said Honestly.

"Well over 50%, some say 70%." Adams said and pointed a finger before starting his next sentence. "Think of the percentage of black men who escape the hood with a pass to the NBA or NFL. I'm no athlete, not at that level, but I found my way. It was hard and I earned it. I got rehabilitated because I could see I had to get out or die. Make money so I could be my own man."

"A lot of blacks have moved into the middle class. The Koreans, Vietnamese and Arabs have had just as hard a time. Look at the Indians, Eastern and native". I said. I knew he was right of course but the statement had to be balanced.

"Hmm,' the bell tolled, 'They ain't a lot of them inside, I know I bin there. Lots of brothers though.

Anyone who gets out of the hood and even gets a medium level job is a hero in my books. At three in the morning though, you walking to the store or even driving you just a nigger and the cops goin to raz you. You can be anything but they figure you for what's happening."

"Your Canadian aren't you?" Adams finished

"Yes ", I admitted wondering how everyone seemed to know my place of origin.

"Your Shatner, he kissed the first black woman on television. Made it OK to kiss a black woman.'

. Hum! 'That was thirty years ago and they wanted
lynch him. He couldn't just kiss her, he had to be
forced by some alien.

Just for your information we knew it was good
kissing a black woman long time ago." He stopp
for a moment and I cut in.

"We Canadians have our problems. At one poir
in Halifax they had an area of the city that was
called Nigger Town. It was as bad as Harlem, Wa
or any of the major hoods, maybe bigger rats." I
explained "The government got religion and
bulldozed the place. Now there are a lot of
condominiums with black people living in them a
of course the name has been changed. We do try.'

"Sure! Readymade projects and you have a glass
ceiling in Canada, ' Adams smirked, 'I know! If
your ass is black it don't go over a certain level.
You can see the job but you can't have it, poor
communication skills right?"

"Not anymore, not with the government backing
anyone who's of colour, to the teeth. You had bett
have a real good reason to fire someone black or n
move them up." God help you if a minority screan
prejudice because they won't believe you if you're
white. I thought to myself. "We're not perfect far
from it. We were a lot more tolerant when we had
lot fewer black faces."

Adams laughed softly.

"At least you're honest.' He paused "But don't you
e tellin me about Watts or Harlem. I been there and
seen them." He said coldly. "In my country,
ney're taking back what they gave us, you know?
ou see all those black lawyers and doctors on
elevision? That's where they're going to stay.
ause they repelled the black professional when
ney repelled the Equality Laws. See we ain't got
ne ability, ain't got the grade average. You try
etting a grade average, where you live, they speak
different language. Your parents are on crank and
ou sleepin in a squat at twelve years old." Adams
nook his head hard like he could see it and didn't
ant to 'And what the hell you know about rats?
et you never seen a rat in your life. I saw one when
was six. I had to beat it off my baby sister before it
e her face. Rats, Hmm." He looked at me and the
yes softened somewhat.

'I don't hate my country Mr. McFurson. You may
nd that strange but I still love it. Just someone got
look out for my people. By 2020 or so 52% of the
opulation in the United States will be Hispanic.
'ho speaks for us then?"
So you're the savior of the black American race. I
ould see it clearly. A black man with a tremendous
nount of cash flow and power who doesn't want

to play the white man's game. Who is still in the
getto even if he lives in a penthouse? Who hadn't
moved on up. He was still down there doing what
he could. The dossier had said he had financed
youth groups, black neighborhood watch, put
thousands of dollars into Black Churches. These
were the backbone of Black communities. His
company was almost totally staffed by blacks. He
provided scholarships to young people out of the
projects, paid tutors when necessary. Organized low
cost loans for black housing. Lionel, Lincoln Adams
was still hitting the rats saving his little sister. Only
the rats were bigger and coloured with hate.

"Let's play 'what if' a little more?" He said after
cooling down some.

"Sure."

" What kind of war do you think the next one will
be, Mr. McFurson?"

"If it's nuclear, crispy critters." Adams did laugh
this time. It was a boyish face now bright with the
full mirth that came from it. He nodded.

"No more nuclear war, Mr. McFurson.
Biological!" He was icy serious. "Do you know why
they didn't go after Saddam? Hmm? They won
Desert Storm. Bush suckered Hussein in and then
clobbered him to keep the other Arab states in

line and to be a hero, of course. The reason the US didn't go after Saddam was, he had biological weapons. You kill him or leave him with no where to go the word goes out. Some fool walks into the water purification plant in Chicago, Philadelphia, or New York's upstate, he drops a little concentrated anthrax into the drinking water. Next morning you got thousands dying. It's the believers you got to watch for, Mr. McFurson." In a moment Hedi's face flashed to mind and the reality struck me hard. The danger was real.

"I thought they didn't go after Saddam because they would have to fight for Baghdad and the Allied body count would be too large'. I offered.

"Old Saddam, he kills fifteen hundred of his own people, a month, just to keep his hand in. Now who the hell is going to fight for him? The army would probably kill him just to stop the invasion. However, that one man gets on a plane comes into the U.S., no one stops him the dogs don't find the Anthrax. I'm no chemist,' He continued, 'but I know you can't stop it with present day methods. I live in one of those cities. Mr. McFurson my people live there too. I don't want any of that shit. Suburbs don't drink out of the same tap." The flight of whites to the suburbs

especially in places like Detroit, was destroying the
tax base and leaving the inner cities to rot.

"I am also a Moslem.' He continued. 'What do you
think of American policy with regards to Israel? I
considered the answer figuring this was going no
where fast.

"They say there are six million Israelis and 30
million taxpayers. The American Jewish
Community has always had a lot of money and
influence. As do similar communities in other
western countries. On the other hand, the number of
Jews in the United States is dropping and
the Americans want the Middle East quiet. The
financial strain of supporting Israel is getting to be a
problem and they want to have some say in the Arab
world." I considered the matter for a moment.

"A lot of Yanks, Canadians and Europeans have
sympathy for the Palestinians. Many of them think
the Israelis are being heavy handed. They figure if
Palestinians got a little land maybe they would shut
up and settle down. Of course they're getting
screwed by their own leaders but that's their
problem." '

Adams snorted again.

"The bombing of the Trade Center Building in
New York,' I continued, 'really scared the average
American."

"They know their government can't do much unless they bring in repressive laws. That won't happen if it has anything to do with gun control restricting movement." I stopped to finish my orange juice then continued.

"The Israelis are going way over the line too.' I shook my head.' This idea of tearing Arab houses down, if owners upgrade them, is nuts. They got lots of Arab prisoners, more or less as hostages. Putting thirteen and fourteen year old kids in prison, just because they are standing there, is also crazy. Mind you, if they're throwing rocks, then that's different.

The Israelis want Jerusalem. Fine! No problem, but they have to cut the settlers back. The problem is that they have the upper hand, militarily. Israel has the bomb. The Arabs won't fight for that reason alone. Not to mention the fact that they are at each others throats continuously and the Israelis kicked the crap out of them the last few times they tangled. Israel's main problem is if the surrounding countries go radically Islamic and they find another Nasser. As long as the US finances Israel, they're OK."

"You have a pretty good grasp of the thing. But What if the Arabs got the bomb?"

"You got to get it to the target.' I said. 'They would need a rocket to get it to Israel. Who would sell it to them?"

"True,' Adams nodded, 'But say that is also taken care of, not long range, but big enough rockets to reach say Europe, not America?" Adams pursed his lips as he asked the question.

"The Arabs would have to buy it from someone. The Russians wouldn't sell it to them their chock a block with Mohammedans in their Central Republics. All they need is to have them with nuclear weapons.' I continued." Say, you were able to buy them from the Russian Mafia. You'd still have to get it over the border. The Americans would know about it right away. They have enough satellites they can tell you when Saddam burps.

"I agree, like you said, us Americas want peace maybe we don't do nothin?" Lionel spread his hands

"That's not possible. The American Army, Navy and Marines are all over the gulf. The Saudis would have a coronary. The Americans would lose the oil, there's no way that's going to happen." I finished remembering Desert Storm and how quickly it had come into being.

"There is not going to be another Desert Storm not

in our life time." Adams said with confidence.

"I don't know. It would make your President look pretty good. He may need something to cover the problems he's looking at." Adams shook his head,

"No way. it be that way. The allies don't want it. The Canadian Government sent one ship and 300 men last time, Bubba called them to play. The British showed up but that's it. All of it was for show but no war. The Japs aren't going to pay for the war this time. OPEC is killing itself. We going to get lots of oil." He was so certain what did he know. I tried another tact.

"Lets say the Arabs were able to get the bomb. They would have to get at least 20 or so rockets, warheads and launchers you're talking Billions to make it work.' I stopped for a moment 'yes billions'. Then I finished my thought. 'The Americans could take them out in five minutes.' Adams watched me amused.

"They wouldn't. What if they miss? You know what a nuclear Aircraft Carrier Costs. Think what it costs to lose one in body bags and prestige. Ain't going to happen. What the hell are the Europeans are going to say? They be scared stiff old Hussein gets one nuke. What happens if he can get to them?

"A big nuclear strike. The US would blow the Iraqis or anyone else who was holding, back to the stone age." I said.

"Won't happen. You know all the water in the Middle East flows through Baghdad. You poison the Tigris and Euphrates, millions die in Turkey, Iran, Syria. Imagine that old cloud floating out over Saudi Arabia. No bombs! at least nothing nuclear. Bubba will have to cover his crimes in a different way. No! Mr. McFurson the Middle East gets real quiet."

"So you're talking a mini cold war" The idea was appalling.

"Right!" He confirmed without thinking.

"What happens if some Mullah has a bad day and pulls the trigger. Or worse, you let the genie out of the bottle, every idiot and his mother has the bomb. You know you can build a small one. The thing will fit it in the suitcase. Park that in the bus station in down town Chicago, set it off, there'd be nothing but a hole, where the city use to be."

"You can't see the third world get ahead, can you?"

"Mr. Adams it's got nothing to do with the poor of the earth. You like living the way you do, don't you? Well I like to live that way too. Lots of food, lots of space, lots of potential. I want my kids to grow up with all the good stuff I have and a future that allows them to stay that way." I leaned forward in my passion, rushing on.

"See, I get a pain every time I hear some idiot liberal tell me we should share the wealth. They're so full of crap it makes you wonder. You and I, we know what real poverty is, I haven't lived it but I've seen it .The liberal, he drives through it every day with the doors locked and the windows up. He goes through red lights in the ghetto. He isn't stopping. He doesn't know squat but he feels bad, guilty about the starving people, so he mouths off about joining the third world.

We know the average man in this world lives in a hut or some one-room hovel with his wife, kids, his in-laws and a pig. That pig is next years little bit of potential. If it has babies, he's rich, if it dies that's it.

I figure when the Liberal who lives in a house that makes mine look like a hole in the ground, moves into a one-room hovel and eats off a garbage pile, I'll move too." I like being where I am and I don't see me giving an inch."

"We absorb 30 % of all the world's resources now, how long do you think the people who have nothing

are going to wait." Adams retorted.
"All over the world the standard of living is going
up, South America, the orient. You know why? The
Americans and the west need new consumers for
their products. They're passing the money around
and it's making more. We all have washing
machines but there big time stuff in the third world.
That's how it's going to change, Mr. Adams. not by
passing out nuclear weapons and hoping no one
pushes the button. I spent my whole life being afraid
of the bomb. My kids aren't afraid, they think we
are destroying the ecology. Good for them maybe
they'll fix it. Until then I will do anything necessary
to keep it the way it is."

"Hmm, more honesty" Adams mused
"How come I'm honest when I say something that
agrees with your concept that the world is stacked
against you. However, if I say that there is a chance
in our Western society is better at its worst then
anywhere in the third world you think I'm lying?"

"Oh!" The bell rang once more 'I don't think your
lying, you're just white. You got to learn you can't
repress people, you can't keep them stupid and
poor. They won't take handouts forever The West
will one day, will find out just how unpleasant these

people can be." Adams waved his hand as if placing this in the future.

"I agree with you that there is only one way to get my people out of poverty, that is, good jobs and a opportunity to live in families again. The last thing we need is more people in the US. Every time a Mexican comes in without papers, the food chain gets longer and the jobs that will take my people out of the hood get fewer. I'm happy as hell to see Mexicans stay in Mexico.

"Why, Mr. Adams you're a bigot." I said with cruel pleasure.

"No shit!' He said with equal candor. 'The Hispanics ain't staying out and that's the truth. I want to hold on to what little, my people got. But I'm not stupid or blind. " He stopped as if to gather his thoughts.

"You remember Somalia, you remember they dragged that white boy through the streets in his underwear, after they killed him. They did that on television. Some cameraman watched that and did nothing. All we Americans wanted to do was feed them fools.

The point is, no one wants us playing policeman. We need to back off and stay home. Put some money into my country and my people, for a

damned change. Foreign aid is just a
hand out. Spending lots on defense just makes rich
white men richer." I tried to cut in but it was as if he
was reading my mind. He held up his hand for
silence. "No question in the past the military and its
technology created lots of by products, which made
my country rich, including the computer. The
Soviets are gone, we don't need to be a supper
power anymore. The only reason we be big assin
about dictating to the world, is to score points for
Bubba.' He pointed forcefully

"You take them soldiers out of Bosnia, them fools
going to kill each other again. They be still fightin
wars that finished in the thirteenth century. None of
that shit is worth one American life.' You could feel
his anger, ' Time to come back home, let the
Europeans handle their own shit for a while. We
been covering their ass since the Second World
War. You stop financing Israel and you see how fast
things get quiet over there.' He sat back and paused
for a moment then started again.

"Between now and 2020 I want my people out of
the ghetto and'in a community with families, houses
and a future. The same future you want for your

kids. The only way that's going to happen is if we realize the people we are trying to help, don't give a damn and be too dangerous to try to control."

"So you're saying we arm the rest of the world and let them kill each other right?"

"Sure, when Pol Pot slaughtered all them people of his. I didn't see some big rush to invade his ass and stop it. We get real selective about where we want to police. Ain't no way you going to see US soldiers in Rwanda. Either you do it even or you let it ride."

None of this made any sense. Then again, what had I expected? My friend Adams, had taken me around the block and told me exactly nothing of substance. The information about his operation in the Virgins at True Love was common knowledge to the FBI and the CIA. He would have to presume I would know. The idea of using the money from the holdups to give the Arabs the bomb was too far out to be believed. It seemed to me an impossible dream too fraught with problems to be feasible. True Love was simple and reflected skill. This concept was crazy; at least I hoped so. No matter what happened I had to stop this man. There was too much intelligence, to much strength of purpose, too much potential for disaster, on a huge scale.

"However, he had tipped his hand. As I said, in spy world it's the little nuances. Never check your watch when controlling a subject. Lionel had taken two glancing looks at his Rolex Oyster so I looked at my Epsylon. It was twenty to nine. What was important about nine A.m.? Well, for one thing, 550 banks and insurance companies opened at nine A.m. sharp on Grand Cayman.

Something else hit me. Adams had known I would be here. He also knew that only his being here would draw me away from the downtown core at a point when I would normally be walking through the very area where the robbery was to take place .He was the only unattached piece of the puzzle. Now at the end of our conversation I could prove nothing. However, I knew I was right.

Point one, could I get out? There were a number of new arrivals on the deck. I didn't think there would be gunplay.

"Thanks for an excellent breakfast." I said standing.

"Where you going? We haven't even discussed product. I might be interested in some of your small stuff." He smiled but this time it was forced and empty.

"I'll see that one of our people contact you. Thank
again."

"Sure you don't want to play 'what if' some
more?" He taunted.

"No, I seem to have found what I was looking for."
I turned and made for the sliding glass door.

Cuttie and his partner had been eating huge plates
of bacon and eggs, while trying to pick up the local
lass, serving them. Both men now stood. I faced
Cuttie, my eyes meeting his dead fish orbs. The
slight smile meant he was ready to finish this. His
hand moved under his shirt. I removed my pen from
my shirt pocket aimed the tip at Cuttie's chest and
waited. The bell tolled a final time.

"Cuttie, Long let him go, He just has a different
point of view." .I heard a newspaper open behind
me. Cuttie looked unhappy, like a dog that had had
a bone taken away, for bad behavior. Long, the
taller man, with the pear face and blank look,
simply sat down. The boss had told him he was not
needed. Cuttie looked at my pen and smiled until
his eyes met mine once more and realized, I would
have killed him. He did not know about the poison
saturated dart that would have paralyzed and torn

his life from him but he knew when a man had
killed, he could kill again. He nodded softly and s:
down.

I moved over to my original table and picked up
my sport bag, feeling much more secure with the
Webley back in my hands.

In ten steps, I was through the lobby and under th
covered entranceway. I took the third taxi in line.
This caused some commotion. I couldn't take the
chance it was rigged.

"Hey man you got to take the front car." My drive
said. I took a hundred Cayman dollars out of my
pocket and held it up to his face.

"Double this if I get to Government House in ten
minutes". I snarled between clinched teeth.

"Sit back." was all he said. The Toyota shot out of
the hotel turned on two wheels and just balanced ou
as the accelerator made the four tires scream. I held
on like a sailor in a hurricane and considered what I
must do.

Chapter Twenty - George Town, Grand Cayman Island, Monday 8:57 A.m.

For A Start

Screaming brakes, terrified faces and faint obscenities followed in our wake. The diver weaved franticly from lane to lane across, around and past, A 1 highway's morning traffic.

A near miss under the wheels of a Mann semi. Caused me, to reminded him, if we were dead, he couldn't spend his money. This seemed to hit home and he complied. We were already coming up on Fort George ,along what was now North Church Street. The light went red at Fort St. and we came to an abrupt stop.

"We gin to make it man!" The driver said in a high falsetto. The adrenaline was pumping.

"Look it doesn't matter now. You get the money . You earned it. Now, take a turn down by the post office along Edward, nice and slow, got me."

"I don't want to get shot, man." I must have been something in my voice, that tipped him off to the danger.

"You aren't going to get shot. I got this guy with another company and he's trying to get the jump on me. So nice and slow, I want to see if his car is on the street."

"Right! Man." He agreed with a nod.

The taxi took the corner on to Fort St.. Moving now past the Assembly Building, then a right onto Edward cruising the Town Hall and library. The architecture was early US, Canadian gothic. The post office made me feel like down town Branford, Ontario. The Blue Royal Post Van reminded me I was in the Caymans.

The major banks weren't open yet. However, the tourists were already coming up from the cruise ship. This was anchored off the harbor against a majestic, cloudless Caribbean sky. I had seen it as we came into the city, out beyond the austere gray of the chapeled HM Customs Building.

I saw the man walking over to the white Mercedes, for only a moment, as he opened the street side rear door and disappeared behind the tinted windows. The beard was gone, but the nose was the same. The hair was different but it was Tisani.

A quick look at the street showed that the five-story block of the Vancouver Confederation Bank was the high ground. I notice another thing there were trucks or vans parked, beside or near the entrances of the major banks on the street. Only four suspect vehicles were visible but then the other

banks were spread out. I could now go to
Bloodworth and Assistant Commissioner
Pointdexter of the RCIPE. The last thing I had
wanted to do was to alert the local authorities if
there was nothing going on but my over vivid
imagination.

"The Government Administration building, now!"
I tapped the driver on the shoulder and we shot
down the street. I made a note of the driver's name
Trevor Manfred. If it hadn't been for his help it
would have been impossible to do anything to stop
this, as Adams had hoped.

In seconds we were past Police H.Q. on Elgin then
up the small entrance road to the admin building.
And the Royal Marine Barracks behind it. I shoved
the money into Trevor's hands and thanked him.

I had a plan or at least the start of one. The
barracks was a single story gray prefab separate
from the main building. Reggie Bloodworth's office
was traditional government brown and cream. A
medium size Argentine flag boasting bullet holes
and dark red stain, which was dried human blood.

The secretary was out and I had just walked in.
Reggie never minded. The man behind the antique
government gray metal desk was a captain all right,
but no marine and he did mind the intrusion.

He looked up at me , evaluated my clothes and immediately presumed I was a lost tourist.

"I am sorry but the Administration offices are at the front." He stood stiffly. His tone was not genial

"Where's Reggie?" I didn't have time for anything and this turn of events wasn't planned for.

" Captain Bloodworth,' He corrected me, moving me up in his pointed little mind, to friend of the aforementioned Captain and therefor perhaps human, 'Is not here." His thin sour face was triangular and had the appearance of having seen everything possible in this tired old world. Above his watery blue eyes, a dark eyebrow cocked like a champion retriever, give his six one height, authority and size. You got the feeling he'd be looking down at you even if you were Michael Jordan.

" Who are you?" He didn't have time for me either.

"I am Captain Nigel Cathaway, detached of the Northumberland Fusiliers. I am filling in for Captain Bloodworth . I am sure if you come back later…"

" Look, you've got the biggest robbery in the Islands history going down in five minutes."

"What!" Nigel snorted incredulously.

" I saw three teams but there are probably more armed with submachine guns."

" Oh! I see." He looked at me as if he had found

something under a rock. He estimated that I was some poor nut.

"Look, I'm Ministry of Defense." I said with growing anger.

"Of course you are." The voice was at once patronizing and condescending. This guy was a piece of work.

' Listen you git.' He didn't like that one at all, a small tick started at the corner of his mouth. 'If one of the local cops out there happens to come along when those mercs go in or exit the banks, you're going to have World War Three on your hands. You're going to need a bulldozer to bury the bodies. Call Lorning over at Admin. He'll tell you who I am. My name is Michael McFurson."

"I 'm afraid I don't have the acquaintance of anyone having that name." but Nigel did and that troubled him. He wasn't going to give up the local Service man. On the other hand, he was uncertain now about me.

"Alright by the numbers then.' I quoted in frustration, 'colour of the day, aqua, 168859 Zebra., Zebra, a line.' He was flustered now, he knew the day code so he should be an authentic British officer but he was uncertain, I might be Russian or something.

It was at this point Lieutenant Jamie Trevers, Bloodworth's second in command, walked in. Jamie had fine combed blood hair and an open first timers face. A faint moustache spread over a wide mouth with gleaming teeth. Jamie might have been a model but his face was a little thin. His nose a little too large. However, women liked our Jamie and it was mutual.

"Ready to leave now ,Sir.' Then sighting me, 'Hello, Mike you owe me a drink from last night."

" Jimmy, great, tell Captain Cutright."

" That's Cathaway." The Captain snapped.

" Who I am. ' I finished. It was Jamie's turn to be flustered.

"Well, you are Michael McFurson.' I'll vouch for you of course. Jamie at twenty-one and new to command was at least quick on the upswing.

" Thanks tell him I'm Lorning's man."

" Oh! I see." Jamie said.

" I wish to hell, I did!" Said Cathaway turning beet red with anger.

"Mr. McFurson is Service. He's responsible to Mr. Lorning who is the head of Governor's Security. He's here on a mission. Sorry, I don't know much more."

"You say they're robbing the banks?" Cathaway was off now. The rest was behind us.

"Yes!" I said. He had the telephone in his hand.
"Which ones?" He had the police on the line.
"The three big ones, including Vancouver
Confederation on Edward and you can figure seven
to nine more. Look, these men are armed to the
teeth, in teams of six. They're ex-American forces
either Nam or Desert Storm. I suggest if Pointdexte
and you guys are going to take them on, to set up
roadblocks on the routes going out of town, then
your people will be dug in and the mercs will have
the choice of surrender or getting popped."
"Popped?" Cathaway repeated.
"Shot, blown away, killed. Sorry, sometimes the
jargon from television gets a little too easy. If they
go to sea, you can have the Seagull follow them."
Cathaway was already getting through to
Poindexter. As I turned to Jamie.
"Where are you going?" Jamie was in full battle
dress with side arm.
"I guess it isn't National Defense stuff. My chaps
and I were off for some target practice, then we'll
do some combat exercises near the Crown Park
lands. Mainly swamp round about the North Sound.
It's standard training. We go out each Monday." He
finished.

"Do you have an extra uniform, shirt and pants." I asked.

"Of course!"

"Good. I need your help."

"Sorry old boy. Orders and so on." Jamie looked back at Cathaway over his shoulder.

Time! Time! Time!

"Listen. How many men do you have?"

"Reggie took most of the two sections with him. Trouble of some sort out on Little Cayman. I have Sergeant Wilson and three men in the Land Rover."

"Ask him if you can help me. Quick, while he's on the phone." I pointed at Cathaway.

"Oh! The light dawned. "Captain Cathaway may I assist Mr. McFurson?! Jamie asked politely.

"What?" the Captain said half concentrating.

"Yes, of course. Now see here…" He continued on the phone.

"Who says you can't learn from your kids. Mine pulled the same thing on me all the time, when they wanted something and needed to get around me." A moment later, we were gone. A quick stop to change. The uniform was a little tight but Jamie was more or less my size. Jamie provided an old Sam Brown holster for my Webley Scott. The young lieutenant was frankly amazed at the age of this antique and offered an automatic from supplies, which I politely refused. I moved my wallet, cell phone and pills over to the uniform, along with 18 rounds for the Webley. A blue beret, without a badge was provided, which looked rather good on me, but I had no illusions. Jamie jumped into he cab of the Rover half ton. I scrambled into the back.'

"Live ammunition, full clips." He said over his shoulder.

"The back of the Vancouver Confederation Bank. Get your finger out." He said to the driver. I heard the Sargent unlocking the ammunition box.

In moments the Rover was hidden behind the bank building. Lead by Jamie and the Sargent, we made the elevator, through the back doors and took it to the top floor. A few moments later we were on the roof.

At 9:02 a.m., three things occurred concurrently. One: the hidden explosive charges attached to the telephone main relays to specific sections of downtown, with the exception of the selected banks, exploded. The telephone system effectively died for police, fire and the government. Secondly: four small dish-like destabilizers started to turn on the highest roofs in the city. These units formed a square in which all cellular communication stopped. Three, a man slowly got out of each of the trucks positioned outside the banks and made for the door.

At the Vancouver Confederation, it was Tom Remington. Tom was blond. His hair was short and clean. He sported the shoulders of a football player. He had served two tours in Nam; one at Desert Storm and lived. For forty-three he was in good shape. Women cadged looks at him as he walked by with the power stride of the Admiral of North Sea commanding. He was dressed casually in a blue polo shirt and khaki Dockers. Clasped in a gorilla size left hand was a new maroon leather briefcase. Opening the main door of the Vancouver Confederation he walked in and immediately made for a side counter placing the briefcase on the arborite surface away from the security camera. He removed a new Uzi silenced machine pistol from the case, turned and, with soft coughs, blew the cameras off the wall. He turned slightly and caught the second and third. Then, with three powerful steps, he jumped on the counter and screamed. "This is a robbery. Do anything to stop it and I'll kill you."
The doors opened as the terrified customers and

bank employees moved toward the corner he
indicated. The second and third members of the
team were in placing 'closed' signs on the doors and
moved directly to the offices. They herded senior
bank people out with the rest.
"Lie face down and be quiet." Tom snarled from
his perch. No one resisted.
The remaining two men came in. They carried the
large canvas cricket equipment bags. They
immediately started to fill these with money. Tom
jumped down and kicked in the door to the side
rooms. In a second they were inside emptying cash
from the luggage and briefcases into the malls of the
five-foot long equipment bags.

The Arab slipped into the bank behind the last two
men. He went through the bank and into the
manager's office closing the door behind him. The
burnished bronze hands removed the printer plug
from the back of the manager's computer. He
opened, what looked like a small laptop and
plugged it into the open outlet. Powered by
batteries, it started immediately. He pushed four
keys on the small board. The result was
spectacular. The smaller computer impacted
commands on the bank's system at a rate beyond its
capacity, and perhaps beyond sanity. The input
commands moved through safety defenses before
they could even react. Once behind

them it cancelled the commands which governed them. This all took place without harm to the system. Other screens elsewhere did not flicker as they might if the system had been hacked. The speed of the commands would have made Bill Gates blush. In a minute the lap top had access to the customer files of hundreds of thousands of accounts, code-names and numbers. In a flash, the lap top was downloading this information onto an optimum capacity disk. This was the same style of disk that fits into standard CD players but with substantially expanded capacity. As each disk filled, it was exchanged.

Meanwhile, the bank was almost cleaned out. The vault had not opened. The men lifted the now full bags. The Arab joined them. They all left together telling everyone to stay put.

Outside, the six men jumped into the waiting blue, Chrysler minivan with glazed windows. The engine gunned.

The Arab walked slowly down the street as if nothing had happened. He stopped outside the Mercedes and the window came down. The package of disks, along with the small lap top was passed into the hands of Mohammed Tiasani, who smiled. The man moved to the back of the large five-ton bread truck parked behind the four-wheel vehicle and entered the rear door.

From our position on the bank building, we passed information to Cathaway at the central radio command with a pack radio. It was poor quality communications at best. By putting out one of the destabilizers, positioned on the bank's roof, we had broken the net. Wilson had found it hidden near the corner of the roof and I had turned it off. The other destabilizers, placed elsewhere, played hell with the quality of our transmissions.

Tisani had to be stopped. What was on the disks I had seen through Jamie's binoculars? I did not know. I knew we were in deep trouble.

"Well, what now?" Jamie asked. It was a hard question. I decided to come clean.

"The man in the white Mercedes all wheel drive is Mohammed Tisani. The disks he's getting have got to be bank account numbers on them. The robberies are a cover. That information he's got, if the banks don't know it's out there, could cost the Crown millions, maybe billions of pounds. Look, Jamie, these hyenas could siphon the money off and the banks would be responsible. Everyone who trusts us will pull their money out. They would be out of here like lightning. No one would ever have faith in a British Colonial Bank again."

"I see." Jamie was troubled. Everything he knew told him he should take on the robbers here. I didn't let him think too much.

"Look! We have to follow Tisani. If we start it here there will be a slaughter. Lots of noncombatants will get killed, but it's your call."

"I think you're right, Harper" Jamie spoke directly to the radio man. "Stay here and continue to signal. The rest of you, follow me." Jamie was going to be a general some day.

In moments we were back at the lorry. We made the corner onto Edward just in time to see the tail of the bread truck disappear down Dr. Roy's street. The chase was on.

Through a maze of small backstreets, we were headed towards Owen Roberts International Airport. This made sense. Tiasani would have a small jet waiting for a quick getaway. He was in for a surprise.

The security people were already putting up roadblocks at the airport entrances. Hopefully, between them and the five of us, we could mount enough firepower to stop the trucks. The over zealous Arabs might even blow themselves up, which would save everyone a lot of trouble.

Tisani didn't make the turn. He went right out on the A2 headed to Savannah and points east.

Chapter Twenty-one - 9:27 A.m., Monday, The A2
Highway Near the Junction of the A5 Grand
Cayman Island.

The Chase

Fortunately the road system on Grand Cayman is
excellent. The ride in the Land Rover, on stone hard
wood seats, was not párticularly unpleasant. The
wind flooded back and balanced the warmth of
wearing battle dress, in eighty-degree heat. Grand
Cayman's populatión had blossomed over the past
few years, people either escaping the rat race or
getting closer to business by coming here. More
then 36,000 souls crowded the three small islands.
This meant a huge increase in building, primarily
along Seven Mile Beach and surrounding George
Town. New homes, like a housing cancer, spread
toward Savannah and beyond. The difficulty in
paradise was that almost 69% of the landmass was
swamp or unusable and the British Government had
decided to keep it that way. Also, there is no natural
water on the islands, which is another problem.
The Rover rushed by small houses, shops and gas
stations that lined the highway. Our concentration
was on the Turtle Bread lorry that was within seven

or eight car lengths of us, local cars filled the gap between. The land here is flat and green. If the game knew we were in pursuit, they did not respond.

I left this part of the situation to Jamie. If he wanted to catch up and start shooting, it was up to him. Taking out the tires on the truck would probably put it out of action. However, the response of say, ten hardened fighters armed with Kalashnikovs, would be devastating, given that the Rover wasn't armored. Also the driver of the bread truck would probably block the road and let the Mercedes escape.

Thoughts flashed through the inner eye of my mind.

Why had the blue Chrysler minivan not moved when we passed by? The emptiness of the van, no movement at all, disturbed me. This of course was unimportant at the moment.

I should call ahead to Savannah, as there would probably be a roadblock at the intersection of the A2, which carried on to Savannah and the A5, which bordered the ocean from South West Point.

The Police at the roadblock would be looking for small vans or trucks not a five-ton bread wagon and two men in a Mercedes.

I took out my phone which was satellite linked and called the police station in Savannah. A calm, deferent, almost bored voice said.

"Good Morning Constable Retin, speakin. What can I do for you?

"Listen this is Michael McFurson, Ministry of Defense. We are in pursuit of a white Turtle Island Bread Lorry five ton and a Mercedes four by four off road on the A2. Is there a roadblock at the intersection of the A5?

"Aw! Mr. McFurson yes, ' Retin had heard of me, 'We got the stand down a few minutes ago. I think it's all over "

"Are your men still in position." I asked

"No sir, you should be passin dem on the A2. They been called back to George Town.

Sure enough two police cars with flashing blue lights and the heehaw siren of Europe screamed past.

"Look how many men do you have there?"

" Well there's me and two constables, comin in from off time."

"I need a road block this side of Savannah."

"I have to get permission for anything like dat. You're wanted in George Town, London time." As

opposed to island time, which tended to be
whenever.

"Well, do your best. We really need you to block
the road. If you can do that the marines I have with
me can finish it up. Look, these guys are armed with
automatics, so I suggest body armor and shotguns
right."

"Sure, you hold the drip at my nose and I run out
and get dem, right now." Retin would be lucky if he
had body armor. His service revolver was probably
the largest caliber weapon in the station. I thought
of having him call the cars back but figured they
would spook the enemy.

"Do your best. A nice semi across the road would
help." I rang off. Not too much chance of stopping
our friends in the column ahead from Savannah. I
saw the Texaco station on the left and knew we
were close to the intersection. The traffic didn't stop
but flowed through. The enemy picked up speed.
They seemed to think there would be a roadblock
there too.

I would have called Cathaway but that would have
had us recalled. He couldn't help, I had all the
Marines on the island with me.

The two largest helicopters had been borrowed by
Reggie to get his sections to Little Cayman . In

short, at this point, we were it.

As we sped up along the straightaway past Prospect point down the A2 which would soon pass through Cave, a small community on Savanna's outskirts. I prayed I would see a flashing red light or a great ugly Semi, parked across the road. Neither occurred.

Sergeant Wilson had been studying me for a while, as well he might and decided to find out what I was about.

As in all armies it is the noncoms that make things happen and they liked to know what it was they are dealing with. He was sitting opposite me.

"May I ask who you are, sir?" he probed. At perhaps forty he was built like a rock. Big powerful hands cradled his Sterling sub-machinegun with it's distinctive sickle clip.

The face was carved from a bronzed material near metal, dusky graying eyebrows overhung his intense brown eyes. The face pored down past a blunt broken nose to a mouth that never smiled and a formative cleft chin

"Mike McFurson.' I said 'don't worry Chief Warrant, I'm just baggage on this trip."

The old combined forces, comes out in the Canadian Military. At one time, they had us all in bus driver greens with mixed ranks. What a mess! When I was in the forces sergeants were Chief Warrants.

His face pursed. "Not Marines them?" he wasn't happy I was play acting in a uniform he held slightly lower than God, in the world.

"Sub-lieutenant, Royal Canadian Navy, Reserve." I looked him in the eye. It became obvious to me that those who have killed share an almost immediate acknowledgement of each other. I believe the message is branded into the windows of the soul. Wilson had been with Reggie in the Falklands. He pursed his lips again. He didn't like it but he would give the Canuck a chance. At least I was navy.

"W'at's it about then?" asked the round headed marine, sitting next to me, called Qlin. Wilson was about to tell him to shut his hole, when I spoke up.

"The people ahead of us robbed the banks in George Town. They're well armed."

"Too bloody right, lets get stuck into 'em." his young, open face with its dull blue eyes turned to his Sterling. He removed the clip and checked it.

We skimmed along the ocean's edge .The soft rollers rushed in to kiss the shore and then lazily tripped back. I longed to be on Seven Mile Beach

swimming or sunning perhaps with Cindy.
Visualizing her naked body in my minds' eye, there
was a sweet melancholy that made my teeth ache
with its intensity.

We were in the Village of Cave a few houses,
shops and pedestrians. In moments we were in
central Savanna. At the intersection before the small
post office, the Mercedes turned left and north
towards New Lands and the North Sound Estates.
We followed keeping back.

Well, here was our chance. Open road and while
homes appeared here and there it would be better
than the upper end Estates with the moneyed
tourists and their children, for a gun battle.

"What do you think Jamie?"

"I didn't expect this, what do you suppose this
Mohammed git is on about?" Jamie asked, he
needed support for the next move.

"I have no idea. Up ahead there are boats, maybe
they want to go to ground in the Estates, grab some
hostages. They could turn on us, there is that".

"Jamie considered the number of cars between the
enemy and us, there were three. Mohammed would
have to know we were back here by now. Having a

shootout over the heads of these locals would be a worst possible scenario. However, we had to do something soon.

"We will follow. They have to come to a stop and then we take them. Wilson set the machinegun on the cab mount. I don't want anyone coming out of the rear of the lorry on two feet."

"Sir." Said Wilson and immediately set the Bren like machinegun into its bracket

"We will probably only get one chance and too much depends on us doing it correctly.' Jamie decided to wait, 'Without any support we can't make a mistake." You're right and wrong lad, I said to myself. Say, they have a helicopter waiting somewhere but I kept my peace. This was Jamie's game to win or lose. I would do my best for him.

"I'm going to call Cooper on the Seagull and see if he can get to the sound, either to block the entrance or come in and head them off..

"Right!" Jamie agreed.

The cell phone call was patched through to the ship by the Island Phone Company. I had drinks with Cooper, he was tall and painfully thin, like the victim of some horrible disease. However, this masked robust health. Blond and hatchet faced, he was what the Scots call a hard man. Emit was tough

and brave as a lion. Heaven help the man who
crossed Emit Cooper. Jamie had told me that
Cooper, off duty of course, had beaten the living
crap out of four Yankee Chief Petty Officers who
had commented on his emaciated structure when
drunk and in a local bar. I could see his sarcastic
smile form as he heard my voice.

"That you Coop?"

"You were right, Mike, lot of people looked bad as
hell but you saved the day."

"Thanks Coop. Listen it isn't finished yet. I'm
chasing two truckloads of Arab terrorists up the
New Lands Road toward the Estates. They're the
ones behind the whole thing. I think they might
have a boat on the sound and thought you might like
to come over and give them Her Majesty's
compliments."

"You doing this by yourself then?" He said
astounded.

"Christ, are you kidding, I got Jamie Trevers here
and the rest of the garrison." Cooper laughed hard.
It was a clipped bray.

"No wonder Cathaway wants you back. You've
stolen his army."

"Borrowed, look, tell the good Captain we're all
right, will you. Just don't tell him where just yet."

"Pointdexter will send men to back you up. Don't be stupid old son."

"This is a military deal Coop, we aren't arresting anyone. These guys see death as a direct trip to Allah. The local cops are good men but they aren't set up for this. We'll just get them killed."

"I see, I'm near the Sting Ray farm. I'll come straight across the sound. Tell me if there are any developments"

"No problem but my batteries are getting low and I don't want to lose our communications."

"Give me Jamie will you?"

"No problem." I passed the phone to Jamie through the open rear window of the Rover's cab and said "Cooper on the Seagull."

"Yes," Jamie started to speak. I didn't listen in but Cooper was giving him a direct order to hold back, Cooper would send reinforcements. He of course was coming. "This was Cooper's call but I shuddered at the thought of the Island police force coming into contact with a well armed military force. Well I had done my bit and now I could just wait it out.

The two trucks made the turn into the North Sound Estates and sped up. We had a hell of a time keeping up. The road was thin and the turns hard. A woman, backing out of her driveway, stopped us cold. They got the lead and we had to catch up. We got to the bottom of the Estates road to find they had disappeared.

Jamie stood up in the Rover's cab, through one of the two roof hatches, to see what was going on. Nothing!

"Perhaps they went on the beach," Wilson suggested. Between the two last houses at the base of the street was a walkway which might have accommodated the trucks but two large steel poles five feet high and about a foot in diameter formed a gate. These were set in the ground to block vehicles from disturbing the beach area.

"Take us down" Jamie snapped. At the bottom of the road we got out and ran to the beach. There were no tire prints but it looked like someone had swept the beach recently.

"They must have gone back up the road, Damn!" Said Jamie.

"Look, at this someone swept the beach but this track is fresh. I said indicating the track of a size nine desert boot. Wilson ran along the track

"Oy, there are lorry prints here." He yelled from about twenty yards out.

"But how?" Jamie took off his beret and scratched his head looking at the poles

Olin threw himself at one post, it didn't move.

" The sand seems to be solid all around but here." I pointed out the slender strip of ruffled sand behind the pole. Olin and I dug in like badgers until we came to the track. I pulled up the bolt and slid it out of the way.

"Try it now." At Olin's touch the pole slid back from the center of the walkway on its track.

"Cheeky buggers." Olin said to no one in particular

While I fixed the other pole Jamie brought up the Rover and we were off again. The sand was no problem. The Rover plowed through.

"The bread truck must have had four wheel drive and lifters to get through this." I said to Jamie who was looking up the beach with his binoculars toward Duck Pond Cay.

"I think I see the bastards. Better yet, I think they feel they've given us the slip" said Jamie very pleased with himself.

We followed staying back. Catching them on the

sand was out of the question. The shore was changing we splashed through more water now the smell of swampland reached us. The beach was giving out. They would have to stop soon. I checked my Weblcy. There were five shells in the revolver leaving the barrel chamber open, so I didn't blow my foot off.

"They've disappeared again. Bloody hell!" Yelled Jamie.

"We'll get them." I said.

"Ambush I suspect, Sir." Wilson suggested.

"Yes, of course. Stop the Rover." Three men jumped down and disappeared like ghosts into the mangrove swamp lead by Jamie. Olin and I waited with the Rover.

Ten minutes later, Jamie walked out of the swamp and motioned us on. Wilson was wiping his knife.

"There were two of them ", Jamie said trying to sound off handed. his knife was also crimson. Jamie had joined Wilson and I, in losing a little bit of his soul. Killing might be necessary but it was never easy. The first time is the hardest. You remember that one.

"They went in there. ' Jamie motioned toward the swamp, 'We'll follow as best we can. Call Cooper and tell him what is going on."

I did.

Chapter Twenty-two - 10:10 A.m., North Sound Grand Cayman

Bloody War or a Sickly Season

Death is something that is put away from us. Jamie and Wilson did not look at the two bodies lying beside the entrance of the hidden road. There was no bravado.

A friend of mine, Bernie Stats, had a father who was a mortician. This was the reason no one would play with him. Bernie once asked me, what people were going to do with Grandma's body after she was finished using it? Would they kick it down the stairs into the basement?

"No! They call my father," Bernie said, 'and he is kind and he helps the whole family through very tough times. Then they ignore him when they see him at church because he reminds you you'rer going to die too.' Bernie was a good friend and still is. This situation on the other hand like Bernie's quiet pleasant, unimposing father, brought mortality to the forefront. Jamie now knew we would have to kill all of Mohammed's people or leave them alone.

I knew fear again. Up to now, it had been fun. The chase was exciting in a distant kind of way but now it was very real.

Jamie came over and stood beside me, he looked older and a little drawn. It is hard to confront death when you are young. The realization that you might be next is even harder.

"You don't have to come you know." He said quietly.

"You're going to need me. Anyway look at all the luck you 've had. Hell, I'm your mascot." He laughed then and it was good.

"I'm sorry but I had to give you the option. After this you take orders instantly."

"Yes, Sir."

"Right! On the Rover."

The road was dark as the trees closed in, the wind was blocked and the sweat started to flow down my back. The smell of rotting vegetation and filthy water reached every crevice of the soul as if this was God's reminder that all things go this way. I leaned up to the window.

"I give them fifteen to twenty minutes before they expect to hear from your friends back there, then they will expect us. The Arabs have been back here for months, to work all this stuff out. Mohammed and company, probably have their base pretty well protected." I had my say.

"Yes!' said Jamie, then thoughtfully, 'I didn't know you were a Sub-lieutenant."

"That was long ago and far away, back before they turned over the rocks." I kid.

"They didn't dump you, did they, cashiered? " he asked uncertainly, it was an ugly topic.

"No, I'm still in good standing."

"Right, Wilson will take orders from you. If something happens to me."

"That's high praise." I said honored that an old timer like Wilson would give over to me.

"No, old boy, that is rank." Jamie said succinctly "I'm afraid Wilson would take orders from a log if it had rank and could give directions before he'd take over himself."

"Sic Transit Gloria," I said and Jamie laughed a clear clean laugh.

"Yes, so passes glory." He agreed.

The road was poor but passable. The amount of work, back braking and long, that it had taken to create this wonder amazed me. An engineer had

come in and worked out a way though the swamp.
Men had laboured to complete it. Hiding at the
sound of a plane or a boat where the road came
closer to the water. With poor or no tools they had
carved it out of the stinking morass. I wondered if
any passing tourist had died to keep the secret.

"The road did a bloody Houdini." Snarled the
cockney from his place behind the wheel.

The road ended at the water. A pond of stagnant,
water covered with green filth, spread for a good 40
yards. The smell was breathtaking. I got out with
Jamie who stood by the edge.

"They might have gone up stream." He suggested.

"Not through those trees. Maybe its shallow
enough?" I took a thin branch and stuck it into the
scummy liquid. It went strait down.

"No." I moved down the shore and just before the
trees the stick stopped a foot under the water. "Its
here." They corduoryed the road.

"What?" asked Jamie.

"They corduroyed it. Laid logs under the water so
if someone found the road they'd think it stops
here."

We eased the Rover across and up the other bank.
Wilson and Olin went across first with Jamie in the
lead. Then we followed with the truck. If there were

to be an ambush it would happen now.

Your head moves by itself. Every noise no matter
how small gets instant reaction. I believe this
situation calls up long unused sensitivity directly
from the pit. Some men believe they can smell the
enemy. There were no shots. This meant our friends
were too busy for that sort of thing or didn't think
we would follow them.

A few miles later, I smelled the sea once more and
knew we were near Little Sound below Booby Cay.
The trees became less dense and the ground firmer.

Jamie stopped the Rover and we jumped down
weapons at the ready.

"Time, I think for a little reconnoiter." Jamie said.

"You want me along? It will sound like your
walking your rhinoceros."

" Sorry, rank. Old boy." Jamie Ordered

"OK."

We started out, the marines moving with quiet
precision. All Reggie's exercises in this stinkhole
were paying off. I stumbled along behind making as
little noise as possible. We slithered through the
mud within a few yards of the camp.

On the far right the bread truck and Mercedes were
covered with nets. Camouflaged tents were almost
chameleon

like in their surroundings. Two reinforced
machinegun positions and guard posts in the trees
watched for intruders. These were not manned or
we never would have come this close.

By the shore was a glass bottom boat. After all this
swamp it took a second look to realize it was really
there. Thirty feet long and painted bright blue it sat
on the shore at the end of a small dock like a
mirage. Yet it was identical to others that carried
tourists into the environmental zone while watching
the fish population below.

The Environmental Zone was a sneaky way for the
British Government to palm off this swamp as a
tourist attraction. The immaculate, white awning
was held up with a metal frame. Small lights were
spread along the awning, giving it a celebratory
effect.

Brilliant, what a perfect way to bring in supplies
and personnel disguised as tourists. What a brilliant
way to leave the island. Set sail across the sound
like a boatload of tourists and make contact with a
boat or ship out beyond the reef. Cooper wouldn't
even bat an eyelash. The plan showed Tisani's
abilities to the full. The steel poles, hidden entrance,
the corduroy road, all subtle little ruses just difficult
enough to put off pursuit with minimum expense.

"How many do you make it?" Jamie whispered.

"About twenty-five, I think?" I suggested

" Wilson" Jamie asked.

"Yes, Sir." Wilson agreed he was a man of few words.

"The tall thin prick with the beard and the hollow eyes is Hedi. He's the one who worked me over on St. Thomas. The shorter one with the bag is Mohammed." Mohammed's bag had to be the reason for all this. Being long and rounded it would hold the disks. The two leaders talked and looked out at the Sound while the other men got ready to leave. We had just caught them.

"Lets go." Said Jamie

We moved out and returned to Olin and the Cockney at the truck.

"Call Cooper and tell him the situation."

I took out the phone and dialed. There are moments when your life changes. This was one of them.

"Damn, the batteries are dead."

"No!" said Jamie grabbing the phone. It wouldn't work for him either.

"You sodding thing." the Young lieutenant snarled and threw the cell phone away.

"Right,' Jamie was all business, 'Wilson your the flank. Stay out here, when they come for us and they will, you prag them."

"Yes, sir." Wilson took the box of grenades and made off.

"Olin and Lane the machine gun and the ammunition. McFurson the raft." Jamie grabbed the other ammunition box.

I picked up the dark green rubber package that expanded out to a 12-foot rubber inflatable raft and carried it, following the Marines through the trees to the left. Finally, the leaves parted and we were on small sand spit with a fallen tree across it. Jamie must have spotted the position with his binoculars while we were looking over the enemy camp.

The tree provided solid cover between the enemy and our selves. It was at least four feet in width and solid. It had been torn out of the soft soil by one of the many hurricanes over the past few years.

Olin and Lane set up the machinegun. Jamie was spaced slightly land ward of them and I was the flank behind the roots of the tree. We had about a twenty-foot field of fire on the land side. This field of fire was not great, but better then nothing. Looking over the log we were one hundred yards from the tour boat, which was broadside to us. The machinegun should be able to pepper it.

Jamie had it all well worked out. If he could puncture the hull of the boat our friends would be forced to escape back down the road. Wilson who had the box of grenades, was stringing trip lines to them across the road. They would be concealed on strategic trees, at this very moment. The trucks would trip the wires as they went through, that would finish the enemy transport. The police or Reggie with the rest of his two sections would find the survivors and polish them off. That was at least the plan. It was the best possible concept from all angles at the moment.

I was strangely calm at the prospect of battle. I remembered a movie I had once seen where an over zealous iguana had told his partner, he had always wanted to face great odds, in a desperate battle, for a brave cause. What no one told the iguana was, that last desperate stands, were fought, by poor sods that were stuck in it, because someone had screwed up. If you won there were lots of medals. If not, no one remembered.

Jamie had put our backs to the wall. That was his job. If the enemy came and they would, the only one who would get out of this would be Wilson. Good for him. I had almost fifty years, that wasn't a bad run. The kids and the wife would miss me. I would miss them. Then I realized I would miss nothing. To hell with it maybe they would get in the trucks and run.

Then of course we would be off to support Wilson.
Maybe we would all live forever. At least the air
was clear; I could smell the sea and see paradise
under a clear sky. The world was momentarily
beautiful beyond words. I said a short prayer,
thanking God for the day. Then I turned to the task
of war. The fear returned like the beginning of a
sickness.

Jamie looked over and I nodded. I held the Webley
Scott, with its new skeleton grip. I had a fellow up
in Dunville, back home, put it on because the old
one was too flat and needed a lot of work to be
accurate.

I took aim at Hedi and braced myself against the
tree.

Jamie dropped his raised arm and all hell broke
loose. The machinegun roared into action. Spurts of
water appeared around the boat as shells impacted
on the hull sounding like of a jackhammer. I fired
but missed as Hedi dropped to the ground with the
first shot. The incoming was almost instantaneous
and heavy. In battle you forget everything but firing
your pistol. The noise is terrifying. The smell of
cordite wafted back from the Bren.

Tisani's tour boat stayed afloat. An armored hull
prevented sinking but there was penetration, she
was taking water. The surface of the tree exploded
into

chips as bullets hit the trunk looking for the four of us.

Fifteen, or so, AK 47's chopped away at us. Olin turned the machinegun on the mound from which the opposition was firing. One went down. I fired my Webley and raised dust near the defenders. One attacker actually stood up to shoot. I fired and he whirled around and didn't get up.

They were moving forward now. Three men were working on something on the far right of the mound.

Under heavy cover fire ten khaki clad fighters moved toward us, slithering across the ground into the underbrush. They would now try to flank us on my side. I wish I had something other than the Webley. Jamie was at my shoulder.

"Take this,' he passed the Sterling into my hands 'Lane's feeding the gun."

There was a yell. It was Olin. I looked around the roots to see Lane fall, a good part of his head blown away. The sand was splattered with his brains.

Jamie jumped over Olin's leg, as the private continued to fire short selective bursts. With one hand he reached down removed Lane's identity discs from around the fallen man's neck and placed them in his jacket pocket. These actions occured like Jamie had been doing it for a hundred years. I turned around to the low, sickly looking grass

across the small killing ground. I emptied the
Sterling's clip into the grass, at root level. That
brought a scream, a curse and a death struggle,
which was visible in the grass. I put a stop to it with
a second short burst. My hand disengaged the sickle
clip and mechanically put another into the Sterling.
You never forget how.

An Arab half stood to lob his grenade. I had no
time to fire, mesmerized like some budgie in the
gaze of a snake. I looked death in the face.

Olin swept the grass with 50 rounds of 7.62 NATO
ammunition. The grenade man went backward in
mid throw, the mini bomb landed just in front of
him and exploded.

A second explosion further down the log, on the
enemy side, sent wood splinters in a semi circle that
maimed more of our friends in the bush. We were
fortunate to be on our side of the tree. Wood is
much worse than mental for peripheral wounds.
However, offered the choice, I'd rather neither type
of sliver imbed in my lilly white. The second time, I
heard the unmistakable cough of a light mortar. Its'
shot was long, shrapnel whizzed by from our side of
the log this time. I took a look to find both Olin and
Jamie still very much in the fight. This was good
but the Mortar made the calculation one of time
until they found us. I drew a bead on one of

the crew, just in time to see two black projectiles flip into the mortar position. The twin explosions and following Sterling fire meant that Wilson, that beauty, had jumped the opposition on the flank. The reaction was immediate the enemy chased the retreating Wilson toward the road. Pressure on our front didn't slacken. The boys in the tall grass seemed to be beating a hurried retreat. I figured they had been called back to get in the trucks for the ride out. Unfortunately they only got out of sight behind the mound and created a more concentrated fire. Their objective was, it seemed, to keep us pinned down. I wondered if they had another mortar. Bullets passed uncomfortably close. The zip and crack of live ammunition plastering the trunk closer and closer to me was enough to cause a sane individual to burrow under the heavy log and hibernate until this whole mess was gone.

Jamie was back.

"What do you think?" He got that far and I saw it. There was an explosion of bubbles as the sub blew her tanks and bobbed to the surface like a prehistoric cork. Looking like a large sand shark out of water. The old conning tower was crested with twin fifty caliber gattlings. The weapon rose to aim and I grabbed Jamie, dragging him behind the roots.

An explosion of bullets turned Olin into strawberry mush and the machinegun into a twisted pretzel of metal. The guns then started to chew the log up as we trembled behind it. The force of the impacts was so strong and so targeted that the log was pushed across the sand two or three feet with us before it. Then it was quiet. It took me a moment to focus after the roaring.

"You asked what I thought, ' I said " I think we're royally screwed.

"Do you?" Jamie asked shakily

"That's the advantage of age. I been there and this is it."

"Olin is dead, I've lost my command." said the young lieutenant.

"Rank, old boy." I said, then more kindly, "You did your best. Your people knew what they were getting into. You didn't lead them into a trap.

"What exactly do you call that." He indicated the surfaced submarine with his thumb

"We should have all been dead coming across the corduroy bridge. You did good, at least we know where the sub is. The thing now is to stay alive so we can tell someone."

"Wilson is out there, we must help him." Jamie was already figuring how to go into the teeth of disaster. I figured Wilson had bought it. I hadn't heard any Sterling fire over in his direction for a while. Maybe he was wounded and gone to ground? I hoped so he had saved all our lives.

It would seem; I was the first to see everything today.

"We got someone else to save." I pointed behind Jamie out over the sound, to a uniquely beautiful and dreadful sight.

"My God!" Jamie whispered.

Across the flat water of the Sound, with white froth ripped from the ocean by her bow came HMS Seagull. A hundred feet long, thirty feet wide built long ago as a fast customs chaser. Seagull was born for speed. Now as she approached two giant Royal Navy battle flags unfurled in the wind. It is of these things, that a navy's pride is made. Back from her knife like bow the "A" battery stood, a Bofors Multi. The barrel of this weapon could be depressed so that armor-piercing shells could be used against surface targets or hydraulically elevated to fire on aircraft. Immediately behind the gun's three man Cayman crew, sat the gray wheelhouse with Cooper in his chair and a bosun at the wheel. The wheelhouse being circa forties something, looked rather antique and a little funny, crested with a range of antennae and radar. In gun tubs, abaft the wheelhouse, were two twin machineguns. Seagull's small stack now trailing an enormous plume of smoke as laboring engines ran full out to save us. On the stern was a heavy fifty-caliber machinegun on a hydraulic stanchion. For accurate aiming the gun and man seated on it, moved as one. She was formidable all right but the submarine was hidden behind a small treed island, which stood like a ship parallel to the coast.

If Cooper came straight in after the sightseeing boat and the grounded terrorists, he would pass the island at speed. This would place him broadside to the submarine's bow and its' torpedoes. The twin gattlings alone would tear the gunboat to pieces. Jamie was speaking again

"We have to slide out to the swamp under the cover of that sand dune." The dune was almost non existent.

"Says the thin guy." I bitched helpfully. Jamie smiled.

"Right! We bring the life raft. Get down along the shore till we are on the other side of the island where the sub can't see us. Then a short paddle out to warn Seagull. We will have some flares in the raft. All we have to do is make sure we don't get killed."

"Yeah! And pray Cooper stops."

"Yes! Look Mike. I can call you Mike? "

"Sure unless you want to dance."

"No! ' He smiled slightly in a whimsical way. "My wife Natalie is here in George Town would you see her if I'm not able to." I became serious this was important.

"Sure and I'll write letters to everyone's families too. If I don't make it, ask Lorning, he'll get you in touch with my old lady up in Canada.'

'Well! Bloody war or a sickly season, eh!" I spoke

the words but they caught in my throat.

"Yes!" Jamie nodded at the grim toast that since time immemorial, had been given, by the youngest officer at every Royal Navy mess dinner. It is a reminder that promotion is based on the death of a superior. Only sickness or battle caused this opportunity. It is the bond of the navy and every officer knows it.

"You first, I don't want my fat carcass in your way." Jamie slid out and moved across the twenty or so feet to the trees. I watched the grass for a return engagement with Mohammed's people.

Fifty cal slugs spraying the log a second time the huge piece of wood turned with the force of the onslaught, fortunately, it was to the right and cut down my distance to the trees. I could tell you I was terrified but if you have never been in the path of an oncoming tree shredder you wouldn't understand. As quickly as it started, the gattlings were silent.

"I immediately began to slither over the sand to the mud at the base of the trees. I just pulled myself in. When the sub did a complete fan of the area, shredded leaves and twigs rained down on us but the aim was short and off hand. The sub had lost interest in us. It wasn't hard to figure out why. The Arab ground personnel were firing everything they had at the Seagull.

Cooper would have the beggars and the sub would have him. The island's proximity and the lack of depth were probably messing up his radar. If we could get Cooper to stop he'd have the whole bunch trapped. A lighter shade of turquoise in the water over the entrance told me the submarine would have to come out on the surface over the shoal hidden beneath.

The next few minutes were the worst I have ever lived. We hauled our guns and the raft up the coast over the entrails of trees and ground brush. Wallowing through mud holes and dead water to my waist, made me gasp for air, weighed down with my sopped uniform, the Webley and Lane's Sterling. The pains in my arm were a reminder of an old body misused. Jamie stopped.

"You all right?" He looked concerned.

"Yes!" I lied, you got some water?" "He handed me his canteen and I downed one of my high blood pressure pills from its plastic package. Jamie made no comment.

"Let's go." I got up groggily and we pushed on.

In few minutes more we were beyond the Island, out of sight of the sub anyway. It was about as far as I could have gone. I stood heaving

Jamie pulled the plug on the raft and it expanded to full size in seconds. We threw our gear in and pushed off. Paddling was almost worse but at least I could sit. I had paddled a canoe but this was purely physical labour and very hard. The current for some reason seemed to move into the area where the submarine was hidden and we had to fight that too. After, perhaps five minutes we were in the middle of the passage trying to hold our place waiting for Cooper.

The sub must have been warned from shore. Computer directed, the Gattlings fired a long burst. The majority of the bullets hit the trees. A small number overshot our air bubble. The remainder hit Lieutenant Jamie Trevers in the back and legs. The sick sound of a cleaver hitting meat brought me around. I put my arm around him as the raft deflated and sank. He was dead. His eyes open but sightless. The blond head tilted back to reveal a foolish smile as if he had finally gotten the great cosmic joke. I closed his eyes, took off his disks and removed

Lane's from his pocket. I then pushed off from the rubber coffin. The current slowly pulled me into the entrance of the killing fields.

Chapter Twenty Three - 10:30 A.m., Little Sound. Grand Cayman

Fire and Water

The water was warm or at least tepid. I floated along until I caught a brain coral and steadied myself on it. At least I was now stationary, a few feet from the little island behind which the submarine was hiding .The current pulled at me requiring that I join the other flotsam in the small bay behind the reef.

Seagull came on, I could hear her engines thrum, the bow wave was extended. She became close enough to see the gun layers faces by the Bofors.

I yelled as loudly as I could, waved my arms and broke the plastic flare which popped into the air with a red rocket like effect. For a moment I was standing at a park in Ivanhoe, Ontario watching part of a Victoria Day fireworks display with my kids; the next I was ducking deep to escape the bullets of ten or so AK 47's. White bubble paths of the projectiles filled the water around me like minisubs. One cut into my arm just below the shoulder, not seriously injuring me but smarting like hell. I

resurfaced, just missing Seagull's bow wave. I
watched the gunboat's Bofors empirically blow two
or three of the hidden gunmen to Allah, with a little
bitter joy. What happened next was the most
horrible and fascinating thing I had ever witnessed.

  Seagull slowed as she came to the channel. All of
her guns were trained shoreward and the Arabs
where taking a really evil hiding. Bodies were
maimed or tossed in little heaps but the purpose was
served and it was the Arab's turn to crow.

  Abdula Ada was the computer technician on board
the Sand Darter. He had set the Gattlings in place
and helped work out the difficulties of the hydraulic
system. In an off limits, little harbour area of one of
the neighbouring islands, the Darter got its coat of
sand coloured paint. Finally, he had inset the eye
hand control for the high tech weapon. Thin,
delicate wires stretched from the computer's control
system up into the wide view camera mounted on
and targeted to the Gattlings, on the conning tower.
At the moment Seagull passed the edge of the island
into view, it was he sitting in the hydraulically
operated control seat below the guns. His eyes
centered on the Bofors gun, the barrels of the
gattlings whirred, moving slightly to point at exactly
that half foot of

space. Pure technology is magnificently horrible in reality. Abdula pushed the fire button down on the joystick, as if in a game store simulator but there was no simulation. The roar of the Gattlings drowned out every sound in the world. From my position in the warm water, I watched in fascination, as the bullets hit their target.

The Bofors crew died as one man. Their bodies ground up like minced meat and thrown overboard like scraps. The sweep of the Gattlings now touched the wheelhouse. Cooper had only seconds to realize his mistake. He and the bosun were cut in half. Chunks of the wood and metal flew off in all directions. The right twin machine gunner, closest to the sub, was next .The heavy cased bullets popped through his armor tub like it was constructed of butter. I saw blood flow out in an angled spout, like water from a ruptured canteen. The stack was sheared and the fifty on the stern that desperately trying to hit the Gattlings missed and died.

Seagull's left side twin twenty now started to fire. I looked back at the sub and realized that three of her crew were on deck. Two were by the base of the conning tower and one standing by the rear hatch all firing Uzi or AK weapons at the gunboat. The Caymaner behind the twin twenties was well trained and hit what he could see. One man, below the con, fell and the other tried to lift him up. The crewman, who had stationed himself near the rear hatch, went backward over the side as the bullets hit him. He seemed to have attached himself with a long safety cord to the hatch. The wire, extend out as he disappeared with a splash.

Abdula now brought his guns to bear on the remaining gunner and slashing off the top of the gun tub with a steady stream of shells. This sent the twin mount into the air with the gunner's hands still attached. The Gattlings stopped.

All was silent. Nothing moved on Seagull. She drifted, the engine room without orders had come to full stop. Abdula now started at the water line and hammered the entire length of the hull pealing back the thin metal like the skin of a tin can. I heard the gurgle as she started to take water. I could only speculate at the appalling havoc wrought below decks. The Gattlings stopped once more. The Seagull remained motionless, crippled and as if dead.

In this all-encompassing silence, this ear shattering silence,. I moved my hands slowly while kicking to stay on the surface. I thought that I should make for the Island and find a large tree. The buzzing noise,

which should have been the aftermath of the attack
on my shattered ears, got louder. I could identify
cruiser engines. The tour boat was stationary. Hedi
and his remaining troops were placing boxes of
explosives into the bow of the pleasure craft. The
blue boat, with its perforated canvas now turned its'
nose toward the helpless Seagull. The engines were
getting louder. Oh! God! Some poor unsuspecting
boat owner was coming to give assistance. I turned
to wave them off, having drifted in past the island,
as the current gently pulled me toward the bar.

A thirty-foot Robin's egg blue sports fishing boat
with the long sail fish sea rods in place, stormed
past me. Parallel to the now motionless Seagull, her
crew of five began to fire. The distinctive blast of M
16's cut the air and Hedi's men who were cut down
on the wallowing tour boat quickly responded. They
didn't have to. Abdula once more touched the firing
button in the air-conditioned submarine and the
little boat was racked from stem to stern. The gas
tanks are not armored on ocean going fishing boats.
The explosion was shear, hot and terrible. I saw two

of the would-be cavalry, jump just before their boat went up.

After a moment, I surfaced again. One of the two survivors was floating face down. The other was clinging feebly to a piece of wood. They were both dressed in blue overalls.

Pieces of cruiser fell all around me. Hot metal hissed as it hit the water. At this point I started to believe I had survived this long for a purpose. That alone kept me going. What was I to do? Getting to the island and finding a place to hide might be a start. Someone had to inform the government about the submarine. If it got out of Little Sound we had nothing between here and Bermuda to stop it. Our North American Fleet was based there and would have the ships to track and sink a pig boat.

On the other hand, I thought I might swim over and help the guy from the cruiser. The enemy, of my enemy being my friend concept having a certain validity in this case.

The sub was moving. It sailed forward at half speed directly toward Seagull then turned toward the beach. Behind its sand body, skimming along like a paravane, came the dead Arab sailor still attached to the hatchway by the safety line. I judged the distance and took a couple of strokes, as he

passed by I grabbed him. I was at once face to face
with the corpse. My weight flipped me under the
body, so that my mouth and lungs filled with water.
I shoved and rolled him over, mad as hell that, I was
being drowned by a dead man. I got on top and was
riding behind the sub just as we came toward the
man on the floating wood, which looked like the
stern bench of the ill fated cruiser. His body just
went under as we came in grabbing range. A single
hand lifted skyward like a last appeal. I hooked my
arm out and caught his body under the armpits. The
weight just about tore my appendage off at the
shoulder. I somehow strained every muscle and
pulled him to me. The blond head was small.
Christ! It was Cindy looking like a drowned kitten.
The pinched, lifeless features, closed eyes, she was
dead. No!

I hugged her to me. A little more water came out
of her mouth; she coughed and gave a small pushing
motion. She wasn't dead.

"Wake up, Wake up!" I screamed in her ear, she
blinked but far away. I couldn't hold her.

I reached around the line and grabbed the front of

her overalls with one hand, somehow maintaining
my perch on the dead man. I pinched her under t
arm. She screamed water came out of her mouth,
then she vomited, but she was awake.
"You bast...!"; she garbled fighting mad.
"Grab the line or I'll lose you." I yelled back.

Her small hand fastened to the wire mechanical
The other followed, we rode the corpse around in
circle. Then, as the sub slowed, our momentum
brought us close to the hull.

"What are we going to do?" Cindy asked comin
back to reality. She realized what we had been
sailing on at this point and was going to scream b
I put my hand over her mouth.

"Listen, we are going to climb on board and ma
for that hatch. You still got your side arm? " I
removed my hand at this point.

"Yes. You figure we're going to take on the wh
crew?" Her eyes were wide.

"I don't know but something."

I shoved her up. She was weak and couldn't ge
her booted foot up. Rule one, cut the boots off or
you're in the water. They fill and weigh a ton. I
reached down and slashed them off with my
pocketknife, thank God she had them navy laced
Meaning the lace required a single cut to remove

the problem. Now she got up. I put my hand on the center of her backside and pushed, sprawling her on the deck. It took all my remaining strength and I had none, to get up. We sat there for a moment breathing heavily on the burning hot sand coloured surface. I drew the Webley Scott, still tied around my neck on its lanyard. She was armed with a new Italian made, NATO standard forty-five, which she tipped with a silencer no less
. On the other side of the ship passengers were being taken aboard. We could hear the small boat bump at the sub's side and Mohammed's voice as he shared a joke with one of the crew.

Two things were obvious; One, there wasn't a lot of crew or the deck would be crawling with them. Second, the twin Gattlings were the only armament outside of small arms. Or more correctly, they couldn't spare the men for more. A crew that small would be strained by the loss of two men. I had seen the two go down.

We moved to the hatchway. Fortunately the camera director was on top of the Gattlings and we

were below its line of vision. Even then the watcher
was occupied with the still formidable Seagull.

My other worry was Hedi and the tour boat, which
was now moving toward the Seagull slowly,
because of the water she had taken on. Hedi was
busy with wounded from Cindy's attack. No one
was watching the sub. Anyway, the hatch blocked
their vision.

I looked into the hatchway. Below was an escape
chamber for the stern torpedo crew but the bottom
hatch to the two man capsule was open. I could
make out the edge of light through an open forward
hatchway to the engine room; the rest was dark as a
tomb. I moved Cindy into the hatch top and came in
with her. There was room; she watched the bottom
of the ladder while I cut the corpse loose.

The Darter glided forward. Her engines picking
up-tempo. The ship had a good strong heart.
Someone loved those engines. For a ship that old
she purred. We turned again in a long and wide
semi circle. I could hear the hydraulics of the
Gattlings whir as they turned to stay on target. The
sub came to a stop on an angle the bow toward the
entrance of the bay.

We were just in time to witness the last act. Hedi
and his remaining crew made for the British warship
with caution. This was for good reason. Lolly
Megins, senior cook rating, was making ready to
provide a greeting. Saved by the cast iron stove in
the galley, he had waited to see what would happen
when things had quieted down, he went out on deck.
Covered from the sub by the superstructure, he
might have made for shore in the lee of the ship.
However, Lysander Megins was a Caymaner and
that is fighting blood all the way from Captain
Morgan. Lolly, still wearing his apron, moved
toward the bow of the ship. At the edge of the
wheelhouse, Megins surveyed the scene. He saw
Turner, the chief gunner and his men were dead,
gone from the Bofors. Men Lolly had known and
drank with now only smears on the deck. The
Arabs coming toward his defenseless ship. The sub
was farther away and busy, with a boat along side,
the Gattlings were directed toward him but he
figured he could get to the loaded Bofors. He knew
how to fire it. Cooper had everyone do every one
else's job, to the momentous disapproval of the
crew.

Lolly judged that the tour boat would be along side

in minutes. He breathed deep, then ran to the gun. Behind it he pushed the gear and brought the muzzle to bare on the tour boat. His foot hit the trigger pedal and the gun jumped.

Railing and canvas disappeared from the tour boat. Hedi grasped the edge of the boat in agony. A four-foot section of the railing had impaled his lean body to the stern of the blue hull.

He breathed out one last time, as the man beside him screamed "Allah Ackbar", and pushed the button on the electric detonator to the cache of explosives in the bow of the blue boat. This occurred as it gently slid under the bow and nudged the Seagull. At that point the tour boat and most of the gunboat including Lysander Megins, disappeared into a rain of flying metal and wood. The sub was far enough away to miss most of it. The way was now clear. The engines gunned and the Sand Darter moved majestically forward.

Abdula, in retribution for the loss of Hedi circled the ship with his Gattlings and shot anybody that came into view. Even our recent craft was torn to shreds by the concentrated fire. Had we been in the water, we would already be dead. His next action was to hammer the island and the shore as the remains of the gunboat sank from sight. When the sub came even with the island, nothing was alive in the little bay. Once over the bar the Captain would surely submerge, that would mean someone sent back to check the torpedo room hatch.

I looked down to find Cindy passed out against the side of the escape hatch. Nothing I did would get her back this time. It had all been too much. I quickly closed the outside hatch submerging us in stygian darkness, then gently let Cindy down to the torpedo room deck beside the open forward hatch. It was completely dark with the exception for the light that filtered in around the partially closed hatchway. The entire torpedo room was stacked with merchandise.

I lifted Cindy's dead weight over my shoulder and squeezed back between the stacks of crates to the actual torpedo tubes at the far rear of the ship. Here she was softly laid on the deck behind the boxes. On checking her pulse, I found she was OK, just out cold. Then with the forty-five automatic in hand, I waited for the enemy crewman.

Chapter Twenty-four - 9:12 A.m., George Town, Grand Cayman.

A Little Bit of Reality

Constable Edward Land walked confidently over to the blue Chrysler mini van. It was parked illegally before the Vancouver Confederation Bank. He did not intend to ticket the van. It was a beautiful day and the tourist was to be helped.

Edward had been with the RCIPF four years. He had never drawn his side arm. He didn't expect to. The baton was much better for his work. Actually the number of Americans who visited the Caymans and their passion for guns tended to be the greatest risk.

He knocked on the glazed driver's window. Then stepped nearer expecting the window to open. He was reflected in the glass; his slouch hat with its red band faced with Island Seal, the standard, blue long sleeve shirt with its uncomfortable dark blue tie and dark blue pants, a black service belt that was worn tight to the body so as to be unobtrusive and non-threatening. The twenty four-year-old face that looked back was sharp and clean. He smiled at his reflection, then realized he would also be smiling at the tourist. Catching himself he frowned, 'don't be

fawnin on these people'. He told himself and tapped
harder, still no reaction.

He reached for the door handle and it gave
outward.

They were dead. He knew it. He had seen the dead.
How did death get in here, in the car? Carbon
monoxide, maybe? The big blond man with the
crew cut looked up with sightless eyes as if in
surprise.

It was then that Edward started to blackout, luckily
he stepped back and shut the door before he fell to
his knees. It was like the devil had cut his windpipe.
He heard the cruiser stop behind him; two flying
squad officers were helping him up.

"Don't open the door." he gasped pointing
vaguely at the van and passed out.

6:51 PM, George Town

The room was silent, large and white painted. Air
conditioning hummed in the background. Paintings
of the Queen and Prince Philip looked down
benevolently at the long polished mahogany
conference table. Sunlight beamed in from the four
large windows opposite. The day was almost over
and yet it was warm and beautiful. When Ridley

had left London hours ago, he couldn't remember how many, it was raining. Granny had sent him to the airport in a police convoy. The government jet left immediately. He had spoken with Granny on the way and read all the information as it came in. One stop, to change planes in Bermuda. Then over the gulf, flying here to Grand Cayman and the scene of the crime.

What an appalling mess! In his time Leonard Ridley had seem many but not this bad. He looked out into the garden with its flowers and wished he were out there working quietly or better at home taking care of his roses.

Ridley removed his heavy, black framed glasses and dropped them on the table. His face was thin and hard. The cheekbones protruded like boulders. The nose was wide and rock solid, as was the jaw, manufactured of the same material, prominent and powerful. Above it the mouth looked out of place wide and thin lipped. However, under the solid protruding forehead with its gray eyebrows were two intelligent penetrating blue gray eyes. He wears a Bradley, light weight blue cotton suit with a gray Armeini tie, even given the island heat. Brooding like a summer storm, Ridley considered what he must do.

As Assistant Director North American Section it was his decision. Granny, who faced endless problems at headquarters over this thing, would back whatever he decided on.

Leonard wondered if Granny would survive this. God help him, God help us all. He thought fervently

Good old Granny, lying in his chair as was his habit. When asked what he would do if they demanded his resignation? Responded.

"I will, old darling, tell them to stuff the lot and become security man on the Turks and Caicos. I will take my lucky ball and turn my back on this place. In leaving I will say a prayer for the next poor sod to sit in my place.' Then more realistically, 'Not to fear Ridley, I 'll be here until the Second Coming. Who else would pull the thing off with such verve?"

"Go out there and see what can be done." That was Leonard's farewell.

The Governor's private secretary, a pretty red

headed girl with a beautiful figure was standing
outside the French doors moving from one foot to
the other like she had to spend a penny. Ridley put
his glasses back on smiled and nodded. 'Go to the
Loo, love don't tarry on my account.' She smiled
relieved and raced off to get the others for the
meeting.

The door opened and Reggie Bloodworth was first
in, his face like a hurricane trapped in a bottle.
Lorning was next looking downcast and old.

The Governor's Assistant, Ainsworth, the nervous
bureaucrat frightened that some of this didn't rub
off on him. Priggish and affected, an oval face with
small features and a miniscule mouth, he might be a
problem as he spoke for the Governor. The old boy
was still in England and wouldn't be back until this
was over. Lucky bloody him!

Captain Bailey of HMS Brittany was next, dressed
in whites. The new cruiser was on NATO exercises
off the Bahamas and had made directly here at top
speed. A rugged, weathered face with a strong jaw
and eyes that seemed to be farming their own
wrinkles. He looked perturbed, wait till he left.

Poindexter walked in heavy, round, with a large

bully's, ruddy mustached face. You're perfect major blimp. Dressed in open neck khakis, he eyed Ridley coldly, before sitting down.

Finally Cathaway, Ridley felt real sympathy for this man. On holiday doing a favour for Reggie whom you didn't say no to. Then this! Well let's see.

"We seem to have a spot of bother gentlemen." Ridley started when they were all seated.

"A spot of bother,' Snarled Poindexter, 'You've a bloody comedian. I've got sixty bodies in a hanger at the airport. Sixty Americans killed with poison gas. Sixty! " He reemphasized the number.

"I've lost four men including Lieutenant Trevers." Said Reggie with a steel edge as if he might come over the table at any moment. Ridley was unimpressed, sitting at the head of the table alone. The others bunched up at the other end.

"Not to mention the little mater of Seagull and her crew." Bailey said blandly from the far right corner.

"Ten bank robberies." Ainsworth simpered from across the table, 'the banks are in frenzy."

"One robbery." Ridley said in a voice that was so low they had to stop and concentrate to hear it.

"One robbery?" Poindexter looked flummoxed, as he should.

"Yes, one robbery. The banks have been told. The six men who committed it were killed in a gun battle with the RCIPF. The money twelve thousand Pounds was recovered" Said Ridley firmly.

"You're bloody Joking." Poindexter's background was showing. His great lion head braced for the attack. Sod that for a start, thought Ridley.

"No, I'm not joking. If this lot gets out, that we had ten successful robberies in one day. No one will ever trust an Island bank again. We will loose the deposits at our financial institutions the substantial return from this as well as other territories. We will also probably have them go independent. Not to mention all of us looking like a pack of idiots."

"It was that McFurson Johnny, that buggered this all up. Why didn't he come to me?" Poindexter whined

"We told you this might happen, " said Ainsworth straightening in effeminate correctness.

"I have no time for this,' Ridley didn't miss a beat. 'This is what is going to happen."

"Pick six of Poindexter's collection of bodies put them in one óf the trucks. Then put some holes in them, or I'll do it myself."

"I'll take care of that," said Reggie,"

"Good, tonight we'll have a little get together for the local press. Lots of free drink, that should get them in. It will be an evening for the Officers of Brittany only in for the night and so on. While the press are at the booze up. The marines will load the remaining fifty-four bodies into a container and run them down to customs then out to the Brittany. I want them sewed in canvas and weighted Navy style. Tomorrow Bailey will take his ship off the shipping lanes and have a nice quiet burial at sea. Everyone on board is National Secrets period. If you don't think you can trust them, just the petty officers."

"I'm not here to clean up your mess." Bailey made to protest but Ridley's face was uncompromising. "The North American Fleet Command has already sent you a message to this effect."

"What about the bloody Arabs?" asked Poindexter.

"They were left where they were found?" Ridley asked

"Well, yes."

"Good! Take their finger prints and DNA samples, following that they become landfill."

"Christ!" Said Poindexter in exasperation.

"Haul a power shovel out there and bury them. But no markers."

"'Trevor's and his men were killed in a motor accident." Ridley continued eyeing Reggie for reaction

"What!" Snarled Reggie, he half stood and Ridley felt real fear.

"They of course will receive the DSO, posthumously. We thought of saying they had been in a fight with the robbers but then some git will wonder what the Marines were involved for. Too many questions, I'm afraid. However, it might work better that way. I'll give a final answer before we give out the press release. The release is just for local distribution.

"And Cooper?" Bailey inquired sour faced.

"The Seagull will sink in the storm tonight, ones expected, with all hands." They of course will also receive whatever medals the Navy deems acceptable." Seagull was a local defense ship. As such was owned by the territory but came under naval supervision, Ridley left Ainsworth and Bailey to work that one out. Bailey gave him a unique look somewhere between hate and respect for the size of the lie.

"No one will go along with this, you must be potty." Chimed in Poindexter. 'What about the explosion?" He asked

"Fuel explosion on the American fishing boat,

petrol fumes and a spark happens all the time."
Ridley closed that door hard.

"Oh! The Americans took their people with them
didn't they?"

"Yes,' said Ainsworth, 'the super Hercules from
Panama had come in and left with the CIA bodies in
a large crate. They didn't like it. Not one bit."

"Good."

"How do you cover enough small arms fire for an
invasion. We've been getting calls all day."
Poindexter wouldn't leave it alone.

"Trevors and his people were out on maneuvers
just with a lot more men. He was scheduled for
maneuvers wasn't he?"

"I think,' said Cathaway quietly, 'You would be
better to have two robberies if you want to make it
stick. The people from the other banks will think
it's them."

"Good, a constructive thought. But then we have
twelve bodies too many" Ridley shook his head.

"No the same six men, just two different robberies."

"Yes, that will work fine, wait timing will be a
problem. Perhaps not!"

"Excuse me, if I rain pee in your poop, old sod but
do you actually believe anyone will swallow this
abortion? You're fabricating it as you go on," asked
Poindexter.

- "They had better,' Ridley turned on his tormentor
His voice was cold with anger, the face was of a
man who was beyond the point of compromise.

"There is very little press on this Island, what ther
is won't be overly upset with a bank robbery or two
No one was hurt. The money recovered. What is
more important the Americans won't twig to it.
They have bank robberies daily. It would be news i
they didn't happen." So that aspect of the problem
will pass. We won't make the BBC News World
Report. Fortunately, for all of us, most of this
happened in a swamp. If those bastards, you towed
in dead, had been interrupted in their little fiddle
you'd have half the free world press here. With Dar
Bloody Rather examining you bum for boils.

You'd have bodies all right, women and children
caught in the crossfire. With your young constable
recovering in the hospital praged for a start.

Just another though what do you think will happen
to tourism if we have open war in the streets?"

"So we are agreed, two robberies, six men, Trevor
and his people a little over exuberant.
with the ammunition. An unfortunate shipwreck an
Trevors and his three men killed in contact with the
enemy. The marines coming back from maneuvers,
cut off the robbers and when they seemed to give
resistance, killed the lot".

"You're mad." said Bailey honestly. 'The people in the banks will talk. Too many witnesses are involved. They might accept the swamp story. I think the bank robberies are a little too much. What if the government sponsored the robberies as a sort of test for preparedness? After all you recovered all the money.

"No, I thought of that, too involved, they would want to interview people, ten is outrageous but perhaps I will take it under review. I should mention, all your department heads have agreed on this plan, or rather my developing the information going out."

"It would be better if you used the Arabs, they're at least shot up." Suggested Cathaway.

"I suspect,' said Peter Poindexter in a calm and reflective voice, 'I've always hated lying. I became a policeman to uphold the law. Why not tell the truth and the hell with it."

"Poindexter,' said Ridley in a more reasonable voice, 'what has been worked out here is in a way the truth. We are admitting that the robbery occurred, as Bailey says we have the money. The men are dead. Whether we shot them or they died of some nerve gas they will be no more dead. However, if your men or the marines bring them down then we give a warning to anyone else with a similar plan.

Bailey, Bloodworth, I would like to tell the world how bravely you're chaps fought. If we do that their sacrifice is lost. They died to cover our mistakes. I will not publicize that and destroy the very Empire, as thread bare as it might well be, they died for.

The real hero even if he didn't come to you Poindexter is McFurson. He told us all and we thought he was round the bend, needed some rest. He warned us at the end and died with Trevors."

"I could have sent in my heavy weapons team." said Poindexter.

"Yes, but he didn't know we had one." Lorning said shaking his head. A little information disruption thought Ridley.

"Now I want to know what happened?' said Ridely, having placed the matter of the banks and swamp behind him.

"Peter you were first on the scene. Why were you so late?"

"The bloody water hazard,' recounted Poindexter, 'we put one Cortina into the pool. It took us ten minutes to find the markings on the tree and figure out where the bridge was under the water. Meanwhile, of course, all hell was breaking loose. You could hear the grenades and the mortar. Then, of course, we came in slow.' he paused as if he could see the battlefield again, 'there were bodies all over the place".

"We almost missed the Sargent he was well hidden.' Poindexter looked at his notebook. 'Wilson. He of course is in the Hospital."

"Well that is some good news, then." Said Ridley

"I spoke to him,' said Reggie morosely, 'shot in the stomach, he isn't expected to make it."

"I see." Ridley wasn't passionless; he hoped the Marine survived.

"The sergeant told me McFurson went with Trevors.' Reggie said, 'he didn't have to, Wilson said, Jamie gave him the option of staying behind. It seems he was a Sub-Lieutenant in the Canadian Navy." This alone would not allow McFurson to refuse in Reggie's mind.

"Trevors tried to destroy the boat the bandits were going to escape in. He wasn't successful. Wilson took out the mortar when it started to fire. After that he was wounded and retreated firing until he held up and the Arabs were recalled.

He heard the fifty caliber machineguns. Perhaps they were on the island opposite? I don't know. There is almost nothing left of Seagull she was taken apart with plastic. Maybe Bailey can give you a little more detail." Reggie trailed off.

"The divers from the ship feel that a fifty Caliber Gattling strafed Seagull.' Bailey said 'It was American, we found the spent bullets. Normally a gun like that is used on attack helicopters. On two separate pivots either side of the aircraft for balance and computerized for accuracy but in this case the guns seem too close together.

"So you're telling us it wasn't a helicopter?" Ridley clarified.

"There were no sightings of helicopters' answered Lorning.

"Some kind of boat then?"

"No boats were sighted that were not local or accounted for." Lorning put in helpfully.

"Well they didn't disappear into thin air, perhaps they're still on the island?"

"My men did a sweep of the area, there are no trails leading out. The underbrush is too dense not to leave some trail. " Said Reggie.

"I wonder, they've been back there for at least two months or so, no one saw them." Ridley sounded tired.

"We are checking on the addresses attached to the van and the other vehicles. So far there is nothing. The Arabs that rented the locations where they stopped, don't exist. So says the Yard and Interpole." Poindexter added

"How many did we kill out there?" Bailey asked

"There are at least twenty .In the swamp and in the water." Reggie estimated

"Could a helicopter get off the island without our radar picking it up?" Asked Ridley.

"Yes, its' possible, but unlikely." Ainsworth confirmed., Bailey nodded in agreement.

"We found Trevors. The shark and barracuda had been at the body but he was shot with fifty caliber shells,' He paused, ' 'in the back. I think he was paddling out in the raft to warn Cooper about the gun position. Wilson said he saw a flare before he blacked out." Reggie answered another question before it was asked. This was going nowhere quickly.

"Fine, I want full reports from all of you. This meeting never occurred and your reports are National Secrets Act right from the start. Good afternoon gentlemen." Ridley concluded the meeting.

"Ainsworth, draft the press release we agreed on. Please bring it here for a final vetting before you distribute it." Leonard said and smiled at the Assistant who left without comment.

Chapter Twenty-five - 8:00 P.m., The Sand Darter, In The Caribbean

The Darkness

It was silent. The darkness crouched around us like a captive. Silence is a relative thing though. While the engines rumbled forward, the drive shaft below us whirled pushing the old submarine ahead. Within the aft torpedo room, with the bulkhead port battened on the engine room side, the noise was minimal. The senses are intensified by danger each moment is the moment of discovery. Each second is the one before capture or death. The smells of the old ship are magnified, fuel oil, old food, sweat, dust and cardboard from the piles of boxes behind which we are hidden.

I sit with my back to the stern of the ship between the two torpedo tubes. I listen to the door. I listen to the water outside along the hull. I listen for any indication that there is someone, an enemy coming this way. Can they hear my heart pound like a sledge? Is the place bugged? We will know soon as the girl wakes up but I don't think so. My watch scanner says no but it sometimes is not accurate. It misses the newer microphone models. The darkness moves, enemies are in, somehow through the wall.

The mind says no but the senses hyperventilating see what is not there.

In the beginning, I had crouched over the girl, as the sailor in the blue striped shirt ran up the ladder to check the hatch. Then, without a moment's hesitation slid down to the deck and through the hatchway securing the battens on the other side.

Cindy hadn't moved. She had remained comatose and I was afraid she had suffered a concussion. However, when I looked into her eyes with the pencil flashlight attached to my keys, there was no dilation. Later, she slept, the voice of her breathing becoming more soft and balanced. She had moved in her sleep making small sounds like a trapped animal but had not awakened. I should waken her but that only makes the next step come nearer and the sharp edge of that step cuts me even now.

Instead, I searched the compartment slowly, stealthily checking once more for bugs. There are toasters, clothing, boxes of supplies some I can't reach, some, I don't want to. I return to her.

Moist blond hair covers my thigh, my right hand slowly caresses her head. She seems child like. Her hair is soft and smells sweet; a cherry scented shampoo still is entangled in the strands even with the effects of the salt water and fuel oil, which are also there in smaller amounts.

Cindy moans low and I know she is about to wake. I lean down and whisper in her ear.

"It's OK! Its dark because we are in the stern of the submarine, you passed out and I had to hide you, be quiet."

"Do you understand me?" I ask intensely

"I'm dizzy, not stupid.' she starts. Lifting her head away from my thigh, which has gone to sleep in the past hours.

The original plan had been to hold the outside hatchway against all comers until help arrived. A little foolish, perhaps, but functional. Especially if Cindy could keep the bottom of the escape hatch open. No sub Commander, no matter how much a believer, would take a sub down with an open hatch. Tisani would have thrown his people against the hatch eating up time. Time for the police to arrive. Thinking back, the twin Gattling would have made short work of them but perhaps not.

The Arabs might have blown up the ship but that was the risk, perhaps the salvation. That would have made being the only survivor, when better men then myself had gone, bearable. I had to do something for Trevers, Olin and the Cockney, Lane. They were

my men and I would not lose them without
retribution.

Stupid! Stupid! Stupid! I was thinking like a
soldier, not a spy. In my world you used people, the
end was always the means. Yet, we were still alive
and perhaps if the girl kept her nerves, we still could
win. Life was the great dividing line. Alive there
was always something to do, dead it was over.

"Do they know we're here?" Cindy asked
mystified.

"No! I don't think so. I also don't think the place is
wired.' I paused, 'While you were sleeping I did
some looking around. This is an old U.S. Sub called
the Sand Darter."

"Sand Darter, wasn't she in a movie? I mean the
navy used her for some dopey comedy."

"Well, our friends have her now."

"How many?" Good girl you're thinking like an
officer, should I have expected less?

"Less then twenty, I think they lost two men in the
fight with Seagull."

"I remember now, they had a Gattling fifty cal. They
shredded us. Then there was an explosion."

"The fuel on your boat."

"You saved my life." This caused me to look away
in the dark her voice seemed so full of thanks. I
didn't deserve it and didn't want her maudlin.

"Why did you do that?' She stopped looking for words, 'after what I did to you."

"You didn't do anything to me."

"I raped you." It came out so sorrowfully and small, I had to smile. I was pleased with the dark at that point.

"I hate, to destroy your illusions and every other feminists but you don't rape a man like that. If he can't provide the ride, so to speak, the trip is off. Scaring the hell out of him won't cause him to be ready."

"Then what did we have in that hospital room?" Came the snarl.

"We had sex, and keep your voice down."

"Oh God! Hello! I'm too dumb to live." She was beside herself. 'What did you tell your wife?"

"Nothing, I didn't exactly go looking for it.' I slowed down this was going all wrong.

"Oh! Jeez thanks." She retorted.

"Look, I wanted to have you. The lovemaking helped me more then you can understand. You made me whole when I needed it most. It was the best sex I ever' had."

"Really?" She seemed impressed because I was telling the truth and she was looking for a lie.

"Yes, but fair is fair, I never thought I'd see you again.' Then more conciliatory, "Look If it helps my conscience is driving me nuts, so you won."

"You saved me. If it was me, I would have let me die."

"I have grown fond of you."

"How come?" She said on the verge of tears.

"I think it's your cute little feet." She laughed then, I could see her in my mind's eye her face full of light as she giggled The tension was broken.

"Thank you." It was sincere. I was very uncomfortable.

"Look! I wouldn't thank me just yet. We are on a submarine with twenty people who will kill us without thought, after raping you for real." It was time to find out what kind of partner I had.

"I want you to start thinking like a US Navy Officer, Ensign."

"Yes, Sir, I know you rank me." Straight out of my file no doubt. Complete obedience was out; this had to be a partnership.

"No! None of that, we are equals. I haven't been a Sub-Lieutenant since there were dinosaurs. You have the knowledge. You're just out of school and know more about ships. We are partners, OK?"

"Yes, Sir. Michael," She was tentative. I smiled "Mike McFurson."

"MI 6," she completed the sentence.

"Cindy Lou Who, U.S. Naval Intelligence." I countered .

"Cindy Lou Who, I guess that works. " She smiled in the dark and I wish I could have seen it. " Cindy Connors is just about right." She was talking because she didn't know where to go from here.

"Want to hear our options?"

"We have Options?" she said in surprise and I smile again. I would have to kill her if I could, should they get to us. I wouldn't let them have her. Perhaps not, perhaps her sex would be her defense. One thing at a time.

"How many rounds do you have?"

"Two clips and six in." She said immediately.

"Good I have fourteen rounds plus five in the Webley."

"Option one, I started slowly, is when they come and put out the garbage, which maybe tonight or tomorrow night or any other time the door opens we kill them all."

"What?" there was deep breath, she hadn't killed before. It wouldn't work if she hesitated, that was it. One of them starting to shoot and someone pushes

the button and the whole ship goes up. I had found
the plastic, attached to the wall of the torpedo room.
There was enough explosive to level a city block. If
there were one package they'd be all over the ship.

"There is a down side. We have to get them all or
they will blow up the ship."

"You lead and I'll follow. I'll do my best. 'I knew
she would, but no. 'Also a bullet hole will let water
in at the same speed as a 303 round."

"Option two, I been looking around back here. It
looks like someone cleaned out the Norfolk Naval
Base Store Depot. Know what this is?" I shoved the
package toward her. In the darkness she ran her
hands over it.

"It's a rebreather, but better then anything I've
used." Good girl!

"You're right it's one of the new ones they use on
the nuclear subs. It has a ten-hour capacity and a
pretty good record with the bends. I wouldn't want
to come up too fast but it will adjust.' I had her
attention. 'I don't think we have gone below three
hundred feet so far, then she sounded like an empty
pop can under pressure." I said

"The sub gets up close to the surface we baffle the
door solid on our side, set the plastic and escape
with the rebreathers. There is a rubber raft back
against the bulkhead. The sub will go on for a little

before it explodes. We should be all right." She seemed to think this one over.

"If we use the escape hatch, lights will be flashing all over the boat. I think they there might even be an override.' She stopped again; 'It leaves us in open ocean with very little food and no means of communication. I've set explosives, that's spying 101 but plastic is different. What else is there." She seemed to plead.

"Option three, same deal but we shoot the guy who puts out the garbage inflate the raft and set off. The sub won't have time to stop the explosion, should do the job. On the other hand, it gives them a chance to use the Gattlings, which probably have night vision and to disarm the bomb. We won't be able to lock the hatch behind us and we will have to give ourselves a little time to escape.

"Is that it?" She asked.

"No, one more. This one I don't know about its the hardest."

"Option four,' I hesitated. ' I think I know where this boat is going.

"Where?'

There was a noise of metal on metal. I handed her the Beretta and took the two handed grip taught at the range on the Webley. She moved to her side of

the boxes and also covered the door down the lane
of supplies.

"Don't shoot till I tell you." I whispered in a harsh
rasp.

. Nothing, we held our position for minutes nothing.
Finally, I eased off.

She touched me as she passed me in the dark her
hand trembled.

"Forget what I said we never could do it."

"Tell me" she demanded.

"The sub is going back to True Love."

"You mean on St. Thomas?"

"Yes! Option four was to wait it out. Given that
she does ten knots under water maybe nine. She will
do more at night on the surface. She has to come up
for air. It would get her there, in four days. I figure
there is some kind of grotto or installation under
True Love. Once they get there, we get out of the
sub swim out of the grotto and walk over to Coki
Point and call up the Marines." I finished.

"Jeez that's simple. No offense, forget about the
being scared out of my mind all the time. I can't
hold it for four days."

"Yes I know but there is enough K Rations here to
feed an army and bottled water. The packaging is
plastic we empty it out and fill it up. Then we place
it in the garbage. They remove it."

"That's easy for you to say, you can aim." She was thinking
" First, why is this sub so important and two why St Thomas?"

"Well our friends here had some kind of computer control unit. I don't know how it works but I think they got into the customer base at the ten major banks on the Caymans. All the codes and so on. We are talking billions of dollars. True Love provided a perfect place for them to operate out of. On American soil with Government cover and with lots of phone calls going out everyday. Mind you when they do the money transfers they will bounce the signal off of everywhere first. The transfer happens in seconds, if all the information is right. It would be hard as hell to check.

Of course your government is covering the operation because Naval Intelligence is getting information on the transient militias coming in and going out."
I feel her discomfort and knew she had some background, I wondered if it was an American operation.

"The United States wouldn't do this."

"If you say so. Maybe not knowingly anyway."

"Of course the banks will change the primary codes on their own computers but if they start changing everyone's personal codes they are dead. Money will move out of the Caymans like water over Niagara Falls. The Island banks will become ghosts. If it gets out, the British Government will be undermined."

"So we, you and I, are going to die because of money on a computer." She seemed incredulous.

"You're right, no one should have to die for money even when it's billions. Of course, if you look at the skyline of any city, the tallest buildings are banks. They used to be church steeples, You might think we're dying for another god." I said with a nasty twist.

"The money aside, at this point these bastards have killed thirty some odd people on St. Thomas, four Royal Marines, the four people with you, the entire crew of the Seagull and God knows how many people in the George Town."

"They have to be stopped. Killing is its own remedy sometimes,"

"You seem to know." She said.

"Yes, I know. Two months ago I had never hurt another human being. Now I've killed so many I can't remember or don't know the number. I only know I left a young man, a Marine Lieutenant. A man who could have been my son and who I would have been proud to have as my son, dead in a raft because of that computer. He was your age and had a long life ahead of him. They killed him and I will not rest until I take that money back because it's so important to them." I finished. "You're right of course, we can't stay here. Let's look at option two or three." I said finally

"Tell me how four will work." She demanded

"We take the food from the back cases and the water. They haven't touched this stuff, so they have to have lots more and better up front. I figure the forward torpedo room is as full. I don't think this shark has any teeth. We stay back here.

When they put the garbage out, there should be one man. I will move up and look out of the hatch. A quick star evaluation should tell us if we are on course. We know the position of the Caymans and Virgins, if they are headed for somewhere else Option two. If not, I have a laser in my watch. I can set it to signal. I aim the thing out the hatch and send it. If we are lucky a satellite will pick it up.

If so the Marines or Seals or the entire American

Armed forces will show up."

"We sleep in shifts, talk to each other until there is nothing left to say and we will be there."

"And if they find out?" She asked sarcastically.

"Then we shoot it out, set the charges and escape as best we can. I won't commit suicide and I don't get taken prisoner again, that's out. These people have some nasty ideas about obtaining information."

"Can I think about all this?"

"Sure! We aren't going anywhere just yet."

There was silence of a second kind as she thought. I could smell her, feel her presence alive and strong it gave me strength. I felt at least I wasn't alone. Perhaps the greatest evil is being alone. The hardest part of life.

Finally, she came close and cleared her throat as if she didn't want to forget anything she needed to say.

"Have you thought they already know we are here and as long as we keep ourselves prisoners and don't cause trouble they leave us alone. It's easier then stationing guards or coming after us.'

"I don't think so' I said, ' They couldn't have us back here. The opposition is not stupid, option two or three would come to light".

"They could have locked the hatch from the outside."

"I would have heard." I said.

"Alright. We wait till the garbage goes out. If the stars are right fine, then we take a chance. You know if you signal then they just might attack the ship and the Arabs will blow us up." I nodded.

"I have to say that this is the stupidest situation I have ever heard of. Why didn't you just get us back into the water?

"Great carrying dead weight over open deck then into the water. Our friends, forward shot up everything in the bay with the twin Gattlings as they left. We'd be fish food now."

Chapter Twenty-six - 10:00 P.m., Tuesday, Sand
Darter, South of Cuba, Caribbean Sea.

Show And Tell

"Anyway, I just came in from the shower and I
took off the towel, we had this great big golden
retriever. So, I turned around to go to the closet and
Pookies nose was right in my crotch. I screamed! I
mean it was really cold and surprised the hell out of
me. So my dad comes charging up the stairs to save
me. There I am standing naked with the dog. I don't
know what he though?" I could see Cindy shaking
her head in my mind's eye. She had been talking and
I let her.

Nothing had happened for quite sometime. Two of
the crew had come from the kitchen, cursing the
cook no doubt, around eight and placed garbage in
the bags. These were the atomic submarine trash
bags made of heavy rubber like material and
weighted with nonpolluting metal, only the best for
our friends.

I shifted my weight. It seemed quite acceptable
that we were sitting here in our underwear, Cindy in
panties and a sports bra and me in underpants. I was
thankful she couldn't see me. Our clothes still
hadn't dried and the heat was oppressive. We were

cut off from the rest of the boat and the air-conditioning stopping at the closed bulkhead door.

"What was your dad like?" I asked just to keep the conversation going.

"Oh! He was a navy man served on cans off Nam. He always wanted to see his kid become an officer. He made Petty Officer. 'I'd like to salute my kid' he always said. Unfortunately I was it. No brothers to follow the dream. Dad had an accident in the boiler room with a steam hose. After that he had a landscaping business. The Navy gave him a pension but his health wasn't too good.

Then I decided to go into the Navy, Annapolis. I worked real hard got great marks missed a lot of parties.

When I needed a sponsor; dad went to his old skipper hat in hand and asked what he could do. This guy was a big shot in some defense industry. He knew this Senator; it was in to have women at the Academy that year. So he gave me his blessing. and we had a lot of pictures taken together. I didn't mind, I got to be a cadet."

"Pretty rough huh." I said thinking that basic must have been hell for her.

"Oh! Yeah, rough is not the word. Being small

didn't help. I could handle the hazing but the touching really got to me. However, Mr. McFurson I got great knees and real good non-sight accuracy, the guy's left me alone. I threatened to deball one in his sleep and they really pulled back then."

"I would think that would do it." I said helpfully.

"Anyway, after four long years I graduated. Good marks too. There were moments, I can tell you. I cried a lot at night in my pillow so no one could hear. Then one bright shiny day, I threw my cap in the air and my dad got to salute me." She sighed deeply as if it was now hard to talk.

"My mom and dad were going to the Golden Lion for groceries one Saturday and some asshole ran into them. Drunk! He didn't get a scratch but they died." The pain in the voice was twisted and deep.

"There are no words." I said thinking of my own father dying of cancer. Lord God forgive me but sometimes a bullet would be merciful

"So how did you get a sweet berth like St Thomas." I probed to get her out of her memories. I knew she was crying and I didn't want to hold her knowing what proximity might do and being afraid of not handling it properly.

"I think Mr. McFurson that might be a national secret.' she said pompously sniffing, 'but seeing we both are probably going to die anyway. One of my teachers asked if I had considered intelligence as a career. I figured it might get me on a ship faster, intelligence officer on a cruiser or something big.

Someday, I am going to be Captain of a destroyer Sub-Lieutenant. Then you can salute me." I knew she would be. Cindy had the strength of purpose that comes from fighting for everything you get.

"Next thing I know, I'm going through spy school and then right out to that international hell hole of espionage, St Thomas in the Virgin Islands.

I mean it is beautiful but unless you're into chasing drugies and don't want promotion, God is it boring. You can swim, sailboard and it's great. It's like living in a postcard. Sometimes I wonder if it's real, if I'm real. Then you came along and really screwed up my life."

"How so?" I asked with equal pomposity

"They wouldn't give me anything important to do just paper work. Finally Ken, he was my team leader, it was him who threw me overboard before the explosion. He informed me there was this

courier coming in. British and no great shakes.
He's tame, he said but you follow him and report in.
Good practice right?" I didn't like being
characterized as a wimp but after all I guess back
then, he had a point. I also figured he was more to
Cindy then mentor but I kept my peace.

"So you were 'on the job,' in the police
vernacular." I could see her panties as a splash of
lightness in the dark. I was thinking of her bum and
the way her flanks moved when she walked naked
across the room. Please forgive me I'm human.

" I decided to find out what you were doing on St.
Thomas. Find whatever you were carrying and bring
it in. That would make them stand up and take
notice."

"Unfortunately they teamed me with one of the
other girls, she was the lookout and real lame. I told
her to whistle if you came back."

"She tried, I heard her." I offered.

"You are a real creep do you know that?" She
really wasn't mad. I laughed and she got serious.

"Do you know how bad my life got after you
spanked me." Her voice got to be brittle cold.

"You deserved it. You're lucky, if I wasn't some fuddy Brit courier you'd be dead by now. Also, just as a side bar you were going to ring my chimes weren't you?"

"Yes! God I wish I had! I expected you to grab me. No one ever spanked me before and I didn't know what to do, it was too fast and humiliating.' She seemed to mull it over for a moment then let me have some really interesting information. 'They didn't tell me but they had a camera on your room. Fortunately, we were covered by the partition so they couldn't hold a film festival with me as star. You really screwed them up when you changed rooms they practically had to cut down a tree to get you back in angle. They got some really good pictures of you and miss 'look at my perfect ass'. You with your eyes at tummy level." Great how do I explain that one if someone slipped a copy to the wife? I am sure Granny had some footage, nothing like NATO cooperation

"Yes! I wasn't as lucky as Pookie." I said. Cindy actually laughed

. "Oh! You're a scream. It wasn't funny. I got to be

Ms. Patty Wacs and you would be surprised what really disgusting pictures there are on the Internet, of girls having their butts tanned. I'd get them casually left on my desk or attached under a file, bastards! Every stupid crack, butt and ass joke they could come up with. I mean I really paid for my mistake. I wanted to kill you." She really meant it and it made me ashamed and angry at my own stupidity.

"If you knew how hard it is just making it without being a woman.

Later I figured if I had sex with you I'd do you more harm that way. My career was finished.

Then Ken helped me. He fixed the report to say you attacked me and I fought you off, offered to have me transferred to a ship. No black marks or anything I think he felt guilty. He got me into the mess in the first place," I thought Ken wanted her out of the way. She was an embarrassment and a sexual problem. I wondered if good old Ken was married? I also thought the report that went with her wouldn't help her. Slowly, she would be passed down the line until she realized there was no future and left.

Well, she was the last one standing right now and if we lived, she would be a hero. I'd make sure of that. She needed a chance not a transfer; I would give her one. Also she was wrong it wasn't Ken's fault it was hers. Cindy would have to start taking responsibility for her mistakes.

"Everything was set to go, then we got ordered to the Caymans." She finished

"So it was you following me."

"You knew, with all the cars and things. I don't believe you."

"Sorry, it's second nature, after a while, Yes I knew but you were good."

"I guess they figured I at least knew you and could meet you again if they needed information." That was purely mercenary and honest. She left out they knew we were romantically involved. They would be watching at the hospital and probably had film of us in bed. They knew I loved her. Yes, I did in an old man's way, grasping at last chances.

"I really can't figure out why you saved me." She said to herself more then to me.

"Your dad would have come for you if you were hurt, like if you were in the hospital" I knew it was wrong, when I said it

"You're not my father."

"No! You're right."

"Wait a minute you went to Red Hook that night they nearly killed you. You went to help me?"

"Yes well, they said you were in trouble. If my kid was in trouble, I would have gone. You really had me fooled. I never suspected you as an agent." I stopped to think over what was about to happen.

" I don't want any crap about how I almost got killed helping you. What I did was purely stupid. I gave away everything we had for nothing. I make mistakes too you know."

"You must really love me." She said in that woman's way when they will do anything for you.

"No! Not that way. Well maybe a little. Listen when you get to my age." I started but that was as far as I got.

"Don't, your not old. Old men aren't capable of what you did. We're partners remember. I don't need you doubting yourself and putting my ass in jeopardy. I understand that's all. I'm here you can depend on me like steel. Balls to the wall Sub-

Lieutenant we don't have time now." As all women, she was right. She had fire I was glad of her as my partner.

The wrench of metal on metal spun us around. We had our guns in hand and at the ready. I sensed the cold determination in her. The lioness is always the killer in the pride.

The man was alone. He went past the garbage and started digging in the boxes. Taking something out, the sailor tore the wrapper from it. He ate greedily in silhouette from a cache of candy bars he had found. After about three he stopped and shoved the empty papers into the garbage bag. He burped, broke wind and scratched then climbed the ladder. I heard the bells forward, the telltale sound of tanks being blown. She was surfacing. The sound of the water outside changed. It sloshed along the hull now as we cut into a light squall.

No stars too bad but we would see.

The hatch opened and water sluiced down to make a pool on the deck. The chocolate sailor swung up on deck. Soft moonlight explored the darkness with silvery fingers. I could breathe sweet air, fresh and clean. Looking back momentarily I saw Cindy her nostrils large to catch the life giving air,

blinking at the soft light looking like an Elfin
Princess radiating not washed in silver light. She
smiled and it made me want to take on the world.

I moved forward to the edge of the boxes while she
covered me. I looked out of the hatch, only the night
with its net of stars looked back. I could see the
constellations. We were south of Cuba heading in
the right direction. I turned the dial of the watch
until the pinpoint laser flashed out a tiny speck of
red. I pointed it at the sky and pushed the inset
button. The Morse Code message shot up into
infinity. I tried to move the direction around
listening for the tread of the seaman. I heard his
boots and backed up quickly. This placed my behind
square into Cindy's stomach. For a moment we
looked like Keystone cops and just disappeared
behind the boxes as the garbage man climbed back
down and grabbed the first bag and mounted the
ladder once more.

I stepped forward and flashed the laser upward.
This time Cindy moved back covering the bulkhead
door.

The Chocolate Sailor almost caught me this time,
his footsteps hidden in Darter's, increased speed on
surface. Twice is enough. I backed to our hiding
place and crouched down beside the lioness. The
sailor went up again and her highness goosed me.

"You stupid!" I started but I smiled too and she was playing. 'Don't do that again." I said gruffly.

Finally, after a short time the sailor, a heavy, black silhouette came back down, closing the deck hatch and cutting off the sea air. He took some candy bars from his trove and made forward battening the hatch behind.

We stood poised to meet a quick return, for a long time then finally sat back and relaxed. She turned and I snapped her bra. It was too good a chance not to take.

"Creep!" she whispered, but she giggled too. This was going the wrong way.

"Get some sleep." I 'll take the watch. The words were rough and brought her back to reality. She lay her head on my thigh and was asleep immediately.

Chapter Twenty-seven - 2:00 P.m., London,
Headquarters, Her Majesties Secret Service.

Revelations?

 The sun had consented to come out; watery true,
thin true, but at least bright and pleasant for a day
late in November. Sir Mortimer Brae held the
corner office atop a ten-story office block across the
river from the old residence of the Secret Service.
This one, of course, had none of the dreary charm of
the old bureaucratic piles normally defined as good
enough.
 The loos worked here at least, as did the elevators,
a pleasant change for Granny Staters. He entered the
fascia offices of Montgomery, Benthill and Durham,
Barristers and Solicitors. The girl at the large
armoured oak veneer desk waved him past. There
was a soft whoosh as the gray four-inch titanium
door pulled back to give him entry. Mounted
cameras watched his advance through the halls.
Various doors, which doubled as cut off points,
directed him to the rear of the floor. Among

other little niceties was the fact that the entire floor
had an anti-gas and virus defense system. North
American Section did not. The European section
had it; perhaps he was being petty. Of course he
wanted to survive a gas attack; he was obviously
being selfish.

His progress took him past numerous offices
where he was greeted with a variety of reactions
ranging from smiles to downright incivility.
Nothing like rising to one's level of incompetence
and being told by those who hadn't of their undying
hatred. Office politics, especially in these lean days
got worse and worse.

Granny wondered, if someday he too would
occupy the corner office. It would nice to be
nobility. Sir Theodore, that would be grand, of
course there was the old army lower ranks dictum.
'Don't call me Sir, both my parents were married to
each other.'

Staters came to the mahogany desk of Paula
Fanner, Sir Mortimer's secretary, who gave him a
special smile. Paula had a wonderful body to go
with the rose coloured skin and shoulder length
black hair. It had been a pleasant and fulfilling
affair, which he enjoyed, even though now it tended
to be a hindrance.

"Shall I wait?" Granny asked smoothly.

"No! I believe he will see you now."

She pushed the button under her desk and the heavy walnut door opened inward, automatically allowing Staters to pass into Sir Mortimer's Office.

As the door closed behind him with a soft click Granny considered his surroundings. The room was large, as large as his office and the boardroom together in the court. The two corner windows faced with bulletproof glass and electrically gaused for privacy allowed the sunshine into a separate world. Granny stepped out on eighty-ounce carpet, which was light gray with a royal blue trim paving the way to a large workstation made of Chestnut. This wooden masterpiece gleamed with polish and glistened like an ad in a furniture magazine. The matching highboy, which concealed a well stocked bar, held up the far wall. Cream paint covered the room.

Sir Mortimer was watching the funerals of Travers and his men. This had been recorded earlier. In general, funerals were not the thing of Staters life. Grieving widows, a lot of people looking uncomfortable. The mumbled 'sorries', quick glances to see how others were responding to the situation. The reminder was clear that your turn would come. Granny had attended too many funerals. He had hoped he would be shot and hurled down some chasm somewhere. Getting old and having a funeral seemed the two greatest crimes in the universe. Of course it was necessary for those left behind but it was a bloody waste of time for the dearly departed.

Granny studied Mortimer once more. Fit, of course, perhaps forty-five at a guestimate, officially he was fifty. The Knight-errant had a long oblong face with pouting lips and small effervescent eyes that seemed to take everything in at once. His nose was a cartoon character slash. His eyebrows were non-existent and Mortimer's hair had receded to a point where he was forced to play hide the spot.

The suit was from Burbery. Dark blue and beautifully tailored. The tie was a Brooks Brothers yellow with yachts on it. The tie was a gift from a friend in the Americas. The tie was boisterous without being offensive, as ties should be. It was a statement.

Large, hairy hands rested on the wood. You would think the man was a gorilla from the neck down. At the moment, they were busy playing with a pen, rolling it back and forth on the unmarred surface.

The cuffs of a creamy, white, silk extended the
perfect length beyond the suit sleeve, sporting
cufflinks with the Brae Crest, six green strips, righ
to left, topped with a helmet and a unicorn's head
glistening in gold. The telltale bars sinister, stated
the family had been added to without the
inconvenience of marriage.

"This all seems to be going well, Granny." The
voice was surprisingly deep and calming.

"Yes, the press seem to have lost interest." Granny
agreed. Pictures of full dressed Marines in white
helmets stood by on the television screen.

"It all seems well laid on." Mortimer said to
himself or rather the telly screen. His heavy finger
hit the off button on a control panel, which also
encompassed the two computers that flanked him.
Bray sat back in his soft brown leather chair, hands
folded on his stomach.

"Sit down, dear boy, ' Granny sat deeply into one
of the plush leather chairs across from his superior.
A magnificent painting depicting the Battle of
Trafalgar stretched across the wall behind Sir
Mortimer, Victory, Nelson's Flagship, seemed to
crown the head of the Secret Service. Sir Mortimer
was an appointed head, of course, never been in the
field. The department heads had been there, no need
for him to go.

The problem was that there had been too many moles. Better to have an outsider that could be trusted. There was a moment of silence as the senior official gathered his thoughts.

"What did we find in the swamp at Little Sound?"

Granny would answer in short simple sentences, as was the custom. Decisions were based on information. The best decisions on the most concise information. This was Mortimer's rule; those who broke it beware.

"The Arabs are from a group of countries. All over the Middle East. Two or three of one or another nationality but nothing decisive."

"Hand picked then?" The peer queried.

"Yes! We believe so." Granny confirmed.

"That is nasty, so they're working together then. Well it had to come, didn't it?"

"The angle of the heavy weapon they were using seems to place them in the middle of the lagoon or over it." Granny added helpfully.

"So some of them did escape then. With what I wonder? Unfortunate our man McFurson hadn't survived."

"He did,' Granny let the bomb drop as blandly as possible but he couldn't suppress a smile.

"You've found him?' Said Mortimer incredulous, "Where?"

"On the enemy's submarine in the Caribbean."

"What?"

"We received a message on the Interstat Van Laa
Satellite. A Dutch communication company owns
The message was from a watch laser in Morse
code." Granny shook his golden head. Good old M
Furson, you couldn't kill him and he was right 90%
of the time, what an asset. The Dutch Secret
Service, you remember Uan Derland?' Sir Mortim
nodded. 'Sent the message over this morning."

"Has he got the crew at gun point?"

"Not quite, It seems the submarine has no
torpedoes, at least in her stern. The room is full of
equipment from the navel stores in Norfolk,
Virginia. It seems an enemy team was secreted
aboard the submarine. That was before, it was sen
to be disassembled. McFurson and the young
American Ensign are hidden amongst the boxes.
Each time the crew opens the stern hatch to off
board the garbage he sends the message through th
opening straight up. It is by pure luck we picked th
up.

The Dutch Satellite makes the rounds that way to
send their television programming to the
Netherlands Antilles."

"Good lord, and they haven't found McFurson?" The tiny eyes seemed very concerned

"Not as yet." Granny looked at the yellow flimsy, 'He says the enemy has a very advanced computer invasion device. It seems this was used to get into the bank computers on the Caymans and removed the personal codes from a vast number of the secret accounts. McFurson says billions."

"Wonderful! Did he say where they are going?"

"As a matter of fact he did, True Love in the Virgin Islands." Granny let the information sit in the air.

"Which ones?" demanded the head of the Secret Service.

"Theirs, seems there is a grotto under the house. Once the ship arrives at the base, it should be the weekend. Sunday they will pull off the largest bank robbery in the history of man." Granny's smile was Cheshire.

"Wait a moment. Start somewhere and end somewhere." Sir Mortiner said irritably.

"The submarine is the Sand Darter,' Staters started. 'I suppose that this unit was used to replace an older submarine, which was headed to the nackers yard. The Arabs were already aboard. They might have gotten on board later but I think it was an inside job.

At any rate, they faked a sinking while under tow and moved the ship to a point where it was painted. By the way it is now sand coloured. The Gattling guns were placed on the coning tower. That would be about the height from which the guns were fired at Little Sound. We think that it might have been done in one of a number of places but nothing for sure." The look was apologetic "While Trevers and his chaps were bravely stopping the tour boat which was to carry this Mohammed git and his friends out to the submarine, the Sand Darter popped up in the lagoon. They never had a chance."

"So that is what did in Cooper?"

"Yes."

"Do we know where this ship is now?"

"Yes, pretty close if she stays on course. I suggest you ask Bermuda to send two Frigates and the nuclear submarine Landsend down. "

"Do the Americans know about this?"

"Not that we know. The Dutch don't have our codes. The message was addressed to the London cut off address en clear."

"If we sink it our problem ends." Brae made his first solid statement of the conversation.

"True, we could sacrifice the two personnel. Should we wait, then we have the information back."

"The Americans could get hold of it."

"The Americans monitor everything. If they wanted the information they would already have it or whatever portion they needed." Granny stated flatly.

"I see.' Brae thought for a moment, 'If it isn't retrieved they could use it and say we missed the target or it was gotten out some other way. It wasn't was it?"

"We don't know, quite honestly. I feel it would be a remote possibility."

"What if they aren't going to True Love?"

"Then McFurson and the girl will blow up the ship and escape. He says he has a plan."

"This wouldn't be a set up, would it? To hold us off attacking the ship?"

"I think not. Why give away your position and the method you used to escape. It's too far fetched. There is really no point. I believe the message and the situation are authentic." Staters said firmly.

"If they catch McFurson we are in it." Sir Mortimer was gloomy.

"They will simply change course radically, at that point, I suggest we dispose of the ship." There was no hesitation in Granny's voice.

"It would be nice to bag the lot of them, they have a great deal to answer for."

"I suggest we send a team of SAS people in just after the boat arrives. That way we can try to take the whole group. Perhaps it will allow McFurson and the girl a chance to get the information and hold it until we can get there. I want the SAS people acquainted with their photos. I would like McFurson back in one piece."

"What about the Americans? After all they might not know about this whole situation. They won't like us taking action on their plot."

"Last minute thing, no time for confabs, done before they can say much. They certainly can't make a lot of noise about the end result." Granny pooh poohed the problem.

"No! I suppose not." Brae agreed. 'I'll consider the matter over dinner, after calling the Admiralty for the ships. I expect the Sea Lord will be stubborn, perhaps they have some units down in the Caribbean already. They aren't happy with us over the burial at sea after the Cayman fiasco."

Bugger the senior service, Granny thought but said nothing. If Cooper had done his job this would already be over.

"I will think about your suggestions but it strikes me that the Sand Darter's demise might be a better solution. We could never change all those codes and if anyone puts that information to use I can't imagine the proportions of the disaster. No I'll have to think on it. Call me at the club when the Navy makes contact."

"Yes, Sir." Said Granny he considered the Victory and wondered if McFurson knew what he had done.

Chapter Twenty-eight - 3:15 A.m. Thursday
Morning, the Sand Darter, South West of Puerto
Rico, Caribbean Sea.

Terror

Your face massages the rough, dirty metal that is
the hull of the submarine. You're breathing in such
a small area is low but in soft gasps. You sweat; the
water runs down your body like rivers. Every noise
is intensified like fingernails on a chalkboard. You
need to relieve yourself but you do not move. The
light is hard at first, your eyes are not used to it, like
a mole, you are blind, it takes time to focus. After
four hours of standing pressed against the hull with
the voices of the workers behind you, the rattle of
every tool, the least movement makes you tense and
wait to die. Perhaps you want them to find you, then
it will end. Let it end! Cindy, how is she on her side
of the sub? Not found yet? Not yet!

We are sitting at deck level, one minute listening
to a new grinding sound in the spinning propeller
shaft below us then, as if it were a child, it screams,
then snaps. The ship slowly comes to a stop.
Crewmembers are in the door. The lights blaze
shocking our sensitive eyes. We are apart, she at

one end of our two foot by 20 foot enclosure, I at the other. This is as it has been each time but this time we are separated and the men are there. At the end of the boxes, each looks at the other once, eyes scream fear and then each of us, slides between the boxes and the hull. The decision is to hide; perhaps we only know concealment now. We no longer have the determination to do anything else.

The Arabic is loud and angry. The boxes on my left are shoved back against the hull, pallets and all, as the engineer curses and waits to get the cover off the shaft opening.

The boxes on the other side of the ship are moving too. Finally it is my turn. The power, which three well-muscled men can heave a stack of loaded shrink wrapped boxes is amazing. My ribs are compressed the air blasts from my body. The boxes compact against me. I am crushed like a butterfly in a glass presentation disk, like a rose in a book. I hold the gun. It points toward the entrance to my cubbyhole. The first face showing itself will be blown off.

There are utterances of surprise; the weight is increased, my body will not give. I place my hands on the wall and push back slightly to relieve the excruciating pressure. How will she survive? Cindy might weigh a hundred pounds dripping wet. The

pressure slacks. I cannot speak Arabic but the
statements of surprise are obvious. I hear the
footsteps moving around the corner toward me. I
raise the Webley Scott once more for the last time.

"The voice calls angrily the steps stop. I realize the
speaker is tapping the bulkhead support, which
extends from the hull to form an arch. This he feels,
is stopping the boxes.

He gives an abrupt order. There are grunts of
revolt then I hear the boxes being shifted. The pallet
behind the one covering me is removed. Now there
is almost no pressure. I must hold myself up with
one hand on the arch and another on a bunk
attachment; the bunk long ago removed for use
elsewhere. I cannot trust the boxes to support me. I
put as little weight on them as possible

I hear the boxes pushed back on the other side. I
imagine I heard a stifled cry. There is no reaction
from the crew. No more boxes are moved. The
space must be enough to pry the heavy metal deck
plate up and off.

The engineer grunts with disgust. I wonder what
has snapped. Maybe this is it. They will evacuate
the boat and we will be left in our tomb.

But no, he drops into the cavity I hear water
splash. A second man joins him. The captain joins
the group or perhaps an officer, the voice is hard

and demanding, the engineer speaks with respect.
The officer speaks or rather spits a single word then
commands in a more reasonable voice as if he is
cajoling. The Engineer replies, upbeat but
guardedly.

It starts then, the waiting, the heat, the need to
urinate. You say the rosary of the fingers. Each,
'Our Father', each 'Hail Mary,' is distinct and
fervent. You say it again and again in your fevered
mind. Thirst strikes. You look down and see the
water bottle you brought with you at the corner of
the boxes. To reach down would be disaster, you
look up, down. You count the bumps in the metal.
Tears come unbidden and unwanted but they come
created by frustration anger and fear.. Self-loathing
or self-pity you concentrate and stop their fall
afterward you feel drained and worse.

Perhaps they will not find you. Someone leans on
the boxes and almost knocks them over. They are
righted with help, the group laughs at the their
clumsy associate, your mind screams.

The part comes out an hour and a half later. You
hear it hit the deck, it wakes you. You tremble on
the verge of sleep and disaster. The engineer curses
the offending part. He then picks it up and takes it

away for repair. The men work on cleaning up and
getting ready for the reconstructed part, water is
hand pumped. The sluicing of the liquid almost
makes you foul yourself.

Would they smell the urine, if I lose control? No
you hold it. The pain in your lower abdomen numbs
after a while. You try to understand the low guttural
speech; you fantasize the conversation is about
women, football other things. Your mind slowly
turns inward into daydreams. The mind hides, afraid
to be found you hallucinate and fight to control both
sanity and body.

The Engineer is back, he curses them for being
lazy, I suspect. Finally, it is done. The order is
yelled forward, the engines start, the shaft whines
into action, it works. The cheers are for the engineer
who yells them back to their positions but the voice
concedes his pleasure.

He sits there for a while, watching the shaft. After
what seems an eternity, the plate is replaced with a
crash. The footsteps leave. The door is closed. The
lights go out.

I breathe out and then in. I move toward the
entrance. In the coal dark, I move the pallet back a
little to get out. The pallet makes a screeching noise
across the metal deck In the stygian ink I expect to
meet an enemy, there is none. I grab for the bottle

of water and drain it selfishly. I then take care of other business. I grope forward in the dark, colliding with the boxes the crew have moved into our space and almost fall.

The tower of boxes stays erect but I wait for a moment to make sure.

Heaving, I move the boxes at least along the back wall just enough space to get through and move to the other side. Near the corner of the boxes, I whisper.

"Its me! Don't shoot, please."

There is a small animal, childlike noise on the edge of sanity. I move the box she is unable. Cindy falls into my arms. She cries, deep, hard, gales of weeping, her whole body vibrates with her sobs, her contorted face pressed hard against my chest. I promise myself we will die rather then be separated again. Finally she wrenches out all her fear and terror. Calming down she does not lose her grip on my shirt. I think how lucky we were to have donned our clothes after they had dried.

I leave her for a moment to stand guard while she handles her problems.

Afterward she melds to me while drinking with one hand holding the bottle the other attached like iron to my shirt. Cindy displays the actions of a three-year-old, who has suffered a terrible fright. I take one of my high blood pressure pills. The second one I've taken. The first, chewed and swallowed, dry during my captivity behind the boxes. Slowly my body calms.

One A.m. Friday, The Sand Darter, The Leeward Passage

The ship slowed. I sensed it more then felt it at first. Cindy was partially awake lying on my chest resting on her stomach, her legs stretched between mine. We cannot see down the boxes and I don't care if they come, we fight this time. I watch the garbage side to see if the door will open.

My fingers gently massage her back she had taken off her coveralls, the heat was far too much. My shirt lies on the floor near by. Her bare skin is moist but soft; I sculpted the contours of her back gently, sensually. Her body moved languidly, little purring sounds escape her throat. I stretched my hands down following the indented spine to the small golden hairs that cover the shield at the small of her back, until my fingertips contacted the tight elastic at the top of her panties. Slowly, I pushed the white material down frightened she will react negatively. Cindy seems to stop breathing for a moment as if she is considering a major decision. I move my fingers in millimeters forcing the elastic before me over the full spread of her buttocks until the crumpled cotton made a tense line above her thighs.

Her bum is full; I had not really appreciated its round perfection until that moment. Following the slope of her buttocks to the top of her thighs. She lifted herself to allow the panties to slide off her front where they were trapped between my pants and her skin. A feline movement follows as she settles pressing her pelvis into me.

I brought my fingers up and under her flanks toward her stomach. She shuddered and her breath flowed out as an almost silent sigh, in parallel with the sensation. Her arms removed the sports bra, full breasts slid out against my chest. The nipples were hard and extended. Cindy places one leg over the other and pushes down again this time masturbating to intensify my touch.

The ship jolted softly as she increased her depth. Cindy raised her head like a lioness smelling the air over her litter.

"She's going to bottom," she said in a soft gasp." As women will, she was off me and had her pants back on in one movement. By the time I got off the deck and reached for my battle dress shirt she was already in her coveralls and armed.

Sand Darter hit the sandy bottom with a limited force but both of us were bowled over by the jolt. The cargo remained solid and while we untangled ourselves, I realized the deathly silence had taken the ship. It was so intense I expected the crew to attack us. I could think of nothing else that would cause this silence except they were leaving.

Captain Fitz-Roy of HMS Landsend stood opposite Braddly, the sonar ratting, who tapped with what seemed mach one speed at his computer. The interior of the nuclear submarine was cool and comfortable. The wait for his quarry had been almost restful after the orders for immediate departure received less than two days ago in Bermuda.

While the submarine made ready and awaited the SAS people who came in sporting their beige berets and carrying every leading edge piece of equipment known to the War Department. This elite unit stepped gingerly aboard and disappeared into their bunking area with almost no noise at all.

A second addition to his crew was a different matter. Reggie Bloodworth, having stopped on his way home to change planes made contact with the base and had heard what was up. Secrets were non existent in the Navy sometimes. The regular marine lieutenant assigned to the mission came down sick and Reggie presented himself to Fitz-Roy's hard-eyed evaluation. Fitz-Roy realized he had a top-notch man in Reggie and grudgedly gave permission for him to come. He knew Reggie had an iron in the fire with respect to this particular situation. His participation might be mute however, if the First Sea Lord gave Fitz-Roy a go ahead. The Darter, her crew, the two spies, the information and the problem it represented would become so much wreckage. The divers would have to go in for the data the ship carried if there was enough ship to search.

Two frigates were searching off Puerto Rico at this very moment but by lying off Hans Lollick Island opposite TuTu Bay, the quarry had come to him.

Fitz-Roy had to be sure it was Sand Darter and not some South American unit on exercise. Braddly was making the evaluation at this moment. The target was stopped on the sea bottom. This made for a poor shot due to obstructions between the two ships but when she came up he would have a lock on from the computer after that The Sand Darter was dead.

"Sir it's her, the outline matches. It's the Arab boat." Braddly had compared standard silhouettes of the Darter class ships, to the one created by the ship's computer as the Sand Darter had passed down the straits, the two were identical with the exception of the deck gun. This was not visible on the copy in the Leeward passage. The USS Sand Darter having fallen on hard times, was settled in the sand a short way off, on the St Thomas side of the strait.

"Number one contact the Admiralty and see what to be done."

"Aye, Sir". Said Dellen his First mate.

A cork antenna went up and surfaced the high powered whine of ultra high frequency. The message was bounced off a number of stations to England. The response was only five minutes in coming. The message had one word on it. " Terminate".

"Make ready to fire torpedo's number one. This is not a drill". Fitz-Roy said shaking his large ruddy face.

Braddly looked intensely at the screen "The target is moving Captain."

"Right, I want a lock Dellen." Fitz-Roy would not take a chance that the enemy had torpedo's in her bow. The possibility of Sand Darter hitting the shark shaped British Nuclear Boat was small but possible. He would take no chances. It must be death, quick as well as sure and he could serve it.

"Yes, sir." Said Dellen as if bored. Nothing seemed

to phase-the Number One, which was why he would make an excellent skipper himself soon.

"Bearing and lock, sir," Dellen confirmed.

"Give me mark and prepare to fire."

"Sir, she is disappearing," said Braddly mystified. "She's gone."

Fitz-Roy looked for a moment at the empty screen dumbfounded. Then he realized the situation. Sand Darter had gone into that hole in the reef at Tutu Bay.

"Get the SAS and the marines ready to go Dellen." Blast and damnation thought the Scot another five minutes and it would have been over.

"Immediately, Sir!," Dellen ran for the stern of the Landsend.

Chapter Twenty nine` - 3:50 A.m., Friday, True Love, Tu Tu Bay St., Thomas US Virgin Islands

The Camel, Through the Eye of a Needle

They had come so far, now only a few thousand more yards remained to the goal. Allah could not forsake them after so much. His crew was smaller by four and these would never come home. Captain Abdullha Kindaani peered through the periscope of the Sand Darter for the telltale signs of lights. The snake like web of lights that indicated the entrance to reef at Tu Tu Bay. This was the most intricate part of the trip. For, once he saw the lights, he must pass through the gap in the reef. There would be little place for mistakes. The periscope although only extended a few feet was powerful enough to see the lights underwater. If his calculations were correct.

All was black, the movement of fish was visible but no lights. The sonar could pick up nothing that indicated a threat. Patrols in this area were few and far between. For the moment Abdullha wanted only to see lights. Then faintly almost in front of him, there they were. How could he not have seen the green glow as it snaked up and down the side of the reef, they had just been turned on of course. This was strange. The lights should have been on for hours.

Below, the men stood quiet as the ship was under silent running procedure. He wondered if it were some kind of warning or a possible power failure. There could be many reasons. Mohammed came up behind him and asked softly what he could see.

"I see the lights, but they have just come on, this is strange, no?" Seaman demanded of the spy.

"Ah,' Mohammed said 'I do not know. Perhaps they did not expect us until now, perhaps someone inquired as to the lights or a patrol boat came by. I do not know. We cannot stay here and the decision is yours." Tisani seemed tired, as if the weight of the thing he had brought aboard with him was slowly crushing him. Abdullha decided to take the chance. There was no other plan. If he failed, then Allah was just, so be it.

"Raise the bubble twenty meters slow ahead, watch the plains well Imer for the slightest fault will destroy us." He warned

The Sand Darter rose from the bottom like a thief and moved toward the hole in the reef. It would come down now to his eye and his judgment. He asked his God to watch over him and his crew. The Sand Darter's bow entered the opening slowly.

Floodlights from above lit the bottom of the bay giving Abdullha a slightly better view. Passed the entrance he swung the periscope around and found his stern was almost through.

"Bring the ship to course 91 degrees port, but slowly." His voice was unhesitating.

The bow moved around blindly in the bay, until the Sand Darter was moving parallel with the shore. She passed the great white colonial house. In the glare of the spot lights precisely set for his entrance Abdullha saw the eye of the needle. The hole in the base of the cliff, which the sea had hollowed out years before the reef took hold. The bottom came up to meet the submarine. The sea had piled the sand back where men had worked for weeks to move it.

Raise bubble two degrees secure to impact." He yelled it didn't matter now the bow of the Sand Darter was already in the opening. Sand scrapped against the hull they were half way through. The impact stopped the ship for only a moment as the Gattlings and periscope jammed under the roof pinning the sub.

"All stop" Abdullha screamed in spite of himself. The boat had a mind of her own, with a cracking noise, a piece of the top of the entrance gave way and fell into the conning tower but they were through.

"Slow ahead, surface." Abdullha corrected with a

long sigh. His men cheered as if they had won the
World Cup. He gave himself a moment. He thanked
his God it was over. Abdullha had done his bit to
form the tapestry of the map of the sweet victory
that was to come, now he could rest.

The water sluiced off the boat as she surfaced. The
hatches opened. Cheers echoed back to them inside
as those waiting in the low ceiling cave under the
hill took up the yelling. The entire crew went on
deck in a mob. At the stern ladder, men pushed and
shoved to reach the top. Everyone made for the
dripping deck. They had been down too long,
against too many enemies, the friendly faces were to
great a lure. Had they not won? On deck they waved
and cried for joy at their delivery.

"It was our turn now. Soft fresh air poured into the
stern torpedo room five or six men had crowded up
on deck and we could hear them cheering and
exchanging friendly greetings to those on the pier.
I looked once at Cindy her pixy face was drawn,
stern and cold. We went over the boxes and moved

quickly to the base of the ladder. The ship had come to a halt and seemed to be tied off to a pier or some kind of dock. In three steps we were through the bulkhead door into the engine room. Only one man stood there he was just shutting down the engines as we entered. His old shambled gray head came around with a happy smile, expecting no doubt to see his shipmates returned, to escort him topside. An inch wide red spot magically appeared on the gray coverall over his heart. The old engineer collapsed, like a sack of sand onto the deck. I glanced back and saw the smoke rising from the forty-five's silencer and knew Cindy had no need for my help anymore. She seemed stunned by her action.

Time was of the essence, I stepped over the corpse, any sympathy I had was gone by now. She followed as we moved down the empty corridors to the officer's territory, we met no one. The curtains at the entrance to each of the officer's berths, were open but one, this I tossed aside, it gaped empty. The ship stank of sweat, dirty clothing, Turkish tobacco and God knew what. At the end of the row was the Captain's cabin. Mohammed's black nap sack, the one I had seen on him at Little Sound in the Caymans, was sitting quietly on the small fold out desk. Beside it was a two-foot long hard plastic container filled with and surrounded by over a hundred silver CD disks. I hurriedly inserted them into the container and stuffed it into the bag. The laptop, open on the desk, followed. I searched the room. He might have made copies but I couldn't find them. There was no other outside hard drive. However, under the desk in a neat pile were the small laptops I had seen passed to Mohammed through the window of the Mercedes a million years ago in George Town, the Caymans. I took two. "Cindy" Take this and put in your pants at the back under your coveralls. Don't worry it's waterproof." She complied. Women can move anything under their clothes, removing bras and other garb without ever being visible. In a second the flat mini-computer was in place.

"Let's go" I said. Stuffing the other one in the bag. We ran back to the stern but met no one. At the base of the stairs I looked at her once more. I had found some jungle camouflage paint and we had both put it on. I leaned forward and kissed her on

the hair at the crown of her head, not to get the
green paint in my mouth. This action was rewarde
with a 'God! What a child you are,' smile that
women reserve for idiots and those males they lov

I went first, up the ladder, through the hatchway,
the Webley in front of me. I reached the top to fin
everyone, the crew and their hosts, were talking al
at once over the port side of the ship. The lights th
lit the cavern were mounted high up on
a scaffolding and were bright. These were, howev
pointed inward toward the tents and working area
on a flat sand floor. I could see a number of
telephones, on a long, portable tables. 'All the bett
to rob you with, my dear.

Sliding out on the deck I made for the darkened
starboard side of the sub, under the chain stanchio
and into the water, she followed. Using the raised
hatch for cover we weren't seen. Our landing in th
water was soft, as we let ourselves in with hardly
splash.

I thought for a moment as to what would be the
best way out but Cindy was off without comment
following the ship to the stern.

I threw shark repellent into the water and

followed. Old Lacy had come to his end somewhere close. Finding the box of repellent, I had brought along a bunch of the green oil covered packages. We went to the end of the ship and around the stern, then up the port side. The next step was to get under the protection of the stone pier, which had been put in place to hold back the water and to form the end of the berth for the Sand Darter. It was a short swim underwater to the berm. Our movements went unnoticed.

It was as we moved along the outside of the berm away from the ship that something bumped me. I turned to see the long silver body of a blue shark, turn only feet away. The fish was at least six feet long and its piggy eyes followed me. As he turned I took the shark repellent pulled the plastic opener and threw it at him. He closed his mouth on it mechanically then opened it and came at me. I was dead. Cindy fired the Beretta and missed but that wasn't necessary because the next moment the shark's eyes bulged like he had had a unique idea, shook himself and veered off. The silver and blue bullet began to shake like he had the palsy, trailing a dark slick of repellent behind him. If he was alone that was one thing if not, we had to get out of the water.

"Now what?" I asked of my companion.

"Over there, its a ladder going up." Sure enough a metal ladder seemed to rise up to the low ceiling at the far end of the cavern and disappear into the rock. Cindy, with her sharper sight, had picked it out from the hatchway.

"OK, lets try." I said gauging the distance to the nearest guard who had moved toward the submarine and the merrymakers. We hauled ourselves out of the water and up onto the berm. Cindy like a monkey, I like a walrus chained to a refrigerator. I staggered to my feet, just as the crew of the sub found the dead Engineer. Mohammed immediately realized he had been burgled.

Bellows of alarm from the crew were voiced by the group on the pier and men ran in every direction to acquire arms with which to hunt us down.

This, of course, as we sprinted to the ladder. The guard closest to me down the bank saw us and raised his AK 47 to his hip. The bullets roared wide but the chase was on. More bullets came whispering across the sand and stone exploding in great gouts. Cindy was at the ladder and up it. Nothing like Annapolis physical fitness in a pinch. I on the other hand, made the ladder a couple of minutes later when they were closer. I stumbled up

weighed down by the waterlogged backpack. At the
same time, I was being told by the pain in my chest,
that this was not acceptable to my over strained and
over worked body. I emptied the Webley in their
direction. The six bullets seemed to make them
think just a bit. That was all I needed to reach the
top of the ladder. I dragged my feet to the second
level just as a solid wall of bullets nearly cut the
rungs in two.

The tunnel was about four feet tall and ran parallel
to the side of the cave. At the other end I could see
the light of a second entrance, like the one we had
ascended. It became very clear that this passage
would become a barrel, to shoot fish in, very
quickly. Cindy scurried along almost passing the
second ladder heading up. This was older and had
rust on it making it harder to see in the dark.

"Here this goes up," she said over the automatic
fire. I came along behind following her voice. My
eyes still trying vainly to see the ladder and opening.
I passed it, then I heard her say with exasperation,

"I'm up here." It was kind of her to exclude the 'stupid' at the end of the sentence. I began to climb just as the first Arab head popped up. I fired the newly loaded Webley at him, missed but made him duck. Up I went, locked a leg around the old ladder and waited for the next orders.

"I can't lift the cover." she said with a cry of frustration in her voice. I moved up and put my hand on the old, wet, metal, manhole cover and pushed. Cindy strained her back taut but there must be a ton on it. I had felt it give, a little, I was sure but cover was a dead end. Arabic was being passed up and down the tube. They would come soon. I had five rounds in the Webley. I carefully took out the cylinder and placed the muzzle of my pistol at the end of the cylinder so that the bullet would pass through the top and out the bottom toward our Arab friends. I pulled the trigger. A bullet smashed through the top of what must have been a kevilar constructed cylinder and exploded the disks shattering them into smithereens of plastic. I moved the muzzle and fired four more times. The disks were fragments. I noticed that the bullets had not gone through the bottom of the cylinder. The holder went back in my bag as I tried to figure out how to swing down to shoot at the attackers while showing the least amount of myself. At that moment there was a metallic scrapping above and the plate was lifted just a smidgen. A very British voice said out of the dark.

"Would you mind identifying yourselves? Please."

"Harry Breakleaf is that you? You son of a bitch get us out of here." I roared. I knew what had been on the plate above and was not in the mood for any more crap.

"Well that's Michael.'. Breakleaf confirmed,' and you my dear."

"Ensign Patricia Warren US Navy."

"Ah, good!" The cover flipped back and five faces looked down red beams of tracking lasers touched us. Hands pulled Cindy out and then me bag and all.

The circular plate was dropped back into place. It looked like a drain cover from above

One of the SAS men stepped forward and asked politely for Cindy's gun. The fact that she was being covered did not help the situation. Once the Beretta was passed over, the belt was requested. She complied but I could see the anger on her face, in the weak space lamp being used by the team.

"Here, you better have mine too, wouldn't want it to go off or anything and here's my webbing." I passed over the Tom Brown Holster.

"That won't be necessary...,"the hooded soldier said taken aback.

"Rutledge will hold the weapons, 'suggested Breakleaf, 'you're good at that aren't you corporal?'

"Oh aye, I make a marvelous bearer." Said a jaunty little man with a wide grin on a lined elfin face and curls of stray hair escaping from his cap. His neutrality seemed to make things easier.

"Hate to break up this little get together,' Breakleaf said apologetically, 'but where is the information."

"I have it here." I said taking the cylinder out and passing it to Breakleaf.

"What!" Said the senior SAS man and Breakleaf together.

"When you guy's wouldn't open up, I put five rounds into the case. Everything in there should be shattered. The cereal like rattle held this to be true.

Breakleaf opened it to find that the bullets had penetrated to the end but miraculously the bottom two or three CDs were only halved or had holes in them.

"Well I tried.' I considered my work and removed the Mohammed's desktop from the bag and handed it over. You'll need this too that's his desktop."

"Do we get a copy" asked Cindy in a low angry voice.

"No, but then those numbers can't be outside our control, sorry."

"This is what they got in with" I gave Breakleaf the smaller lap top." He handled this with interest.

"That all?" He asked

"What, do you want his jockey shorts?" I said sarcastically

"Do you have them " Said Harry with a smile. The thing about friends is, you can get away with that stuff.

"My men will take you out to the ship." The SAS officer said. The command in the voice was enough to pick him out.

"No thanks ' I said, 'I have to walk the lady home." His head snapped around and looked hard at Breakleaf.

"Well orders and all that.' said my old time friend, trying to get the crumbs off the tablecloth.

"There is no way in God's Western Hemisphere I'm getting on another submarine." I said with finality.

"The girl?" said SAS inquiringly to Breakleaf.

"Ensign Warren saved my life and if your pointed little mind comes anywhere near hurting her, I will tear your head off and piss down the hole." I turned to face one of the best killing machines known to man. He raised his night vision equipment and I looked into the coldest, least feeling, most merciless gray eyes I had had the nightmare to witness. Fortunately, he simply looked at me and said,

"We were going to offer escort." In the amused manner, of men, who could do you grievous bodily harm just by shrugging and know it.

"I'll get her home." I said in a more amiable tone. "Long periods in an enclosed place tend to make you jumpy." I changed the subject.

"Right now, you've got sixty odd Arabs down there who have lost any sense of humour they started with." The sound of the Arab voices getting nearer meant they were over their discomfort of following me.

"Don't get the wind up, we'll take care of your friends" For a moment, just a moment, I was sorry for poor old Mohammed and his people. They were trapped and didn't know it. While they had committed their sins knowingly, they were about pay for them big time, to an individual who could serve it up on a scale they never imagined.

- "Just a word in your shell like." I said to Gray eyes. 'they have AK's and probably heavy machine-guns down there, which is one thing. But they also have twin Gattling guns on the conning tower and you're going to have to come across clean ground to get to them. Just thought you'd like to know."

"Is that your assessment of the situation Ensign." He turned to Cindy and I realized he wasn't doing it to get at me but to get the correct information there by having the best chance of success.

"Yes, I think they damaged the guns coming into the cavern but if not you will have real trouble. Also they may have mined the cave

"Sergeant see Mr. Breakleaf gets back on the ship. Rutledge return the officer's side arms once your outside. Corporal, open the hatch. Mr. McFurson perhaps it would be a good time for you to leave unless you'd like to lead us back."

"No, Sir, not for all the tea in China."

"All right then, the exit is straight down the tunnel and to your right. Good luck, you too Ensign." We walked to the end of the tunnel as quickly as possible and out into the sweet night air.

Chapter Thirty - 4:50 A.m. Friday, Near Red Hook, St Thomas, U.S. Virgin Islands

To Touch and Touch Not.

We walked down the hill to the road on bare feet, not feeling anything of the rough terrain. The narrow path we took was flat and even. It was still dark but the first pale light of morning had started on the eastern part of the island. This gave us enough light to see.

Saying nothing we got to the road and began to walk toward Red Hook. The lights of Coki Point shone before us in the distance, the black top was cool beneath our feet.

A fresh breeze swirled around us in refreshing gusts. The pure harmony of the moment with its softly rustling leaves and buzzing insects cleared my mind. The stink and blackness of our captivity on the submarine seemed years away. I thanked God for the morning, the beauty and the girl who walked along beside me in angry silence. I was reborn, made anew, I would never get on a submarine again. I really was going to retire this time. I had had it.

"I'm going to phone the Marines from Coki Point." She said abruptly

"Here is a quarter." I passed her one.

"It won't take Canadian." She passed it back.

"Hold on I have an American one and Tom's Place is right up ahead. There is a phone outside by the door."

"Why are you helping me? " She demanded, turning on me. Her body, in karate attack, position The right fist raised in front of her body the left at her side, feet spread and ready to kick.

"You screwed me out of Mohammed's computer. I was there too you know. I have just as much right to it as you do." she said seething with anger. Controlled now by that overpowering desire to win, a strength or weakness that would someday give her the destroyer she wanted or kill her.

"You want to break into a bank?" I asked

"No." She said irritated

"Then you don't need the numbers.' I said firmly, 'Anyway the CIA or FBI could listen in to that information any time. They monitor everything and you know it. What you have in the back of your panties is worth a lot more." She snarled and kicked. I backed away fast and just in time. Her foot missed my chin by a whisper.

"I mean the computer." She stopped and realized what I was saying was true.

"Oh, Yeah!" She said grudgingly.

"That's leading edge tech. You're people will have a trophy to show off. Everyone will look good, you most of all." I smiled and she smiled back.

"Aren't you going to get in trouble giving the laptop to me?"

"You earned it." I said thinking her government probably had it already?

"That SAS Officer would have killed me wouldn't he?" The question was bland but cold.

"Without thinking 'I said, 'but it would have been done right away if it was going to happen. I over reacted." Did I know for sure? No! Did I know for sure the other way either? No!

"Hell, I was impressed Sub Lieutenant you standing up for me like that." I slouched there like a school kid who had stood up to the class bully for her honour and almost said "Awe shucks twernt nothin.' Until I realized I had almost wet myself, when I looked the SAS Officer in the eye and knew, as always, that money talked and bullshit walked.

"My people won't be happy the SAS went in without their permission."

"I won't apologize for the actions of the British Government. I can't. They did save our lives and cleaned up a big problem for your side."

"We could have done it just as well. " She snapped.

We went along in silence until Tom's Place, now closed. She called, while I waited in the lee of the building. For ten minutes we watched the sunrise in depthless glory. Gold and reds plus other colours only found in a Caribbean morning. Ten minutes later the black government four door arrived with two trucks full of US Marines. I hid in the shade of the building. She got in without looking back. They were off to True Love but that was someone else's problem.

I walked along in melancholy wonder, absorbing everything around me, I had neglected to or refused to see before. I had been blinded to everyday life, my focus stimulated now by almost losing it.

I reached Coki Point and found a cabby sleeping in his van outside a nightclub. It seemed the patrons he was waiting for were already gone and he swore at the closed doors of the establishment.

"You can't trust, nobody, now a days." He informed me.

I gave the driver fifty dollars, to take my plastic bag which, of course, held my Webley and I to the Dolphins. Rutledge had given it back along with Cindy's forty-five but he lost her clips, which put him right off her Christmas list. The cabby eyed me and then said get in. In minutes we were at the hotel.

The desk clerk seeing me in battered battle dress and without shoes or socks for that matter was hesitant at best. To his surprise the gold card worked and he got to be all smiles. Almost immediately I was in a room. I stripped off, showered thoroughly removing four days of grime and slipped into bed to sleep for eight hours.

By Noon, I was awake though. I made three telephone calls in quick succession.

I called the wife through my cutoff. She answered it took a minute or so for her to react. Then it was tears. I wondered if they had told her I had died? I apologized, told her that I loved and missed her, assured her I was all right and said I would be home in two or three days. I would call tonight to talk to the kids. I was in the Virgin Islands. She wouldn't call but it would give her some peace of mind.

"I then rented a laptop from the hotel and tied into the internet. I made up my report in soft code and E-mailed it to a cut off.

Breakleaf called right back. It seemed the Landsend had made an unexpected stop at Road Town in the British Virgins. The personnel I had vetted were home as they were ill. All of this was passed on in soft code telling me the computer disks and the other items were more or less in Granny's hands. He suggested I stop over to his office for my visa. I agreed but had some unfinished business. Breakleaf felt the action might be rash.

I offered to have him sit in. No, it might start bad blood. He would have the package I requested, delivered. By the way the head office had called and was very pleased with my work. I thanked him and rang off. My third call was for a rental car.
Hertz was pleased to oblige and I was on my way.

For four awful days I had one thing that brought me back to sanity each and every time I strayed. It was Hull beach. If I lived, I had promised myself a long sit on Hull Beach. The hills passed by and the wind blew in. I had turned off the air-conditioning. It seemed sacrilegious to waste all that, clean air.

Pure joy overcame me, the freedom to move, to feel and to live was overwhelming. Tears slipped out from pure relief. I didn't care about the tears they were tears of joy and I drank in life like the sea absorbs a river.

The side road was still there. I drove along until stopping just before the white house and there was my spot, my tree beckoned. I wandered through the bracken and walked onto the pure hot sand. I put the boom box down in the shade, placed the red half lawn chair on one of the Dolphins pure white towels and lay down resplendent in my white Dolphins 'T' shirt with pocket size blue hotel mascots jumping over my heart and black Speedo trunks. The hat was

Panama Jack, as always, found on a back shelf of a shop in Red Hook. It was a wide brim flat planter's style and had a black band. I kicked off cheap sandals and lay back. The portable boom box filled the beach with a soft Carib tune. Strange I didn't recognize it. Perhaps it didn't matter.

The beach was as I left it a month or so ago, or was it years? The sun was omnipotent beaming down. Pelicans squandered out. Gulls skimmed the water and disappeared. The endless sea came in soft measure and I relaxed. Made friends with myself anew and liked what I found. I had done my best and won. No one would ever know of course but that didn't matter either.

Another man might have hidden a disk for later. For a moment I had been the richest man on earth. The beach made me richer I thought. Yeah, I know I'm nuts. Oh well so it goes.

A full stomach will do wonders. At a small but clean restaurant in Red Hook I had eaten with Epicurean joy, a large steak sandwich smothered with onions, fries, onion rings and coleslaw. This was followed by two pieces of thick blue berry pie and washed down with endless Coke, cold from the fountain. Thank God! I was on an American Island, nothing like good old Yankee junk food.

I heard her or sensed her, more then saw her, come up. I had not heard the car, perhaps she had been dropped off. It was Cindy, I could never call her Pat or Patty or Patricia. She wore the same string bikini with the red and white checkerboard pattern and the same funny straw hat. Her body moved with the grace of an elfin princess. Cindy's golden skin tanned just enough to make her part of the beach. Over the suit she had a sheer cover that looked like gauze and a picnic hamper over her left arm Her bare feet, I found, endearing.

She smiled, as only she could, with that impish charm.

"Hello, Sailor." She said a little uncertainly, I wondered if it were put on.

"Hello, Sailor." I said and smiled. She looked around as if she were sizing up the place, smiling broadly.

"This beach taken?" her head dipped as if she might be frightened it was.

"No, come and sit." She did spreading the second Dolphins towel then removing her hat and the wrap.

"Gee at least you don't steal cheap stuff." She quipped. I had to laugh, she radiated joy.

"The towels are logged out and I have to get them back."

"Oh for sure." She valley-girled it with aplomb.
"Should I ask how you found me?"
"We happen to own the island sailor. We knew
where you were when you went back to The
Dolphins."
"You came here the last time you were on the
island.' She became serious. 'When they said you
came out this way I figured this is where you'd go. I
guess this is where I wanted to go all morning. I'm
off duty now.

By the way thanks for having the head of the
Secret Service write me that letter of reference. Sir
M. Bray, cool.' She raised her eyebrows as if it was
significant.' I was surprised. I figured on a short
pointed, congratulations to her, from Granny as
requested. To have our noble peer involved was
surprising and highly irregular. "I haven't heard that
many nice things said about anyone, who wasn't
dead, for a long time.' She continued. 'Fine, laugh,'
I couldn't help it. 'Now my boss thinks I've turned
over." she laughed " Actually, he was impressed as
hell. I think I'm going to get my cruiser."
"So you came down here to thank me."

"Yes,' she stopped and thought a moment. Then Cindy spoke, in a low earnest voice. ' No one has ever gone to bat for me like you. No one really gave a damn outside of my Mum and Dad. I don't take compliments well."

"Why not, you're beautiful' She shook her head no.

"I was always squirt or pygmy or shorty." She looked sad and it was real. 'I always hated half pint."

"When you walk your body is a Michael Angelo sculpture, perfect. 'I said softly ' You're like a fawn, everything about you is soft and balanced with just a little vulnerability thrown in. You have the most wonderful smile I have ever seen ' She turned away and actually blushed. 'And, of course, you have cute little feet." She really laughed now.

"Great,' she said hitting me lightly on the shoulder, 'Other, women get Bruce Willis, I get a subie with a foot fetish." -

"I beg to differ, you have nice ankles and small, well formed feet. Most women have these huge gnarled things' I gestured with my hands, 'growing out in all directions. With toes wrapped around each other or growing out the sides, Yuck." We both laughed " Of course you do have chubby little toes." She laughed again.

"Shut up.' she said trying for royal hauteur. 'Don't

say chubby, my butt is chubby."

"You have a spectacular behind, a phenomenal behind, you may have the best behind in Western Christendom."

"Like wow, and to think I only sat on it, up to now.' she aped 'You put women on pedestals don't you?" She said frankly.

"Not very many." I countered.

"You're a romantic Sub Lieutenant."

"True.' I agreed, 'Guilty as charged."

"I love you" she said huskily and hugged me hard.

"They will be watching you know." I warned

"You flatter yourself. They don't give a damn about you. They're mad as hell about your boss taking care of his business here though." Fine, I'll believe you, I thought. They have me on film anyway they really couldn't do much worse.

"So you don't want me anymore?" I started.

"Crap, I want you because you're you. They don't care.' Then seriously, ' I know you'll go home to your wife. I don't want a relationship sailor. I want to have fun for a little while, then its done. I'm not stupid. I don't want to cling to you." Frank and to the point, that's my girl she was hugging me harder.

"I smelled her hair and was inundated with the scent

of cherries or rather cherry blossoms.

"You smell good"

"I took a bath," she said.

"I knew there was something different." she laughed then

"Rat.' Then more quietly, 'hold me please.' she calmed like a kitten. I realized that for all the bravado, she was still a young girl who had faced death for too long and had dealt it for the first time. I held her and kissed her on the forehead again

"Jesus, Can't you do anything right" she said and kissed me on the lips. I was soft, sweet and pure, I only partially returned it.

"The wife?" she asked.

"The Wife!" I answered

"Then you don't love me anymore." She said matter of factly with a shake of the head but with some sadness underlying the bland presentation.

"I like you a lot and I definitely sex you, especially your "A" battery.' she giggled, ' I thought you hadn't noticed "and made her breasts sway, happy as a lark. Women love to have their breasts complimented.

"I love you,' I started, ' I guess, because you gave me so much and I can never pay it back. You gave me youth for a while. I can't thank you enough." Now that's brilliant McFurson. A toss in the hay, in a hospital bed yet, unbidden, a mountain of guilt, your privates almost turned around to face rearward and you're thanking her. Then there was the Sand Darter but was that just the danger, the need for closeness?

"I didn't give you anything but seeing you don't want to play, we can eat. "She indicated the hamper and sat on her haunches. "I got wine and crab salad sandwiches, big ones' she gestured with her hands to show me the size and Hostess cupcakes for desert. The ones with the squiggles."

"Sounds great." I said

"It should, I cooked it myself. "She giggled at her own joke.

"Get out of this business." I suggested.

"Why?" It was as if I had hit her.

"Because you have a heart."

"You have a heart too," she said little girl like.

"Yes, but I'm just a courier, remember. You're going to be out there with the sharks. Hearts are too important for this sort of thing. No one appreciates them and all they do is get squashed. "Get your cruiser and sail away."

"Aye, aye, Sub-Lieutenant." She saluted with great intensity then half smiled to see if I would join her. I did of course.

"So I'm going to get fed, am I?" I asked.

"I think maybe at your age, you can feed yourself."

"That is why the nuclear family is going to hell."

"All morality aren't you? Am I amoral?" She said cocking her head

"I should certainly hope so." I said with conviction and she giggled.

"So you met the great moral challenge, all the money in the world and you didn't keep it, any of it." She corrected herself.

"No." I said, wondering why I didn't even think of it.

"I got this vision of you handing over a bunch of shattered Beach Boy disks and walking away with it all."

"I guess if you are honest then you are honest. I know it sounds kind of stupid but I never even thought of it. I was too busy chasing after you and not getting killed. I guess I'm just a dinosaur too old for this business, knowing too much, maybe not enough, about myself." This was going in the wrong direction so I changed the subject"

"Food, woman."

"Listen sailor, you want to eat, we eat but be good or no desert.

"First, I have to go potty so you don't look "
"I promise."
"Good." She got up and went to look for a likely
spot or to report in. God, I hated knowing so much.
At least I had no false concepts and being with her
was fun. However, It was time.

I stood and walked half way to the water. I
removed my hat and shirt. Finally my trunks,
for a moment I was naked and alone in paradise.
The soft island music was behind me on the CD. I
stepped out into the water it was warm and inviting.
When it got waist high I began to swim long easy
strokes straight out over the aqua blue water beneath
a friendly sun. The waves started a little later. I
would swim on forever or at least as long as it went.

Then well that would be it. Too many things were
there. I could not go back, I had broken my word. I
was finished and couldn't know when that film of
Carma and I, would come to my house in a brown
paper package. What would I tell my wife? No, I
couldn't. This was better, easier. I had left the note
with my folded uniform, in the room.

Number 18 was paid for until tomorrow no one
would come in until eleven in the morning. The
note was a goodbye, for my wife and the kids, a
thank you to Granny with the reason in soft code.
He would understand.

All of it nice and simple, my body started to warn me. I was out too far, was putting too much pleasure on it. I didn't care. The end was close the water was harder to push against. My high blood pressure was acting up I could hear the buzzing in my ears.

I felt the bump and turned in terror. This was supposed to be a nice quiet end, not some horrible slashing, blood soaked, screaming disaster.
It was her, Cindy, stark naked short golden hair down on her face. The eyes though, looked at me intensely, through me. I looked away ashamed.

"You came out here to die." She said it coldly. "You didn't care if we knew."

"I thought no one gave a damn." I said defensively.

"Why? You won. Your boss must be happy with that. Christ it's your wife.

"That too' I conceded.' All those men died, I was the last, the only one to survive. I broke my word. You're so beautiful, this is so beautiful, it will never be this perfect again."

"Oh great and what am I chopped liver? "She said and snapped me out of it." I was there too you know. Maybe it would be good to stop thinking about yourself for five minutes?" She was nagging and knew it, she stopped and made up her mind on what she should do.

"We were both on that ship we both hurt but on the

inside. It will take time to come back to where we were. You've got to try."

"You're what, twenty-one you've got forever I don't."

"Fine let's swim. I don't care when you can't go any farther I'll try to bring you back." she set her jaw with determination.

"Why?" was the only thing I could think of to say.

"Because I love you." she said simply. I was overwhelmed with pride and love and other emotions too graphic to explain. For a long time I just looked at her angel's face.

"Let's swim back.' I said finally,

"Have you ever dance naked on a beach?" She smiled impishly and we started back. It was hard I almost didn't make it. I stayed on all fours heaving like an old horse at the waters' edge. Cindy squatted beside me imitating a pagan goddess. She would not help, that would take my pride. I would do it myself that was the Navy way, the way she had to do it.

Instead she told me about why the US Navy acted as the main intelligence agency on the islands.

"See,' she said between gasps. Cindy was played out too.' Denmark used to own the Virgins but the US Government got scared in 1915 or something that the two royal families, the Danes and the Germans, you know, like Kaiser Bill, anyway, that they would get too close together and maybe the Germans would use the Virgins as a submarine base under Danish neutrality." Her soft hand moved the wet hair from my forehead, 'You OK?' It was a kind and loving gesture. I nodded and she continued. "Well the Danes had about two hundred men on the islands, mainly local militia, for police work and so on. So one morning Charlotte Amalie woke up to find two thousand or so Marines all over the town. The Government made the Danes an offer to buy the islands. I think, it was about sixteen million. So the Danes looked around, not too many options and sold the place. Seeing the navy took the islands, we ended up governing it for a while. Security for the place became a Navy job and you know how things don't change easily, in the military bureaucracy. Which is why I'm here all these years later." I was in love, at my age. I was in love with a crazy woman in transition, who needed me.

Finally, I stood solidly.

"Want to dance" I asked

"Who gets to lead," she asked with a sarcastic smile.

"Me! 'I said
"That will be a change." And to a soft island song
we waltzed, sky clad beneath the sun.
   I stopped for a moment and held her sweet face in
my hands.
   "Looking at you is like drinking sunshine."
probably the dumbest line I had gotten off all day.
   "Yeah, that's me fresh squeezed orange juice with
a chubby butt." We both laughed and I kissed her
soft mouth holding her to me. She hugged back and
then wrapped her legs around my middle like a
gymnast almost knocking me over.

Chapter Thirty-two - 8:30 P.m., Monday, Home.

Lights in the Window.

I stepped out of the Civic into the snow. It fell in huge twirling flakes heavy and wet for early December. There was no wind but the air was clear and cold. It burned your lungs when you inhaled absorbing the old smells of maple wood burning in the fireplaces and of new snow. The house was still there back from the street, the birch stripped and bare. It had been a long trip.

Cindy came down to the airport to see me off unbidden. She was there in whites with that little uniform bonnet sitting on the top of her head. She looked very special and I went over, which she didn't expect having thought she would just wave. "You look terrific." I said with a smile, it was catching. She had a new bar on her salad of medals.

"Get away from me or I'll cry." She said with tears welling along her eyes.

I hugged her and she me.

"I love you sailor'" I said

"I love you sailor." she echoed. The tears rolled down her face from her huge bright blue eyes.

"I'll come and visit on your destroyer."

"Oh, yeah! I'm definitely going to let you on board you'd probably steal us blind."

"Good bye, sailor." I said as they called my flight for the last time.

"Good bye, sailor" She kissed me, it was full and meant to last. I returned the kiss we locked there for a moment, until some malcontent whistled. I was gone.

I'll always remember her trying to get her hat back on and waving at the same time.

On the Caymans Reggie was at the exit door to meet me. We shook hands. The Captain had an iron grip.

"I have letters here for Lane's and Olin's families, didn't know if it should be to the mother or the wife." I gestured feebly.

"Lane's mother, Olin's wife and daughter Sarah." Reggie said off handedly, as if it were peripheral but he had seen them and the memory was still too real.

I finished the letters and passed them to Reggie.

"You'll see they get there?"

"No fear of that.' he stopped, 'about Jamie?"

"He and I dragged the raft out beyond the island and went to warn Cooper. Jamie got it in the raft when they fired through the trees. The raft sank and

I swam to the island and tried to warn Cooper. He didn't stop. I fired the flare, waved my arms and everything. He had a bead on the Arabs and he chewed them up pretty good, before the sub opened up. This is between us.' He nodded, ' My report will read he was too far in when I warned him. Screw the brass, he did what was right." I changed the subject.

"So how was your cave exploring expedition.?"

"Oh, reasonably successful. The boat won't be going anywhere soon it has a rather large hole in it."

"That's about what I expected."

"We didn't bring Mohammed back, decided to leave in a different direction."

"Gee, that's too bad."

"Our other guests are visitors of the US government, one of those hostels they have."

"Good they will be safe there."

"I brought your luggage down made sure it was placed on the plane as you requested."

"I have to see Jamie's wife" I said 'Then I have to stop off at Government House"

"Well Reggie it's been a slice." I finished.

"It's been good knowing you too. A word in your shell like, old thing. Don't bugger about with the SAS they have no sence of humour.' as you're want to say' He smiled. 'Michael I hope our paths cross again."

I said the right things to Jamie's wife. She was plainer than I would have expected but exceedingly gracious. The house was being packed up for return to England. We both felt out of place and time. I made it as short and painless as possible on both of us. She cried in the end and thanked me.

Wilson was in bed with tubes still coming out of him but he was making progress and would rejoin the unit. He wanted to stand when I came in, you could see it in his face. I was an officer, just a Canuck, but still.

I wished him well and he told me he would serve with me at any time if it were convenient. High praise, from a Sergeant of The Royal Marines.

Government House was a different thing altogether. The Governor was not available. I was met by Lorning and went through my abbreviated report with him. It would be his problem to sell it to the Governor, who wanted assurance the problem was solved. Lorning and I weren't going to be friends but he gave me a weak handshake and we parted on good terms.

A convoluted return through Canada, to make sure
I wasn't followed and home. I had gifts from the
Virgins and Caymans for Christmas. It was hard to
believe it was only a couple of weeks away. Jamie,
Olin and Lane would not raise a pint or hear the
laughter. Perhaps where they were it was better? I
hoped so.

Wally was pleased with his brochure.

Granny was happy.

Adams was still breathing, to the best of my
knowledge, for how long I wondered. The real
people, the ones with money walked away from
problems like that.

During an evening drink with Breakleaf, I found
out why Bray had been so gracious. Planning my
death must have made for a bad conscience. He of
course would have been right to destroy the Darter
and I held no grudge. Harry also admitted the SAS
mob had cut power to True Love thereby turning off
the lights and giving Landsend, a better shot.

The Americans who watched my little play act out
on the beach would think I was nuts and discount
me. Well, you can only hope. Rutledge was out
there about five minutes away when Cindy showed
up. He had an extra scuba tank. It worked out

anyway, at least I hoped so. Instead of being dead by drowning and reborn. I was nuts and even wimpier than before. I didn't figure in Cindy. She was either the greatest actor in the world or I was the luckiest spy ever hatched, we would see.

I am now a line spy but I will still be a courier. I was going to retire but maybe I have what it takes after all. I hope my wife has a good sense of humour.

The film of Carma and I nose to well…, was destroyed or so Breakleaf said. Granny had nothing to do with it supposedly. The local Navy Security Chief thought I was dead on the Caymans along with Cindy and his yeoman destroyed my cinematic first attempt, with other information. The mistake was only found after the fact and after my leaving the islands. This precluded a camera team at our little luncheon so, the dance on the beach was not recorded. The wine was Californian and not bad.

Am I different? Perhaps! I will have nightmares, they say from the killing. The reflections will come back.

I have a friend in the US Navy or perhaps not. In my world it always has to be, perhaps not. Those who trust too much die hard. I shall have to pack

my heart at home when I am out and about on her
Majesty's service.

In the windows the lights shine brightly, trees
twinkle, hot food is being served. The family and
those on the street rest comfortable and secure
because of the Trevers and the Cindys and the
Breakleafs and myself. We are not perfect and the
line is thin.

Somehow we must continue to win because these
people that we love, that we defend, live in a
bubble. They are so padded against the outside they
have no understanding of the world I have seen and
know. That is not their job nor should it be
their worry. Until I and Granny and Lorning fall
there will be a line in the sand and our enemies must
beware for we will accept no quarter and will die
before we give up our way of life.

My fat dog is barking, having dragged himself up,
remembering my footsteps perhaps.
The door opens and everyone comes out to hug me.
I hug back.

·   End it.

McFurson will return in Covet Not.

Thank you for reading my book.
George V. Henderson

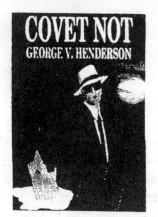

FROM THE PUBLISHER

COVET NOT
$9.95Can

SPY NOT
$9.95Can

WASTE NOT
$8.95Can

georgev_henderson@hotmail.com